OBLIVION

Book Two of The Interference Series

A.F. Presson

Plantation House
PUBLISHING, LLC

Copyright © 2021 by A.F. Presson
Plantation House Publishing, LLC

First Edition September 2022

Paperback ISBN: 978-1-7372433-9-7
Hardback ISBN: 979-8-8456761-2-2

www.afpresson.com

CHAPTER
ONE
MERCY

I could smell his sweat—feel the heat of his breath from fifty yards away, as he stalked me from tree to tree. Every part of my body burned under those predatory eyes. His determination to catch me off guard was impressive, but not enough.

Few actually challenged me anymore.

My gift of subconscious interference pushed toward the surface, eager to delve into his mind and discover his intent, but I refused. It wasn't a power I wanted any part of, and I'd made the decision early on to never violate another's thoughts.

So I ran.

Pulling from my elemental power, the air around me vibrated, propelling me through the forest, away from his grasp. The pace of his pounding heart quickened, as if thrilled by the chase. A dark chuckle echoed through the tall pines, as my vision blurred, hazy from his assault on my senses.

I stumbled from the lack of sight, slamming into the rough bark of a tree as a sharp pain ran across my upper arm. All at once, I closed my eyes, concentrating on stealing his eyesight also. If I had to defend myself blind, so would he. I tilted my head back, letting the breeze brush across my face, carrying a hint of his frustration.

I called upon the forest around me, anything I could use to protect myself. A crackle in the air intensified, then a brutal snap broke through the silence as the roots of nearby trees rose up through dense dirt and moss underneath my feet. One by one they swung toward the direction of my offender, knocking him off his feet.

My vision returned, and I bolted once again, the roots rising to form a shield behind me, intertwining into a wooden web. The smell of smoke seeped into the air, overpowering the scent of pines. Roots sizzled as flames scorched the shield, as if angry for their hindrance.

"You can run . . ." he whispered.

I lifted my hands, using the energy around me to spin leaves and debri to obscure his vision while I hid among the thicket. I closed my eyes, sending an image of myself on my knees, yielding in front of him. As the leaves settled, his gaze landed on the vision of me, kneeling on the ground, and he grinned sadistically.

He walked forward, distracted by the faux image I had created, as if he had won. I sprang from the protection of the pines, knocking his feet out from under him with one swift kick. At once, he jumped forward, but I swung my palm out in front of me, calling on the energy around me to keep him in place.

Struggling against the force of my power he clenched his jaw, fighting my hold. His body hovered mid-air in front of me, sweat dripping from his brow to the brown, wilted leaves at my feet. All at once, he relented, falling onto his back, gasping. I stood above him, lowering my hand to my side. "Had enough?"

He clenched his teeth, and I knew he wasn't willing to relent, but before I could protect myself, he kicked my legs out from under me, then rolled on top of me, holding me down. I didn't see that coming. His chest heaved as his eyes met mine. His strong hand slid to my throat—a warning.

"Mercy?" Colton called out from somewhere in the forest. "Are you out here?"

I swallowed, unsure if I should answer. If I didn't, Colton would send Neela to find me.

"Tell him you're fine and you'll meet him at the Domicile," he whispered.

"Colton? I'll meet you at home, alright?"

Leaves crunched under his boots as he shuffled through the brush—I could tell he wasn't far. "Are you sure?" he asked.

I nodded, even though he couldn't see me, hidden behind the thick tree line. "Yeah, I'm sure. I just, I need some time alone."

"Alright," Colton mumbled, his footsteps drifting further away. "Drake is gonna kill me if I come back without you. Sure, piss off the dragon. Sounds like a lovely conversation."

I stayed perfectly still, until the sound of the crunching leaves grew quiet. His hand lightly gripped the base of my throat. "Good girl."

"What are you going to do with me?" I asked, breathless.

Drake smirked. "So many possibilities."

I bit my bottom lip, fighting a smile. As soon as his mouth covered mine, my body melted. The breeze picked up around me and his lips traveled down my throat. I wrapped my legs around his waist and the ground shook as my hands clawed at his back.

"What if someone catches us?" I asked, pushing his shirt over his head. I obviously wasn't too concerned.

"They won't. Everyone thinks I'll eat them. They're keeping their distance." He grinned. "Of course, if they walk up on you naked, it's possible."

My fingers grazed over thin white scars running down his back. He tensed under my hold, and I knew how much the reminder affected him. "It's who you are, Drake. It's your legacy."

"A legacy that frightens every Regalian known to man."

The black of his eyes tinged red, shadowed by exhaustion. Now that he had changed, the dragon fought to be released. It had turned into a daily battle as it clawed at the surface, while Drake ignored the overwhelming need to let go.

"Maybe if they're around that side of you more often, they wouldn't be afraid."

"Mercy," he warned. "The only time the dragon broke free, I bit your aunt's head off. I'm not taking that chance again."

"But I didn't like her so, you know, it's fine." I grinned.

"You know what I like?" His finger brushed the skin along my hip. "These black pants. I can't focus on anything when we're training."

I shoved the fabric down my hips, as he slid them from my legs. "Why do you think I wear them?"

Chills ran up my spine at the sound of his deep, throaty chuckle. "We only have another week, right? Then you'll be officially mine."

I couldn't help but smile. "I think everyone knows who I belong to. You aren't exactly subtle about it."

"So you aren't going to back out? Leave me at the altar?" he asked, as he gently kissed the top of my knuckles. "Sentence me to a life of sadness and solidarity, mourning in a dark cave on the cliffside for the rest of my life?"

I palmed the side of his face, my thumb sweeping back and forth over his full lower lip. "I'd never survive."

His eyes softened. "It's times like this when we're alone, surrounded by nothing but trees and mountains, when I swear I can sense what you're feeling." I took a deep breath as he pressed his palm against my chest and whispered, "Your heart calls out for me, I can sense it."

"How do you know it's for you? Have you seen the new Custos guard? He's packing, don't you think?"

He didn't smile, but I knew he'd heard me by the clench of his jaw. "How?" he asked. "How is it possible?"

I knew exactly what he meant. Allegato matches were connected, but not in sync until after the mating ceremony. That is when the bond would be at its strongest. "I don't know. Maybe because we aren't exactly normal," I whispered.

His palm slid up my thigh, like a hot stone gliding across my skin. "I've never liked normal," he replied.

I ran my lips along his jaw, grinning. "Normal is boring."

. . .

I COULD HEAR THU DANG, complaining no doubt, before I reached the door. The low drawl of his voice, full of annoyance and boredom, as if my delay ruined his entire afternoon. What could he possibly have to do? Torture small children? Regrease his freakishly shiny bald head?

"How powerful can she truly be if she can't tell time?" he chuckled.

I pushed the double doors open with more force than necessary, swinging one off the hinges toward the tall glass windows behind Thu Dang. I threw my palm out, halting the slat of heavy wood in midair, then closed my fist, pulling it back into place. The bolts and screws drifted through the air, gracefully securing the hinges back onto the frame. I smiled in his direction before taking a seat at the end of the table.

"I apologize. I'm afraid my attention was demanded elsewhere."

"Elsewhere?" Thu Dang laughed. "In the forest, I believe?"

I grinned. "Why yes. Would you like the details?"

He cleared his throat, shifting in his seat. "We have important matters of our own to discuss. If, of course, you're ready to focus on the current state of Seregalo?"

"You forget who you're speaking to, Dang," Josiah spat.

Thu Dang chuckled. "Leader of Seregalo or not, she has a responsibility. Last week, we had complaints of Seregalo widows unable to provide for their children because their husbands died in her war."

"Aadya's war," Josiah corrected.

Several elders nodded in agreement.

"Same difference," he mumbled.

"Complaints from last week? Heavens, good thing I check on them every day or they would have starved by now. You're just now bringing it to the attention of the Elders?"

He tilted his head up, peering at me with beady eyes. "Pardon?"

All at once, the doors swung open as Drake and Colton made their way into the hall. I watched as the Elders sat straight in their chairs, some out of respect, and others out of fear. Drake hadn't given anyone a reason to fear him since the war, but they wouldn't forget anytime soon.

I hated that Thu Dang was right, Regalians were terrified of him.

I pulled the reports from the stack of papers in front of me. "Updates?"

Colton stepped forward. "I've visited everyone on the list, ensuring they have food and shelter. The businesses that closed a few months ago are starting to reopen and the marketplace is thriving compared to last month."

"You went alone? I thought Drake was going with you?" I asked.

Colton sighed. "It seems they are still quite skittish of him. They won't answer the door when he comes along."

"I see."

"I don't mind going alone. Drake has been handling the Custos while I'm away. A healthy dose of fear is good for them," he grinned.

"Updates on the units?" Josiah asked.

"Custos have been given an option to resign if they so desire."

"Resign?" Thu Dang asked. "This is ridiculous! These men are powerless and have no use in our land. You think they will stay and protect you? For what?"

Drake stepped forward, glaring at Thu Dang, as chills ran across my skin. Then, he sent me a vision of the menacing old man tied to a skewer, roasting over a fire. I lowered my head, fighting a grin.

I cleared my throat, attempting to get it together. "If they truly care about Seregalo, they will stay to protect our people, not me."

"How many resigned?" Thu Dang stood from his chair, throwing his hand into the air. "How many ungifted do we have to care for because of her ignorance?"

Suddenly, Thu Dang's chair slid forward, knocking his feet out from under him and forcing him into his seat. The intensity of Drake's anger vibrated around the room as everyone shifted uncomfortably.

"None," Drake's deep voice rang out across the hall. "Not a single man resigned."

Thu Dang met Drake's eyes and swallowed, nervously. "You threatened them, didn't you? They fear the dragon will rip their heads from their body. How proud you must be."

Drake teased, "No need. They know I prefer Asian food." He wagged his brows.

Colton cleared his throat to cover his chuckle.

"Is this what we have to look forward to? Your boyfriend threatening to kill us if we don't comply?"

"If that's her plan, it's certainly failing," Josiah mumbled. "You're still talking."

Laughter erupted around the table as Thu Dang's face flamed red. I felt a simmer of resentment, ready to boil over at any time, I just didn't know when.

"The important thing is that Regalians trust us to take care of them. Our people left this land years ago to protect their families. I want this to be a safe haven for all, no matter how powerful. They'll come back over time, but we have to set our differences aside for one common goal," I explained.

"Which is?" Thu Dang asked.

"Protect our people—their families, their children. Help them thrive. It's been a long time since someone put them first."

He sneered at my remark. "Is that what you're doing? By placing a gifted Regalian female over one of our Custos legions?"

"Do you have a problem with that? Neela is smarter and braver than several of our male Custos. I trust my life with her, and I know the people of Seregalo can also."

He sat completely emotionless. "I'm sure we could find a more useful position for her with less of a leadership role."

"If you had an issue with her rank, it should have been brought to the table when we voted on it. If I remember correctly, you didn't say a word."

"Maybe I couldn't get a word in between you and your elder sidekick. You two control the conversations that take place around this table."

I scoffed. "Are you insinuating that we are manipulating the system? That's a serious allegation."

"Yes, it is and completely false, I might add," Josiah responded.

Thu Dang sneered at his remark. "You are all alike, bitter and self . . ." He gasped, his body completely frozen in what looked like agony. His skinny pale hands shook from effort as his eyes bulged from the intrusion.

Drake stood, completely focused on the Elder, rubbing his chin back and forth with his thumb as if intrigued by the sight of him suffering. Using his sensory gift, Drake had relieved pain for me on more than one occasion, but I'd never seen him inflict anguish.

"That's enough," I muttered. Everyone in the room

exhaled as if forced to hold their breath, and Thu Dang slumped, weakened.

Drake took a step back, a sign of respect for me.

I glanced toward the end of the long table where Elder Isolette always sat. "Where's Icy?"

Josiah cleared his throat. "She hasn't been feeling well, I'm afraid."

"She's ill?" The feeble woman would always hold a special place in my heart. I recalled my first meeting with the Elders, right after the war. Isolette stood by my side, showing her support in a time of confusion and fear. Ever since, I could always trust her to be a calm and collected spirit in a troubling time.

Another spoke up. "She hasn't said as much, but we can feel her weakening through our connection."

"I see." I bowed my head, focusing on the reports, but not reading any of them. Isolette had become a friend, and guilt flooded me for not picking up on her condition earlier. Drake's concerned gaze burned hot from across the room.

"Is there anything else?" I asked. The room quieted as the Elders refused to glance in my direction. "What? What's going on?"

Josiah sighed. "There is the issue with your sister, Mercy."

"My sister? What issue?"

"Some feel as though she can't be trusted. Her temper and overall disposition keep her at arm's length from just about everyone. The staff is terrified of her."

"That is crazy. Aadya held my sister captive for years. Can you imagine how confused she must be after finding out the truth about our parents? She needs time."

"I agree," Thu Dang interjected, trying to appear unshaken. "Marley has struggled to accept the truth about her family, but she isn't a danger to anyone. She could use a mentor, someone to help her sift through the pain."

"I didn't realize you'd spent time with my sister."

"My duty is to all Regalians, isn't that right?" He raised one brow.

I watched him for several seconds, searching for his motive. "Let's give her more time—see if she acclimates."

Josiah nodded, as if not wanting to argue. "As you wish."

. . .

IT DIDN'T TAKE me long to find the perfect hiding spot. Somewhere I could go to clear my head and forget how every Regalian relied on me for their family's well-being.

Yeah—no pressure at all.

The rooftop of the Domicile had been left unattended for what looked like years, overgrown with weeds and the concrete covered in fallen leaves.

In a matter of weeks, I had transformed the rooftop patio into my very own tranquil haven. Large ceramic pots of mint, rosemary and lemons filled every corner of the terrace, and a wide, double lounger sat on a woven rug in the center, directly under the stars. Few places in Seregalo brought as much peace to my over-anxious mind as my private garden.

I laid on my back, gazing from one bright star to another, mesmerized by the brilliant contrast against the night sky. The scene in front of me slowly dissipated into a vision of beach waves, washing over my ankles as I walked along the sand. Breathing salty air, I watched as pelicans called out over the water, dipping low to skim the surface for fish. I grinned as Drake jogged out of the water, shirtless. He winked.

"If you're going to take over my senses, could you make it less like Baywatch?"

He snickered behind me, and the night sky once again gleamed overhead. "This is new. You've been hiding this place from me."

"Not you. Everyone else maybe."

Drake walked to the edge of the rooftop, looking out over the river. The stars had always brought him peace, something he'd mentioned on more than one occasion. My thoughts drifted back to our nights outside Fremont, arguing over the best views in the garden. It felt like a lifetime ago.

Drake's gift of sensory interference had always been unimaginably strong, but to find out he was the only dragon shifter in over one-hundred years, the newfound gift had taken a toll on him. He fought the change daily, desperate to keep the monster at bay.

"Do you remember the first time we met?" I asked.

He looked over his shoulder and smiled. "You were trying to take my secret hiding spot behind Fremont. The one with the best view of the stars."

I cleared my throat. "I believe you were the one stealing my spot, if memory serves me right."

He shrugged. "It doesn't."

I grew quiet, studying the shadows of the moon. "I miss it, you know—the hustle and bustle of the city, the mystery of Fremont. I discovered myself there, but it feels like I've aged years instead of months. Our magic forced us to grow up quicker than most, and sometimes I wonder how things would have turned out otherwise."

Drake walked to the lounger beside me and laid down, reaching for my hand. "Are you unhappy?"

I shook my head. "Not unhappy. I think transitioning has been harder than I thought."

"Seregalo's magic is flourishing since you arrived, have you noticed? Parts of the mountainside were brown and dried up, and the river had gotten low. The trees are full and the river is overflowing with fish. Part of the reason we've been able to take care of the widows is because the fields are producing for the first time in years. Why do you think that is?"

I knew something had changed. Although beautiful before, Neela's parents said the food supply had begun to dwindle under Aadya's leadership, as if the hidden land had lost its will to live. "I'm sure it had something to do with Aadya. She continued to rule even after another had been chosen. The woman was like a disease. Maybe it was Seregalo's way of saying enough is enough."

"Maybe." He reached forward, brushing the hair from the side of my face. "Maybe it's you. You're strong Mercy, maybe your power is feeding Seregalo. It's thriving, and people are starting to notice. I know you want them to trust you, but give it time. They are seeing the difference, I know they are."

"I hope you're right. I'm going into town tomorrow, so I'm praying it's uneventful. Although they appear to respect me, I feel like I haven't fully gained their trust yet."

"It takes time," he whispered. "You'll get there."

"I think I just need a moment of peace. It's so chaotic all the time."

"We don't have to host the Allegato ceremony this week if it's too much. There's no rush."

I raised one brow. "Having doubts?"

He turned, pulling me against his side and wrapping his arms around me. "You should know better than that. I know you're trying to find your way in this new role, and I want to support you, not add stress. Let's face it, the people of Seregalo, your people, are terrified of your fiancé. Which is probably why some are scared of you."

"A healthy dose of fear is good, right?" I joked. "They'll get used to you, as soon as they learn you aren't going to set them on fire."

"Nice."

Pulling his face down to mine, I lightly kissed his lips. A gentle, rare gesture on my part. He groaned, pulling me against him, then deepened the kiss. He gripped the back of my hair, his lips traveling down my neck. "Come back to my room with me."

"No, we can't. Someone might see us, and I want the staff to respect me."

"I will. I'll respect you so hard . . ."

I laughed, pushing him back to meet his eyes. "You are not just a boyfriend. They need to see us as responsible adults, with something that resembles self-control."

"So the forest earlier was more responsible than the bed?" He raised one brow, as if challenging me.

"No one was nearby! The Domicile is filled with staff, Drake, not to mention family and friends."

"Afraid you won't be able to control yourself? You are kind of loud."

"Can we act like adults?" I grinned, I couldn't help it. Especially when Drake's playful side came out. It didn't happen often.

"Definitely. We should do adult things."

I sighed. "Soon we'll be together every night, not just hidden away in the woods on the occasional training day."

"It was hot though," he said thoughtfully. "I guess I can relish the memory until I have you all to myself again." Drake smiled. "Wanna train tomorrow?"

I zoned out, hearing him speak, but not taking in his words. Every time I tried to relax, it happened, and I started thinking of things I needed to do or that were waiting for me.

He cut his eyes toward me. "You're distracted."

"Just thinking about tomorrow."

"I can go with you, if you want. I don't like the idea of you going into town alone."

I grinned, trying not to appear overconfident. "I think I can handle it."

He chuckled. "Yeah, sometimes I forget who I'm talking to."

We laid quietly on the rooftop, relishing the silence. There weren't many opportunities like this anymore, and I focused on enjoying the private moment, ignoring the nagging feeling that I should have been doing something else.

I blocked everything out, concentrating on the heat of his breath, the rough fingertips of his hands. I could almost imagine we were back in the courtyard at Fremont. My fingers gradually drifted underneath his shirt, circling the skin above his waistband.

"Mercy . . ." he warned.

"Sorry," I lied.

. . .

THE NEXT MORNING, I found Marley outside, sitting alone beside the Seregalo River. Warm rays of the sun reflected off the water, brightening the red of her auburn hair. Her flowy green top fluttered with the breeze as she closed her eyes, her face relaxing in the solitude. In moments like this, she reminded me so much of our mother—what little I knew of her.

"They complain about me again?" she asked, a smidge of humor in her tone.

"Why would you think that?" I sat down beside her, letting the ripple of water soothe me. I'm not sure why I didn't go out there more often, if nothing else, just to clear my head.

"Sorry. Sometimes I can't help but listen subconsciously. Not everyone is shielded like you." She grinned. "When Aadya ruled, I dove into everyone's thoughts, desperate to find a way out of the Domicile. Old habits die hard, I guess."

Her eyes grew heavy, the forced smile graceful, yet sad. I couldn't imagine what she'd gone through, and more than anything, I wanted her to trust me enough to tell me about it. All the years we'd lost created a divide between us that felt a mile wide. I vowed to mend that broken connection, no matter the cost.

"I can't imagine what you've gone through. Don't worry about the Elders—I'll handle them."

"They don't trust me, Mercy. The last thing I want is to make things difficult for you. Seregalo needs you."

"I need you. I won't let anyone rip you away from me again."

Marley's shoulders relaxed, as if relieved. "I didn't know

what to expect with you. The rumors were quite terrifying." Her eyes met mine. "Liar. Manipulator. Murderer."

I swallowed, uncomfortable at the dark tone of her voice. I didn't want to be that person, one whose own sister feared her. "You don't have to be afraid of me."

Marley smiled, a half-grin that could easily be interpreted for over-confidence. "Funny. That's exactly what Aadya said."

Her words hit a part of my heart I didn't expect. Maybe because deep down, the fear of becoming like my aunt lingered. It terrified me to think I had no control of her blood running through my veins. "I'm not Aadya. I want things to be different with us. Our mother's didn't necessarily have the best relationship from what I hear, but we could if that's something you want."

Marley sighed. "You don't need me, Mercy. You have people that love you. I don't think your boyfriend wants your sister tagging along. Plus, Neela watches me as if she doesn't trust me."

I couldn't help but giggle. "She looks at everyone that way."

"Not you." She shook her head. "There's respect and admiration in the way she speaks to you. As if there is no doubt you are all powerful, and she will sacrifice herself to make sure you succeed. She thinks you're the one that will save our people."

"What do you think?" I wanted to understand my sister —know what went through her head on a daily basis. Otherwise, I'd never get to know her.

"Does it matter?" she asked.

"It does to me."

Marley watched me for several seconds, before glancing up at a bird flying overhead. "Aadya told me a surge of power swept our land between the birth of you and I. How do they know it's supposed to be you?"

My chest tightened painfully at her words. What was I supposed to say? That I'm more powerful? That I hold more gifts? That a part of me refuses to bow down to her, as if it knows she's weak? No—I couldn't.

"I don't know."

She leaned back on her elbows, her gaze traveling over the blue sky overhead. "Tell me about them."

"Who? Our parents?"

Marley nodded, then pursed her lips as if the words offended her.

"I never met our mother, I only had moments with her in the trials. Did you ever experience that?"

Marley shook her head. "I came here with the leader of Seregalo, I wasn't required to go through the trials, but I hear they are quite ghastly."

I hated the way her eyes lit up at the words. I nodded, eager to move forward. "She suffered, more than you or I know. For years, she lived outside California, hidden away to keep an eye on you."

"That doesn't make any sense. Why?"

I shrugged. "Aadya wanted you and I. Maybe she wasn't sure who held more power. Maybe she wanted to control us. I don't know, but Mom and Dad put distance between us to throw Aadya off our tracks. It worked for a while. In the trials, I saw Aadya murder our mother, on our thirteenth birthday."

"That isn't true. That is the day Aadya rescued me and brought me here. She said my own mother deserted me. Aadya reunited me with the Regalians, and taught me to use my magic."

"She isn't necessarily known for her honesty." I

muttered, wincing. I hated to hurt her, but she needed to know the truth.

Marley didn't respond, and I felt it best to continue.

"I met Dad in New York at Fremont. He and Mom decided to split up to protect us during the first war, one watching me and the other watching you. They'd swap from time to time, just to be able to watch us grow up."

Marley scoffed. "Nobody watched me. If so, they didn't care about the hell I went through. I guess that comes with being the weaker daughter."

"No, Marley. Mom lived in the woods outside your town, protecting you. She loved you very much."

"I guess we have different meanings of the word. Nothing would keep me away from the ones I love. Nothing."

"I wish you could have seen what I did. The visions during the trials would help you understand. It helped me so much, I can't even describe it. I also visited our Grandmother here in Seregalo. She's asked about you, and I know she wants to get to know you better. Maybe you could come with me to see her."

Marley stood, brushing the grass from her legs. "I'm happy you have closure, Mercy. I really am. But I'm afraid it's going to take me a bit longer." She walked past me toward the back door of the Domicile.

"Marley?"

She stopped in her tracks, but never turned around.

"Please don't take me the wrong way. But when I first found you, you were desperate to get away from Aadya, begging me to save you. Now, it seems as though you are coming to her defense. I'm just a bit confused."

One side of her mouth pulled up in a sneaky grin. "It's

all part of the game, isn't it? If you don't know who to trust, play both sides."

Her honesty stunned me. Marly was confused, completely oblivious to what our parents went through to keep us alive. I felt sorry for her. "I'm here. If you ever need to talk or want some company, I'd love it if we could be friends."

She scowled. "I don't even know what that is."

CHAPTER

TWO

MERCY

T he cobblestone path underneath my feet led to the pristine streets of downtown Seregalo, the devastation from the war long gone, as if it never happened. I hated how the simple task of going into the neighborhoods affected me. The fake smiles and nods from my own people who didn't know or trust me. I knew it wouldn't always be that way, it would take time. I wasn't necessarily known for my patience though.

The small village behind the marketplace housed several small cottages, bordered by bright yellow tulips. The homes were idyllic, each with a neatly trimmed yard surrounded by a white picket fence separating each property. I hadn't seen a single extravagant house since I'd arrived. Even with the intense amount of power in the city, Regalians were modest.

Kids chased each other in the fields, flying kites with no strings. Their small hands glided through the air, guiding the colorful shapes with gifts of energy and wind. I smiled as they waved, losing control of their sails. Children rode their bikes down the street without fear, and grandmothers sat on the porch in rocking chairs, calling out to neighbors as they passed by.

I'd visited the neighborhood before, when Ren first moved in with the Hughes family. Joy and wonder filled the small boy's eyes at the thought of having a home that didn't include a cell door. He'd acclimated so well, I didn't feel the need to come back right away. In fact, I feared it would make things more difficult if he depended on my presence.

But things had changed.

Alycia Hughes had reached out the week before about a change in Ren. He'd withdrawn from them and their two daughters, refusing to eat more than a couple of bites at a time. They brought a doctor in to look him over, but physically he appeared fine.

I also knew Ren had gone through major adjustments at a time when most Regalians were coming into their power. I wasn't sure if that would have an effect on him, but I knew it had to be considered. After knocking twice, Alycia opened the front door and exhaled.

She patted the top of her head, as if worried over the state of her hair. "I'm so glad you're here. I don't know what to do."

I stepped into the quaint living area, where a teenage girl sat sideways in an armchair, reading. The clock on the wall ticked loudly as I searched the room for any sign of Ren. "He isn't any better?"

She shook her head, shedding the flour-covered apron around her waist. "I'm afraid not. Honestly, the girls don't want to go to his room anymore. Madi says there's something not right about the energy."

I looked over toward the young girl with dark blonde hair and glasses. "Are you psychokinetic?"

"Yes, Ma'am," she answered. "I can't explain it though. It feels off. My sister, Kenz, won't get near him at all."

I tried to smile, reassuringly. "Maybe he's just going through an adjustment phase. Is his room down the hall?"

Alysia stepped to the side and nodded. "Last room on the left."

I made my way toward his bedroom, and the hum of energy vibrated around me as I drew near. It intensified as I grew closer until my lungs burned from shallow breathing. The need to turn around and run in the opposite direction grew fierce, and it felt more like a defense mechanism than anything.

I refused to turn around.

When I reached his door, my fists shook from effort as I knocked softly. "Ren? It's Mercy." All at once, the negative force dissipated to a level I could withstand, and my shoulders relaxed. The door opened, just a crack, and one big blue eye peeked into the hall.

"Mercy?"

"That's right. Can I come in?"

He nodded, opening the door slightly wider. I walked inside, shutting it quickly behind me. Ren had all of the lights off and the blinds were pulled closed. I concentrated on adjusting my eyesight in the dark, then took a step back, shocked by the sight of him. Ren had always been small and frail, and since he wasn't eating I assumed it had gotten worse.

I was wrong.

He looked as though he had aged three years since I had seen him last. The top of his head almost reached my shoulders. Dark circles shadowed his eyes, and his short brown hair stuck up in all directions. How was it possible? "Ren— you, um. You've grown since I saw you last."

His chin quivered as he sat down on the end of the bed. "I don't know what's wrong with me."

The small houseplant beside the window had shriveled into strings of brown weed. Broken glass from the lightbulb in the lamp scattered along his wooden desk. "Are you in pain?"

He shrugged. "My head hurts all the time. Nothing helps."

"You didn't tell the doctor?"

Ren shook his head. "He wouldn't understand. Only you can understand."

"Understand what?" I hated to tell the kid, but I didn't understand at all.

His eyes grew heavy, as his whisper slithered across the fog of unease and confusion, "The voices. Make the voices stop."

I swallowed, choosing my words carefully. "What are they saying, Ren?"

He rocked back and forth, shaking his head. "Which one?"

Chills ran through my body at his tone, cold and callous. How was I supposed to respond? "Tell me about your gift, Ren."

The room grew cold and I could feel the energy draining from every pore. All at once, I felt as though I could sleep for days. I placed a shield around me, protecting myself from the unknown force.

"There is no gift. It's a curse—a curse that causes pain. To you. To everyone in Seregalo."

I froze, and fear of what could happen kept me from giving any advice. I realized I had no clue how to help this child, but I knew someone who could. "Ren, I know someone who might be able to help. You have to trust me, alright?"

"No one can help me." He shook his head as if willing the tears away. "They won't believe me."

"That's not true, I promise. I have a friend who helped me, and he's been helping children for years. Do you trust me?"

He began to cry, but never looked away from my face. "I trust you."

"Good." I smiled. "Everything will be alright."

Ren whispered, "It won't. It never will again."

. . .

I LEFT REN'S HOUSE, absolutely wrecked. I'd never seen such a drastic change in someone, especially at his age. I wasn't sure what to do, but I knew someone who might be able to help him.

I walked for hours, going over every word of our conversation. I needed guidance. Someone wise who I could trust. Elder Isolette had constantly been by my side since the war, supporting and trusting me. She offered advice when asked, and never treated me as ignorant or inexperienced. I wanted to visit her anyway since she'd taken ill, and this seemed like the perfect opportunity. Something inside of me relaxed at the thought of her presence.

A variety of brick and rock cottages, similar to the home of Neela's parents, lined the streets, surrounded by large trees and flower gardens. It was perfect—too perfect for someone used to living in Manhattan. There were no naked cowboys, acrobats in the street, or savory food carts. The loud wail of sirens had been replaced by the ripple of streams and songbirds.

I walked further into town, and something dark in the midst of perfection caused my steps to falter, as if eyes were following me. I searched up and down the streets, taking in each Regalian, going about their lives. An elderly man, pulling weeds throughout his garden—not because he had to, but because he found joy in the task. A young woman strolled her infant in the fresh air, humming a familiar lullabye.

Then, a home, maybe fifty yards away, loomed darker over the light and airy cottages I'd grown accustomed to. A greenish hue tinted the top of the copper roof from lack of care, and the paint-chipped shutters hung haphazardly around the windows. One sweep of their palm, and the house would be as new. No, whoever lived there wanted to be different. They were making a point by showing their flaws in the sea of gifted perfection.

A ragged white curtain caught my attention as it fluttered inside of the window. I caught the sight of frizzy blonde hair and wide eyes before the figure quickly disappeared. A quiver of unease prickled across my skin at the sight. I slowed my pace as I walked in front of the cottage, taking in every detail about the mysterious residents. As soon as I passed the property, peace quickly replaced the alarm, and I almost tripped over my feet at the abrupt change.

What the hell was that?

I continued strolling down the sidewalk, smiling and waving toward everyone I passed, but my thoughts kept drifting back toward the dilapidated cottage. I crossed the street toward the Elder's homes on my left, lining the Sere-galo River.

The familiar blue door surrounded by rock was cracked just a bit, as if someone had left it open. I pushed it forward gently, adjusting my eyes to the dark. "Icy? Are you home?"

The living area sat bare, a small quilt folded neatly over the back of a sofa. A china cabinet in the corner, beside the fireplace, housed several ceramic angels, lined perfectly on the glass shelves. I peeked into the kitchen, looking for any sign of her. "Icy?"

"Mercy? Is that you?"

I walked toward the small screened-in back porch where Icy sat hunched in an old rocking chair. Even in the heat of the day, she huddled into herself, as if chilled. I walked back inside, quickly grabbing the folded quilt. She smiled as I wrapped it around her shoulders.

"That's nice, thank you."

Her typically bright complexion and blue eyes had been replaced by fatigue and dark circles. Had it only been a week since I'd seen her? "Icy, what's going on with you?"

She scowled. "Nothing's going on with me. What's the matter with you?"

"Oh, stop." I smirked at her attitude, sitting in the chair beside her. "It's me. No one else is here. You can be honest with me."

"I'm old, Mercy. Damn it, that's enough."

I grinned. "You may be old, but you're still the scariest woman I know. Except your crazy neighbors—you have some competition there."

She tilted her head, confused. "Neighbors?"

"The shabby cottage down the street? Saw some crazy eyes looking through the window when I passed by. That's a dark place."

"Ah, yes. Jules and Creeky. Craziest sisters you'll ever meet. That's saying something considering you and your mother both have demented twins." She laughed at her own joke, but grew serious when she saw I wasn't amused. "Rumor has it they're into dark magic."

"All magic can be dark if you misuse it."

"True, but most Regalians respect their gift. Give those psychos an incentive and they'd sacrifice each other." Her eyes grew wide as she whispered, "Caught Jules running down the street butt naked one night. That crazy blonde hair flying through the wind. That's a sight I won't forget anytime soon."

"She was alone?"

"Her sister, Creeky, was there—videoing." She nodded. "Crazy, I tell you."

"I think I'll keep my distance. I've had my share of craziness."

Icy nodded, sitting back in her chair. "Smart girl."

I grinned, but her words hit me deeper than I expected. "I don't feel smart. I feel ignorant, and unprepared for all of this."

"It seems like things are going well. What has you so distraught?"

"What doesn't?" I frowned. "Our people are still afraid of Drake. I haven't chosen a dress for our mating ceremony yet, and my sister isn't acclimating like she should. She resents me—I can feel it. Now something is going on with Ren, and I don't know how to help him."

"You're putting too much pressure on yourself."

"Maybe." I rubbed my bottom lip with the tip of my finger, thinking about everything that needed my attention. "I don't know."

"Breathe, Mercy. Regalians will settle once they see

28

Drake is here to protect them. He's different, and his gift is not one they are used to seeing in Seregalo. Dragons have been nonexistent for years—they are almost a myth at this point. As far as the ceremony, you don't have to wear a dress at all. It can be private, between the two of you. That's how it's usually done anyway."

"Drake and I were raised around traditional weddings. We both want to incorporate that into the mating ceremony, if possible. I think we'll regret it if we don't."

"So have a party. There are no rules when it comes to this, so stop stressing. Walk up the aisle in anything you wish, say your vows and ceremonial oaths, then have your way with that fire-breathing, hunk of a man."

I gasped. "Icy!"

"I'm not dead, Mercy."

I laughed. "He's alright. If you like the tall, dark, and broody type."

She raised one brow. "Who doesn't? You get tired of him, send him my way. I'll find the strength."

"I'll remember that," I replied, laughing.

"Now, what's happening with the child?" she asked.

"Child? He doesn't look like a child, not anymore."

"Ren? The boy from the dungeon?"

I nodded. "It's unbelievable. Something is happening. Something I don't understand."

She frowned. "I didn't want to worry you, but I wondered what would happen when his gift had a chance to manifest."

"What do you mean?"

"Aadya could have had him locked up for years, Mercy. We don't know how long or why. Do you remember how you were unable to use your gift in the dungeon? His growth, in all aspects of his life, has been stunted by that spell. As if frozen while held captive."

My mouth fell open in shock. "So you think he's catching up, all at once?"

"I don't know, but it's possible." The Elder leaned forward, her eyes sharp. "I can tell you one thing, I can't think of a single reason Aadya would have held a small boy captive unless she felt threatened by him."

"But . . . he is only a child," I argued.

"A child who would grow into a man. A very powerful man," she explained. "Otherwise, why wouldn't she just find him a home and be done with it?"

I sat back in my chair, stunned. Is that what happened? Did Aadya know how powerful Ren would become? It honestly sounded like something she would do. I'd be lying if I said he hadn't frightened me, and I had the ability to shield his advances. Not everyone could.

The same feeling of emptiness washed over me at the memory of sitting in his room. "I felt the life being pulled from inside of me—as if he consumed all of the energy around him. I don't think he even knew what he'd done. His family is scared of him."

"He's too young to understand. That in itself makes him even more dangerous."

"Ren told me he is hearing voices. Do you think he's crazy?"

"Aren't we all?" She replied. "Even so, I'd get the boy some help. He needs someone to talk to, and I don't believe it needs to be the leader of Seregalo. You have enough on your plate."

I took a deep breath and nodded. "I have a friend who hopefully can help."

"Good. Task sharing is a sign of a smart leader."

Already, the weight of the day lifted from my shoulders. I wasn't alone and the reminder brought more peace than anything else could. I sat with Icy in silence, waiting for her to say more, but she never did.

"I know you aren't well. We don't have to talk about it, but just know I'm here if you need me. Anything at all."

"I'm not scared, Mercy. I've imagined the afterlife so many times, it's more like a memory now." Vulnerability filled her blue eyes as she swallowed. Icy's silky white hair had been neatly pulled up by the jeweled comb she always wore. Always classy and elegant, I'd never seen her any other way. Her gaze drifted toward the river and she took a deep breath. "I almost drowned in this river as a child. Have I ever told you that?"

I shook my head.

Her glassy eyes focused on something in the distance, as if lost in the memory. "One early Sunday morning, I lost my fishing pole to a big one. It was the only thing my father had ever given to me. I dove in after it and the river washed me downstream. My elemental gift manifested at an early age, but it wasn't strong. I'm not sure why I didn't try to use it. Maybe I wanted the water to take me."

I considered her words, thinking about my own experience. "I get it. I almost drowned in a swimming pool once. The water came alive around me, and I lost myself in it. I remember the feeling of peace washing over me, like the waves knew what I needed more than myself."

She nodded. "Terrifying, isn't it? Our power has such a strong life of its own, it can convince us to do horrible things, and we feel completely at peace about it."

"Are you saying it was Aadya's power forcing her to believe she'd done the right thing?"

"I'm a ramblin' old woman, Mercy. Half of what I say is bullshit."

I laughed. "Fair enough. So how did you survive?"

Icy grinned. "You wouldn't believe me if I told you. The nightmares still plague me even now. I woke up on the river bank that evening with the worst headache of my life and a white scar across the back of my neck."

"A scar?"

Icy pulled her salt and pepper hair back, showing the elegant two-sided white arrow.

"What does it mean?"

"Have you ever heard stories of the Oblivion?"

"No, I haven't. Sounds daunting though." I raised my brows, intrigued. "Tell me."

"It's an in-between world. One that only the strongest can survive."

"In between? Like between life and death?"

She thought it over, then nodded. "Sort of, except the past, present and future all coincide."

"I don't understand."

Icy turned toward me, her eyes filled with a strange combination of excitement and horror. "The Oblivion is a world where your darkest regrets are mixed with the most inconceivable nightmares. Let's say the Oblivion took Josiah today, he could very well run into my younger version, trying to escape."

"You believe that's where you went? When you almost drown?"

"I know it is. I saw things a small child should never see, Mercy. People fighting inner demons they never wanted others to witness. It was put on display—all of it. I also made friends, who saved my life and helped me find my way home. I owe them everything."

"How did you get there?"

"That is what I never figured out. Do some go there when they have a near-death experience? Why does the Oblivion demand proof we are worthy of returning? Why some and not others? I'll never understand."

"Is it similar to the trials we went through on our journey to Seregalo?" I asked. "That wasn't easy on any of us."

"Not even close, I'm afraid. I can close my eyes at night and still hear the screams from terrified Regalians, begging for death. Even after all these years, not a day goes by when I don't think about it."

"Do you think it will ever go away?"

"I hope not. Nothing has given me more perspective in life."

CHAPTER

THREE

MARLEY

I sat on the edge of Mercy's bed, imagining my scarf tight around her throat, as she gasped for her last breath. I grinned at the thought.

"Don't feel as though you have to come. I mean, if you don't want to, I'll understand." Mercy sat on the edge of her bed, securing her earrings. I watched as she opened the top drawer of the nightstand, reaching for our mother's emerald ring.

My ring.

I hated to tell her, but I didn't give a damn about her stupid ceremonial dress. I'd watched her prance around in our mother's gown the night of the war, and I didn't care anything about watching our new queen celebrate her perfect life once again. I'd rather sleep in the dungeon, with only Thu Dang for company, and that is saying something.

"I'm your sister. Of course I want to be there." I smiled, hoping she wouldn't see through the lie. "Do you think you'll be able to find something in time?"

Mercy sighed. "I hope so, or I'll be showing up in jeans."

"What's the rush? I mean, unless . . ." I glanced down at her stomach suspiciously, raising one brow.

"What? No! Is that what people think?" Mercy's eyes widened.

I shrugged. "It crossed my mind."

She shook her head. "Of course not. It just feels like there is something lurking around every corner. There isn't a reason to wait, and we want our connection to be as strong as possible. Plus, I love him, Marley."

I ignored her declaration of love and emotion, worried I'd become nauseous. "Is Grandmother Monroe going also?" Ignorant, old twit. It's all I could do to sit and listen to her nonsense about the sacrifices her perfect son made for his family. Too bad he couldn't be bothered to raise his own daughters.

Mercy smiled. "She's meeting us there."

I clenched my teeth, fighting the need to scream. "That sounds lovely." Just what I needed, more family time, as if I hadn't dealt with enough from this psychotic bloodline. All at once, Neela and Nora burst through the door with their too-bright smiles and perfect silky hair.

I hated them.

Neela had surprised everyone with her cunning ability to research and plan strategic investigations. Although not extremely athletic, her intelligence had made her a vital part of Mercy's guard. I wanted her gone.

Nora was weak and emotional. She spent most of her days teaching Regalian children and ogling Caleb, her mate. I didn't see her as a threat and didn't waste time worrying over her part in my plan. No, she wasn't a priority.

"Time to pick out a dress!" Neela sang in a high-pitched voice, then she leaned forward to whisper, "Guess we won't be buying white."

Mercy's mouth fell open. "Thanks, Neela. Besides, it isn't an official wedding so I can wear anything I want." She turned toward the mirror and took a deep breath.

Nora stepped behind her, propping her chin on Mercy's shoulder. "Which is?"

Mercy smiled. "Red."

Times like this reminded me we were sisters. How can we be so alike and different at the same time? I cleared my throat, reminding them of my presence. Sometimes, they carried on as if I didn't exist at all.

Mercy glanced up and smiled. "What do you think, Marley?"

I nodded. "Red it is."

. . .

SEREGALO WASN'T KNOWN for being the fashion capital of the world by any means. Most Regalians traveled to Dublin for their clothes and accessories, but Mercy insisted on shopping at a dress boutique midtown. She wanted her ceremonial dress to come from her own people.

As if they care.

The small shop sat on the corner of the street, across from the local pub. The wide glass windows showcased multiple mannequins in evening wear, standing under long strands of string lights. Lanterns sat along the ground, lit by magical flames blazing orange and red.

A tall thin woman with pale blonde hair pulled back in a strict bun walked toward the door to greet us. "Miss Monroe, it is an honor to meet you."

I rolled my eyes. I couldn't seem to help myself.

"The honor is all mine, Mrs. Whitman. I've heard so much about your designs."

"Please call me Bree." She smiled.

The bright light of the store assaulted my eyes—a gleam I wasn't prepared for. The silver floor shined brightly, and everything from door handles to chandeliers had been diamond encrusted. Sewing machines against the wall worked diligently by themselves, creating Mrs. Whitman's designs. I had pictured an old lady in a floral mumu, chastising Mercy for the edgy dress she desired.

Well, this is disappointing.

"I have several designs picked out for you, and of course I can do them in any color," Bree continued. "Follow me."

Neela and Nora drifted toward the clothing racks while I followed Mercy to the dressing room. Not quite in my comfort zone, I stood awkwardly outside the curtain, shuffling from foot to foot while Bree handed Mercy several gowns to try on.

"I imagine this is what girls feel like when shopping for prom," she called out.

I scoffed. "You never went?"

"Um, no. I tried not to put myself in those situations if I could help it."

I sat on the sofa, curious about her comment. "What kind of situations?"

She stuck her head outside the curtain and frowned. "The kind where I'd be laughed at. Or lose my temper and hurt someone. Those are my only memories of high school." She shrugged, then disappeared behind the black drapes once again.

Her words stunned me. I'd never heard much about Mercy's life, but I knew it had to be better than mine. "I'm surprised. I thought you would have been the prom queen, for sure."

Her laughter rang out through the store. She pulled the curtain back, showcasing a dark blue, one-shouldered gown covered in diamonds. The top of her cleavage spilled over the neckline and the hem stretched tight around her backside. I frowned at the sight.

"Heavens. That looks painful," a familiar voice called out from the front entrance.

Every head turned toward the front where Grandmother Monroe stood, scowling.

"Got something that shows less of her . . . assets?" she asked.

I grinned at Mercy. "Or more."

"This is my granddaughter, Mrs. Whitman. Keep that in mind."

Mercy laughed, but grew serious at Mrs. Whitman's unamused expression. "I'll just, um, check in the back."

"You do that," Grandmother replied, turning to join Neela and Nora.

Mercy bit her top lip, fighting amusement. "Did you ever go to prom?" she asked.

"Not really my thing."

Once again, she stuck her head around the curtain. "Why not?"

"Not many foster kids get invited. Especially when you can't afford a dress."

"Foster kid? I thought you were living with a cousin in California?" She shook her head. "I don't understand."

"That's what Aunt Isla told our neighbors. I guess she didn't want them thinking I belonged to her."

Mercy sighed. "I'm sorry. It appears neither one of us

had the best upbringing." Her eyes grew sad, and I almost felt sorry for her. "I've been thinking about my mom, or our aunt who pretended to be my mother. She's been there since the beginning, you know. Good or bad, she'll always be a part of me."

"Funny. I rarely think of Aunt Isla at all. I guess we aren't as alike as we thought." I raised one brow and smiled.

Mercy stepped forward, whispering. "Did you feel it? On your thirteenth birthday, did you feel it when our mother died?"

"Feel what?"

Mercy's forehead wrinkled from concentration. She opened her mouth, but closed it again as if struggling to explain. "A loss. As if a vital piece of my heart had been ripped from my chest."

I scoffed. "Vital? Certainly not to me."

"Marley, you don't underst—"

"Try this one! It's lovely, don't you think?" Grandmother Monroe stepped forward, clutching a strapless black gown.

Mercy tilted her head. "I'm not sure it's right for the ceremony, but I think it's perfect for the dinner tonight."

"Dinner?" I asked.

She nodded, her eyes wide with excitement. "Neela is planning a celebration dinner tonight for us." Neela grinned brightly across the store at the mention of her name. "Everyone is invited, right Neela?"

Neela faltered, then plastered on a fake smile. "Yeah, of course. Everyone." She turned away, frowning toward Nora.

I knew exactly what that meant. She had no intention of inviting me. Neela had been suspicious of me since day one and I refused to let her drive a wedge between me and Mercy. She had to trust me, it was the only way I would get what I wanted. I deserved a future, the same as anyone else. I deserved Drake, even if I had to fight for him.

Mercy beamed. "Will you come? We can pick out a new dress for you while we're here."

"I wouldn't miss it for the world. I mean, you are my sister after all." I smiled, giving her a solid wink. "Drake is going to be my brother soon, so I should definitely get to know him better."

"Aw, Marley. I would love that. It means so much to me. Thank you."

I stepped forward, reaching for her hand. The emerald ring shined underneath the light overhead and I clenched my teeth. "Anything for you, Mercy."

...

I BARELY MADE it out of the dress shop without losing my damn mind. Even if I wanted to, I couldn't describe the amount of hate I had for those people. Even my own grandmother looked at me as if she didn't trust me.

I would always be the black sheep compared to my sister.

I declined Mercy's offer of an annoying brunch filled with celebration mimosas and fake smiles. Bile bubbled inside my throat at the thought. After hiding away in my bedroom for over an hour, I could still hear the cackling of alcohol-induced hens downstairs. I lost it.

I snuck outside, desperate for peace and distance from everything that made my skin crawl. An hour through the streets of Seregalo turned into two hours, and I found myself wading deeper into the forest behind the stone cottages across town. I hadn't explored this area before, but immediately decided to visit it more often.

There were no voices, only the chirping of nearby birds, and the whisper of a gentle breeze, nudging the heavy limbs of old trees. I sat on the bank of a crystal clear lake, covered in lily pads, enjoying the silence.

A wave of heat washed over my skin, from fingertips to my neck, as if sitting in front of a furnace. My nerves were on edge, but I didn't know why. I stood and stretched my neck to search the trees around me. Curiosity spurred me on, and before I knew it, I found myself searching the woods for the mysterious presence I knew was there.

I walked for almost a mile, and I would have given up except the sensation began to intensify. The heat became almost unbearable, and sweat poured from my brow. I almost turned around, but the crashing of a waterfall ahead caught my attention, as did a ferocious growl.

I stood on the bank, maybe twenty feet above the water, where the waterfall fed the lake. Huge silver-lined rocks piled haphazardly on both sides, creating a protective barrier around the deepest section. One of the most beautiful sites I had ever seen in Seregalo, and it had nothing to do with the scenery.

Drake, in nothing except briefs, kneeled on one of the rocks with his eyes closed. His entire body shook, pouring sweat. He and Mercy had perfected their subconscious shields, and the last thing I wanted was for him to know I lurked in the woods, watching his struggle. So I concentrated on shielding myself, so he wouldn't sense me.

I wanted nothing more than to run to him, hold him and get him through whatever caused him pain. He groaned, gritting his teeth against the onslaught, fighting a battle I didn't understand.

"Do you know how long I've been searching for you?"

I cringed at the sound of Mercy's voice, ruining my peaceful day. She needed to turn around and leave him be —give him space to breathe.

"Go home, Mercy. You don't need to be here," Drake growled, shaking and sweating.

She stood on the bank beside him, shaking her head. "Why did you come all the way out here? Are you hiding from me?" she asked. "I could barely feel you from the Domicile."

He shook his head. "Trying to put distance between me and that damn cave."

His entire body tensed, and I realized the dragon had pushed forward, desperate to be free. My heart hurt to see him in such agony.

"How's it working for you?" She raised one brown, putting a hand on her hip.

"Don't be a smart ass," he snapped. "You need to leave."

"You want me to leave?"

"I want you safe. There's a difference," he choked out.

Mercy carefully hopped from rock to rock, making her way toward him. He sat on his heels, clenching his jaw at her proximity. "Mercy . . ."

"You need a distraction." She stood in front of him, and lifted her shirt over her head, throwing it on the bank. "Let me help."

"What are you doing?" he asked, narrowing his red eyes. "You're playing with fire right now, and I'm being completely literal."

"You would never hurt me, Drake. I don't think the

dragon would either." She slipped her shorts down her legs, standing in nothing except sheer panties.

"How do you know?"

His chest heaved, as his rage-filled eyes devoured every inch of her. I balled my fists at her gall, demanding complete attention over everything I'd ever wanted. I couldn't even enjoy a walk in the woods without her showing up, seducing a man who could barely stand.

She climbed into his lap, but he refused to touch her, gripping the rock as if it could keep him from reaching out. Mercy pushed his hair from his forehead, and smiled. She leaned forward, pressing her breasts against his chest and grazed his lips with her own. His body relaxed under her hands and he groaned.

"Have you been drinking?" he asked around her mouth.

"Just a little. Would you like to take advantage of me?"

Drake's hands wrapped around her, pulling her tight against him, then slowly drifted inside the seam of her panties, pushing them lower with his thumbs. "What kind of man would I be to take advantage of a tipsy woman?"

"I have no qualms about taking advantage of you," she replied, shoving her hand down the front of his shorts.

Drake hissed, throwing his head back.

I bit angrily on the side of my tongue, the taste of copper filling my mouth at the sight of him, completely relaxed in her presence.

Or, at least in her panties . . .

Drake turned, with Mercy still straddling him, and slid into the crystal lake, the dragon forgotten. I watched as he licked and bit her skin, tasting every inch of her he could reach, while he fumbled with his briefs. He pinned her up against the rock, and she gasped as he thrust forward, over and over, their groans echoing in the trees around me.

I didn't look away. I took in every detail with jealousy and rage, determined that it would be me—one day. I would be the one who satisfied him. He would hold me tight, eager to spread my legs and take everything I offered. Mercy had just upped the stakes in my plan to take everything away from her.

She didn't even know it yet.

...

I REACHED for the copper handle of the shower, turning off the faucet. How long had I been in there? No matter, I couldn't imagine anyone had noticed anyway. The day had been hellacious—consumed with the mental image of them naked together, not to mention all of the praise and gratefulness over my pathetic sister. For what? Drake was the one who killed Aunt Aadya, not her.

The memory of Aadya's blade against Mercy's neck brought a smile to my face. If it weren't for Drake, she would be dead. Why did everyone think she was the chosen one? Why did they owe her for their freedom? I paused, my hand still gripping the copper handle of the faucet. When was the last time someone praised me? Thanked me?

I shook off the thought, pretending I didn't care. Why would I? I'd never known any different. I pulled the thick white towel from the hook and quickly dried off, throwing it to the floor. The air cooled my hot skin as I padded across the sleek black tile, completely naked. I stood in front of the mirror, wiping a streak of condensation from the glass.

Sometimes I searched my features, wondering who I looked like the most. I'd always been curious as to why they gave me away if Mercy was the one in danger. Was I bait? Were they using me to throw Aadya off Mercy's trail? Did it matter? I combed through the tangles of my long red hair, catching a glimpse of someone behind me in the reflection of the mirror.

Thu Dang stepped into the doorway of the bathroom, his narrow black eyes meeting my gaze in the glass. I didn't bother covering myself, I had a feeling I wasn't his type anyway.

"Did you have a lovely afternoon with your sister?"

"Screw you," I snapped.

His tongue clicked against the roof of his mouth, as if I were a disobedient child. "Now Marley, I only wanted to check on you."

I smiled. "You say that like you care."

He leaned against the frame, crossing his arms in front of his chest. "You know I worry about you. You've been through so much—things your sister would never understand."

"But you do?" I raised one brow, turning to face him.

"Of course I do. You know you can always depend on me." His eyes traveled down the front of my body, more out of curiosity than desire. He reached for the robe hanging beside the door, then offered it to me. "I respect you, Marley."

Had anyone ever told me they respected me? Why would they? I pushed toward his mind, searching for the smallest crack to slither my way inside and discover his secrets. The man had a wall stronger than any I'd ever come across. Subconscious interferers were experts at shielding their thoughts.

"Why?" I slipped my arms into the robe, tying the belt across my thin waist. "Why do you even care?"

"This is my land, my people. I want what's best for them."

"And you don't think my sister is the answer?"

He shook his head, completely relaxed. "I don't. Most of the Regalians in our city have never been outside our enchanted land. They are ignorant of the real world and need someone to protect them. Someone who can show them the way, whether gentle or not-so-gentle." One side of his lip pulled up in amusement, as if the thought excited him.

I tilted my chin higher. "You think I'm that leader."

"I do. You're smart and cunning. You're harsh, but I believe you'll show mercy when necessary."

I turned toward the mirror once again, staring at my own reflection. Was I that person? Could I be strong enough? "They will never go for it. The Elders will never allow me to step into her shoes, even temporarily."

"Let me worry about the council. I've been around Seregalo long enough to have collected years of scandalous evidence on over half of them—at least enough to sway the votes your way."

I took a deep breath but didn't respond.

Thu Dang stepped up behind me, placing his hands on my shoulders. "Don't doubt yourself, Marley. You were born for a time such as this." He swept my wet hair off one shoulder, lovingly. "You remind me so much of Aadya."

I turned, mere inches from his face. "I'm not my aunt." Pushing him aside, I stormed into my room, sick of being compared to everyone around me. They would learn.

He smiled, walking into the bedroom behind me at a

leisurely pace. "No, you aren't. You're more determined. Less emotional. That is what makes you so powerful."

"And how do you expect me to dethrone a woman who owns the heart of not only Seregalo, but the only dragon we've seen in over a hundred years? You don't see the problem?"

"Marley, our people have only known her for a matter of months. They respect her out of fear. And honestly, they do not know any better."

"This is treason. We could be cast out for even thinking it."

Thu Dang grinned, then shrugged one shoulder.

"How?" I asked.

"Pardon?"

"I know you have a plan. You're cunning and sneaky. You've probably dreamt about this since the day Aadya died. How are we supposed to get Mercy out of the way?"

"With help."

"Help? Who would help us?" I asked.

He leaned forward, dropping his voice to a whisper. "I have friends."

"No, you don't."

"You got me there," he chuckled. "I have allies. Gifted allies."

I stepped forward, unimpressed by his so-called allies. "We're all gifted, Dang. What makes them so special?"

He pursed his thin lips, tilting his head from side to side as if contemplating how to answer. "Their gifts are a little more . . . how do I say this? Sinister. Yes, that's a good word."

I stepped back, surprised by his admission. "Dark magic."

"You say dark—I say resourceful." He grinned. "They're

all gifts, Marley. They've just learned to utilize an untapped power we haven't."

I paced the room, thinking through every available option. I wanted her gone, more than anyone, but I knew I couldn't do it alone. "Why would they help us?"

"They want something we have, and will do anything to have it."

I tilted my head, trying to figure out what he knew. "And that is?"

Thu Dang replied, "Not important right now. Just let me know when you're ready to bargain, and I'll make the arrangements."

I turned toward the window and stared at the gardens below. Vibrant pink and white peonies surrounded the property and covered the fields around the domicile. Such a beautiful scene in the midst of my wicked thoughts. What would his allies do to Mercy? Kill her? Did that bother me? Should it?

"How will I know?" I glanced over my shoulder, meeting his eyes. "How do I decide it's time?"

He took a step toward the door and grinned. "You'll know." He stopped before leaving my bedroom and nodded, gracefully. "You know where I am." Then the door shut so quietly, I barely heard it.

I fell back on the bed, exhaling air I didn't even know I held. Closing my eyes, I thought about the last conversation with my aunt before Drake killed her; the day Mercy would be mated to Felix and out of my life forever.

"You have to trust me, Marley. This is your birthright, not hers. She has spent her entire life being pampered and taken care of. What about you? Who's taken care of you?"

I shrugged. "It seems like she cares. I'm so confused. Are you sure? Maybe she's changed—maybe she isn't the person you think she is . . ."

Aadya laughed. "Don't be naive, sweet girl. If you only knew what she was like, the people she has sacrificed along the way. The way she has stolen Drake's heart, when it wasn't meant for her. If it wasn't for her, your parents would still be alive."

"What?" I stepped forward, shocked. "What are you talking about?"

"That's right. They died for her—both of them. Did any of them consider your well-being? No, they didn't. But who's been there for you? Who found you when you were thirteen and brought you here, teaching you everything your parents should have?"

"You," I admitted.

"That's right. You are much more capable than you know. Sometimes we just need someone to believe in us. I understand that more than anyone. My perfect sister took everything away from me, and I won't allow your sister to do the same. She already has your mother's dress, that wretched twit."

"My mother's dress?"

"She demanded it, Marley. She wants it for the mating ceremony today."

"I see." My fists balled at my sides.

"She has your mother's ring also, the one meant for you. It's too powerful for her—we have to get it back."

I fought the tears, determined to stay strong. "I'll take care of it."

Aadya stepped forward, smiling like a proud mother. She cupped the sides of my face and whispered, "You'll follow in my footsteps one day, Marley. I'll make sure of it. But you have to trust me." Her green eyes gleamed against her pale skin, her red lips plump.

I nodded. "I trust you."
She muttered, "Good girl."
"I won't let you down."

I OPENED MY EYES, staring up at the crystal chandelier above. "I won't let you down, Aunt Aadya. You have my word. Mercy will pay for what she's done."

CHAPTER
FOUR
MARLEY

I delayed going to Mercy and Drake's dinner as long as I could. The chatter from dinner guests drifted upstairs to where I'd hidden in my bedroom. The silk of my pale green dress clung to my skin as I stared at my porcelain complexion, so different from my sister.

Mercy favored our father, from what I could tell from his pictures. I wasn't fortunate enough to have any actual memories of him, but his olive skin and dark hair reminded me of Mercy. I hated everything about them—their similarities and nauseating bond they shared.

"Marley? Are you coming?" a voice called out from the door.

I turned, my spine stiffening at the sight of Mercy in a tight, black strapless gown. The smooth, flawless waves of her hair fell over one shoulder.

I hated her.

"I'm ready. You look beautiful," I forced out, as if the words were painful. "Has everyone arrived?"

"Almost. There are so many people I want you to meet." Mercy's eyes brightened.

I cringed at the thought of faking pleasantries. "Lovely."

She held her hand out for mine, and I gripped her palm without hesitation. Immediately, my skin began to crawl from the contact, and I wanted nothing more than to put distance between us. But I wouldn't give her a reason to suspect anything other than my love and devotion. We walked downstairs, hand-in-hand, into the main dining hall where a long rectangle table had been decorated with white cloths and silver china. Red roses covered every available surface and moonlight shined overhead through the glass paneled ceiling.

My eyes instantly found Drake, standing in the corner alone. The dark suit fit his muscular frame perfectly with a white dress shirt, unbuttoned at the neck. He looked good enough to eat. His dark gaze traveled around the room, as if studying everyone, always on guard.

If he only knew.

Mercy caught sight of Neela and Nora, and released my hand. I watched as she clung to her best friends, her sister forgotten—just as I knew I would be. Straightening my shoulders and pushing my breasts forward, I strolled toward the tall, dark dragon in the corner. Halfway across the room, he did a double-take, watching me prowl forward. His intense gaze focused, as if trying to determine my motive.

He couldn't read my mind, but he could sense my feelings. I imagined his arms pulling me against his chest, his wet lips traveling across my naked skin. I thought of sneaking to the adjoining room, where he would have his way with me—nothing except a wall between us and the party. Heat flooded my body at the image, and I took a shaky breath.

"What are you doing over here all alone?" I pursed my lips, stopping directly in front of him.

Drake cleared his throat, glancing around as if uncomfortable by my boldness. He nodded, politely. "Just waiting for Mercy. You look very nice, Marley."

My nails drifted along the bare skin of my chest, and I grinned. "Just nice? That's disappointing."

Drake's unique combination of dangerous and light-hearted chuckles excited me. "You know you look lovely, as always."

I leaned forward, whispering, "You should see what's underneath."

His eyes widened as a high-pitched voice called out from across the room. "There he is! Come give Hillie a hug!"

Drake quickly stepped away, toward a blonde-haired woman with blue eyes. I couldn't help but grin at how quickly he escaped my grasp, as if he were now safe.

Cute.

In a sea of elegant evening gowns, the woman named Hillie wore a bohemian-style ruffled dress, the color of tangerines. Clusters of gold and silver bracelets bunched around her wrists and her long hair had been piled haphazardly on top of her head. I hated how beautiful she was with very little effort.

But I pretty much hated everyone.

"Marley, this is your cousin, Hillie. Her and her husband, Quinn, live in Astriawell, not far from here."

My eyes widened. More family? "How lovely to meet you."

Hillie didn't step forward. She didn't wrap her arms around me, thrilled to meet me for the first time in her life. She scrutinized me. Her blue eyes focused as she tilted her head in deep thought. "And you," she mumbled.

I pushed forward, eager to delve into her shallow mind, but surprised when she shoved back, grinning at my effort. Apparently, subconscious interference ran in the family. Her wall didn't feel as strong as mine, but impressive considering she hadn't put forth much power. I realized quickly that Hillie only used her power for protection, like Mercy.

Ignorant—both of them.

"If you'll excuse me, I need to catch up with Mercy. I'm sure we'll be seeing each other again soon, Marley."

"I'm counting on it," I replied.

I spun to continue my assault on Drake, but he had slipped away to play the devoted boyfriend to my sister. Guests were scattered along the room, laughing and drinking as if there wasn't a care in the world. Nora snuggled tight against Caleb's side, and Neela stood proud beside Mercy with a glass of champagne in hand. Drake wrapped one arm around Mercy's waist, whispering something in her ear to make her skin flush.

Selfish, spoiled brats. Every one of them thought they'd had a hard life. Not every Regalian had a Fremont to learn from. Not every Regalian had someone to care for them or protect them. I hated them. I hated them for how easy their lives had been. I hated how they thought they were better than everyone else. I hated how they put Mercy on a pedestal, worshiping her every move.

Anger stirred inside of me at their happily-ever-after, as the bitter taste of jealousy coated my tongue. My confidence wavered as a flutter of unease caused me to take a step back. No. I refused to cower. I refused to allow anyone to make me feel beneath them ever again. Pain and rage fueled my determination as I focused on the intimate group of friends.

A young man, standing a few feet away, captured my attention. He clutched a tray of champagne glasses with shaky hands, and his greasy brown hair shimmered under the lights, parted to one side. I watched as his eyes filled with longing, completely smitten over my sister. I couldn't feel any power radiating from him at all, and that's when I knew—he would be the perfect target.

I walked nonchalantly across the room, focusing on his thoughts. His mind was a buffet of nerdy musings for the taking. It was so pathetic.

I WONDER if I should say hi. Would she notice me? Her boyfriend is standing there, but he doesn't look so tough. I mean, I could breathe fire. You know, if I didn't have asthma. Why did I take this job? There wasn't anything left for me besides the Custos and let's face it, I wouldn't last a week.

She's so beautiful when she laughs. If her dress was a little lower in front . . . man I bet she has a rack. I've never seen a naked woman before. I wonder if she likes cats. I mean all of mine are used to sleeping with me, but I can figure something out if she's, you know, allergic.

I COULDN'T CONTAIN the scowl. Was this guy for real? Shaking off the image of Mercy in bed with this loser, surrounded by cats, I fed him visions of what could be. Daydreams filled with true love in the midst of flowers and felines.

FROLICKING in the lush green lawn together, with wildflowers and kittens at their feet. The warm sun shines overhead as Mercy leans in and kisses him gently at first, then more forcefully. A

smidge of ice cream on the side of her lip that he swipes with his
thumb, while gazing into her hazel eyes. His fingertips graze the
smooth skin of her arms, all the way down to her fingertips he
kisses softly.

I GLANCED at the love-sick fool, standing in the corner behind Mercy. He grinned, enjoying the romantic vision he'd always dreamt of. Swaying back and forth, he succumbed to my every demand, my subconscious power easily controlling him. I whispered, "Go talk to her. Talk to Mercy."

He took a step forward, then faltered, as if deciding what to do.

"Go to Mercy," I demanded, more forcefully.

He slowly shuffled to where Mercy and Drake stood, greeting their guests. Just as another ungifted waitress entered the room, I delved into her mind, forcing her to spin toward her right, crashing into the asthmatic waiter with the glasses. Champagne flew through the air before anyone knew what had happened, covering the front of Mercy's dress. Everyone froze, unsure how to react.

Drake grabbed the young man by his shirt, slamming him against the wall.

"Drake, it was only an accident. I'm fine," Mercy whispered. Her eyes traveled nervously around the room as she cleared her throat. "Will you help me clean up?"

Drake never took his eyes off the guy, but slowly released him. He turned his head toward Mercy and nodded. I watched as he followed her out of the room, unable to keep the smirk off my face. I turned my head toward the heat of an angry gaze. Hillie stood, arms crossed in front of her chest, glaring as if she'd known exactly what I had done.

Maybe she did.

I raised one brow, then grinned. Without another word, I left the dining hall quite proud of myself. My black heels took one step at a time toward my bedroom, as I hummed a cheerful tune. The night could not have gone better. Dinner guests would be talking about the waiter's mishap all night instead of celebrating my sister's bliss.

But my happiness was short lived as I heard voices at the top of the stairs, a few doors away from my own.

Mercy's door sat cracked, where she stood in Drake's arms—his lips traveling down her neck. He gripped a handful of her hair, giving him better access to her skin. "You could have used your power to clean your dress."

She laughed. "But I wouldn't have a reason for you to take it off."

"I don't need a reason." Drake turned with her in his arms, pinning her against the wall. "Soon, you'll officially be mine."

Mercy placed her palms on his face, forcing him to look at her. "I've always been yours."

"I'll take you in every room of this house, anytime I want," he whispered. His hand traveled across her stomach, sliding up her chest to her neck. He tipped her chin toward his lips, then devoured her mouth.

Mercy moaned, running her fingers through his hair and pushing her chest forward. "Just take me. Right now, Drake. I don't care who hears us."

"Your guests will be expecting you to return," he whispered.

Through the split of her dress, she lifted one leg around his hip. "They can wait."

My temper seethed at the sight of them, passionate and filled with desire. Mercy didn't deserve him. Drake's strength and passion required a woman who could handle him, and I knew my sister would never truly satisfy his needs. She didn't know him the way I did. Their Allegato marks could be wrong—maybe they were mistaken.

I closed my eyes, pulling from the connection I'd made with the waitress downstairs. I sensed confusion and turmoil as I pushed her to come upstairs, but she did exactly as I wished. A couple of minutes later, small slippers padded up the stairs toward Mercy's room. I sneaked down the hall toward my room, leaving my door cracked to eavesdrop.

After two small taps on the door, I heard her meek voice call out. "Ma'am? Pardon me, but your guests are asking if you're planning to return."

"Oh? Thank you, Annie. I'll be right down."

The waitress quickly left, and I stood perfectly still, attempting to listen next door.

"You've got to be kidding me," Drake snapped. "You're coming to my room tonight after everyone goes to sleep."

"I can't. I feel cheap sneaking down the hall of the Domicile."

Drake leaned forward, whispering, "But not in the forest? Or under the waterfall? Or pinned up against your wall just now?"

She shoved against his chest. "I was caught up in the moment."

He chuckled. "Mercy, this isn't 1920. I don't think they expect us to wait until we're officially mated. Plus, that ship has sailed."

"Thanks a lot, Drake."

He laughed. "After our ceremony, I'll be sleeping beside

you every night, so I won't pressure you right now. Just know I'll be in my bed, half naked and lonely."

Mercy's giggles echoed down the hall as they turned toward the stairs. "That's a mental image that won't go away anytime soon. Thanks."

"Anytime," he answered, smacking her on the rear.

. . .

THE ABNORMALLY BRIGHT moonlight glowed through my bedroom window as I laid awake. But I guess nothing in Seregalo could be considered normal. Everything here had a polish the real world lacked, as if the sparkle gave a false sense of security and power.

The fools didn't realize no one was safe.

My mind wandered to Drake, alone in his room. I'd seen the way he looked at me, how his eyes roamed over my curves. If he wasn't so well trained in blocking, I'd hear the vulgar thoughts running through his head. He couldn't hide them from me. Drake had fallen in love with me long ago, he just didn't know it.

I shoved the blankets aside, jumping from the bed with resolve. I refused to wait around any longer. For whatever reason, he would be mated to my sister that week, and I had to tell him the truth. He needed to hear the words before it was too late.

I padded across the room in a thin nightgown that fell mid-thigh. Even though everyone had been asleep for hours, I turned the door handle slowly, peeking into the hallway. After closing my door behind me, I quietly walked down the long hallway toward the guest quarters, where Drake stayed until he and Mercy were mated. I didn't knock. After opening the door, I slipped through a small crack, closing the door behind me. I could barely make out his form in the middle of the bed, his breathing even and relaxed. I slid under the covers behind him, the heat from his body warming the silk sheets.

I hesitantly grazed my fingers across the bare skin of his back as he stirred.

"Mercy?"

I smiled as I leaned into him, kissing his shoulder. He knew it wasn't Mercy, but I'd play along. Running my tongue along his skin, I plastered myself against him, needing his warmth. Drake groaned, then rolled onto his back, pulling me on top of him. His hands slid up my thighs under the nightgown. He gripped my hips and thrust against me, showing me exactly how he felt about me surprising him in bed.

I leaned forward, my hair falling around my face. He slid his hand up my spine and as soon as his lips touched mine, I melted.

Drake froze.

I continued nipping at his lips, unable to get close enough, but he didn't move. All at once, Drake sat up, reaching for the bedside lamp. When the orange glow lit the room, he gasped.

"Marley?" he asked. "What are you doing in my room?"

I smiled, leaning down to kiss him once more. "Like you didn't know."

Drake turned his head, refusing my advances. "I didn't, I swear!" He jumped from the bed, pacing his bedroom floor in nothing except briefs. "I'm marrying your sister! How could you do this to her?"

"This isn't about Mercy, Drake. I know how you really feel, and I wanted to let you know I feel the same way before it's too late!"

"How I feel? What are you talking about?"

I took a deep breath, determined to be honest. Did I even remember the last time I showed vulnerability to another? "We love each other, you just need to let me show you! I shouldn't have to hide it anymore."

He took a step back, surprised. "Marley, you are a beautiful woman, but I'm with your sister. I'm meant to be with her—mated to her."

"Did she tell you that? How do you know she isn't trapping you?" I stepped forward, attempting to undo the damage Mercy had caused. "You want me, I know you do!"

Drake stepped forward, cupping my face. "I love her. It's always been her. That will never change, do you understand?"

Something in his eyes turned my stomach. She'd gotten to him—heart and soul. Made him believe that no one else could ever compare to her. My eyes burned from unshed tears as I stepped away. The last tendril of compassion inside of me snapped as resentment filled my heart. I stepped forward to kiss him. He put his hand on my shoulder, holding me in place.

"I think you need to go back to your room."

I bit my bottom lip, my gaze traveling below his waist. "Are you sure?"

Drake nodded, completely unphased. "Positive."

I slowly turned toward the door, but looked over my shoulder before leaving. "If you change your mind, you know where I am."

He didn't respond.

When I shut the door behind me, I closed my eyes and

breathed through pent-up anger. I knew he loved me, but I couldn't figure out why he fought it. Had she brainwashed him into believing he truly loved her? I turned, eager to leave the humiliation behind. I paused at the sight of Mercy standing frozen at the end of the hallway. Her gaze traveled down my body in the short night gown, then cut toward Drake's door.

Deciding to use the situation to my advantage, I adjusted the front of my nightgown and smirked. As I passed her on the way to my room, I brushed against her shoulder. "Goodnight, Mercy."

I didn't make it far. Mercy's nails clawed the back of my scalp as she gripped a handful of my hair, and began dragging me down the hall, away from Drake's room. I didn't scream or shout, the last thing I wanted was for Drake to run out there and witness our cat fight. No—this was between us.

"I've had all I can stand, Marley. I've tried with you, honestly I have, but now you've gone too far," she muttered through clenched teeth.

Anger clouded her judgment and before she knew it, I slipped easily inside her mind, showing her visions of Drake kissing me, touching me, loving me. Mercy froze, slowly turning to look down at me with shocked eyes.

I wanted to hurt her, to plant the obscene amount of jealousy and bitterness I walked around with everyday. I grinned. "Oh, I'm sorry. Still thinking about our night together."

She released me to get a better grip on my hair, and I kicked my foot up, hitting her in the stomach, knocking her back several feet. She gripped the railing of the overlook, and the wood cracked under her hold.

Somebody's angry.

"If you were anyone besides my sister, you'd be dead right now," she growled, shaking.

She had completely blocked her subconscious after that last vision, so I jumped to my feet and smacked her across the face as hard as I could, swinging her head to the side.

Damn, that felt good.

Mercy stood, with her hair hanging in front of her face, breathing hard. I felt her restraint, the power it took for her to control herself.

All at once, the door to my right opened and Neela squinted, as if trying to focus through the remnants of sleep. "What is going on?"

Mercy slowly turned to face me. "Just working things out."

That's never going to happen.

"I can see that," Neela muttered.

All of the resentment I held inside rushed forward. I didn't care that she was more powerful, I wanted to ease into her mind and plant doubt about her relationship with Drake. "Tell me," I teased. "Is he always so aggressive?"

Mercy clenched her teeth, and before I knew it, she gripped me by the throat and held me in mid-air. I kicked, struggling to take a breath as her shoulders heaved from the effort it took to not break my neck. I thought I would mentally torment her, shock her into questioning her Allegato mark. I didn't expect this level of violence—not from her.

Even I was smart enough to know when I'd pushed her too far.

"Mercy," Neela whispered. "That's enough."

Mercy tilted her head to the side. "Is it?" She pulled me closer, her bright hazel eyes boring into mine. The last thing I needed to do was show my fear, and I knew that was exactly what she wanted. All at once, she threw me over the railing, and my body fell through the air toward the marble floor of the Domicile below.

"Mercy!" Neela gasped.

The air rushed around me as Mercy leaned against the railing, watching me fall to my death. I thought she would panic, use her gifts to stop me midway, but she didn't.

She's going to kill me.

Mercy waited until I was mere inches from the floor—from cracking my skull—to throw her hand out and freeze my body in mid-air. I breathed a sigh of relief as she gently turned counterclockwise, and I slowly drifted up through the air, her gaze piercing my own as she turned back time.

Mercy brought me directly in front of her, pausing, as if wanting me to understand how easy it would be for her to kill me. "I think I've made myself clear."

I grinned, unwilling to admit defeat, even in my vulnerable position.

She threw my body back onto the floor of the hall and turned to leave, not so much as another word.

Neela glanced down with wide eyes. "You have a death wish?"

I pushed to my feet in front of her. "Maybe you should mind your business."

I sauntered to my room, like I didn't just have my ass handed to me. I hid the anger and hate, determined to appear unaffected until the door slammed behind me. I slid to the floor, breathing through the panic and embarrassment of what had just happened.

She had taken everything from me. Now it was my turn. I subconsciously reached out for Thu Dang, knowing he wouldn't block me from getting through. I knew he would be waiting for me.

"It's time," I mentally whispered. "I'm ready."

. . .

I STAYED HIDDEN from sight the next day. I didn't want an uncomfortable run-in with Mercy, one that ended in conversations about feelings and family. I would apologize, and she would accept, ending in an awkward embrace.

I don't have time for that shit.

Which is why I asked for my meals to be brought to my room, waiting out the hours until nightfall—until Thu Dang and I could sneak away to meet his allies.

There should have been a smidge of guilt, a small sliver of doubt, but there wasn't. There was nothing left for Mercy or her perfect group of friends. As for Drake, he would soon realize his true feelings, and I would be there waiting when that day came.

Just like always, the brightly lit stars above surrounded the full moon, perfectly visible in front of the pitch black backdrop of the Seregalo night sky. I followed Thu Dang for several silent miles before arriving at a pitiful excuse of a cottage, especially considering everyone else's home had been kept pristine.

This house was in shambles, purposely left to decay in a perfect world, as if it were a reflection of the deteriorating souls inside. Not really a crowd I pictured Thu Dang having drinks with on weekends.

He checked the streets to make sure we hadn't been followed, then paused when his eyes fell on me. "Wipe that disgusted look off your face. Try to remember we need their help," he snapped.

"How am I supposed to do that? I'm always disgusted."

He turned to knock on the door, his pointy eyebrows raised, appearing more prominent than usual. "Try to be a good actress then."

I hated being told what to do.

The rotting door squeaked under the strain of being moved, and a beady blue eye peeked through the crack, cautiously. "Who's there?"

"Thu Dang. I believe you are expecting me."

A gruff voice huffed on the other side. "You're late."

"Late?" He stood up straight, defensive. "I believe I'm precisely on time, Ma'am."

"If you're not early, you're late." Her visible eye focused on him, awaiting his response.

He glared at the crotchety woman.

I leaned forward to whisper, "Wipe that look off your face, Dang. We need their help, remember?"

After regaining his composure, he nodded. "My apologies. May we come in?"

"Get outta the doorway, Creeky! You'll draw the neighbors' attention again!"

"Me? I'm not the one who ran down the street naked!"

A high-pitched voice snickered. "Good times."

The door swung open and the unpleasant odor of cheap perfume and sage assaulted my nose. A woman with frizzy blonde hair shoved the other out of the way, then swung her arm out in a dramatic welcome gesture. Average build, she wore a brightly colored mumu, and one foam roller hung haphazardly in the back of her hair. Her hazel eyes brightened at the sight of me, as if I had the answer to all of her problems.

I wouldn't know where to start with this one.

"Creeky, fetch our guests some tea."

Creeky, a busty woman with silver hair, threw one hand on her hip and yelled, "Don't be tellin' me what to do!" She pulled the fabric of her dress higher to keep from exposing her nipples. She spun toward us with a toothy grin. "Would either of you like a cup of tea?"

I glanced at Dang, afraid to answer.

"That would be lovely, thank you," he answered.

"I brew it fresh daily," Creeky announced, smiling. "Ballock pine or Gizzard lemongrass?"

"Ah . . ." Jules threw her hand over her chest and grinned. "Ballock pine is my favorite. The combination of salt and earth leaves a wonderful taste in your mouth. She has a gift, you know."

I shook my head, confused. "I'm sorry, Ballock?"

Creeky nodded. "Gotta get your protein, right? Nothing more flavorful than pig testicles. Just wait until you try it!" She spun toward the kitchen without another word.

No way in hell would I be drinking that tea. Balls or no balls.

"Please, make yourself at home." Jules danced toward a dimly lit room with a couple of orange and brown floral sofas, surrounding a round, black marble table. Sheer orange, tasseled cloths were draped over lamps, and the appalling scent of burning herbs wafted through the air.

I sat, my gaze traveling to the top of the coffee table where a variety of cards, marked with foreign symbols, laid from one end to the other. A small bowl of black crystal powder sat untouched, as if waiting for the opportunity to release its sinister sorcery.

Shockingly, I was taken aback. I knew myself to be as dark as any treacherous Regalian alive, at least since Aadya had been killed. But a tremor of fear slithered up my spine at what we were meddling with. I leaned toward Thu Dang and whispered, "Are you sure about this?"

"Creeky! Get your ass in here!"

"Shut your face, Jules! You can't rush perfection!"

Jules, the blonde in the mumu, grinned while awkwardly sitting on the sofa across from us. Her wide eyes cut from me to Thu Dang, as if unable to begin polite conversation. She opened her mouth to speak, then closed it. Her observant gaze put me on edge, and I found myself wanting to back out of this insane plan.

"No. You mustn't," Creeky called out from the doorway, panicked. Her eyes bore into mine while holding a tray of glass cylinders. "You're here for a reason, Ms. Monroe. Don't let fear keep you from what's rightfully yours."

I gasped. Had anyone ever been able to penetrate my mind before? I felt violated and weak. "How did you do that?"

Creeky sat the wretched tea in front of me, but I refused to acknowledge it. She turned to sit beside me on the sofa, nearly knocking me in the head with her breasts. "I can do so much more," she whispered. "Would you like to learn?"

"Yes," Jules hissed. "We can teach you."

I swallowed, slightly nervous. "I want you to get someone out of my way. Someone who has taken every-thing from me."

"Sisters are twits, aren't they?" Jules scowled toward Creeky. "I'd get rid of her in a heartbeat if I could." She leaned forward, as if someone would hear. "I tried once, you know."

"Tried? You buried me alive in the backyard! Took me five hours to dig out, it did!"

Jules groaned, as if sick of hearing the story. "You're alive, aren't you?"

Creeky growled. "I'd stay awake tonight if I were you."

"Ladies, if I may," Thu Dang interrupted. "What exactly can you do for us?"

Creeky swiped a glass of tea, turning it up like a shot. "What is it you want? Dead? Kidnapped? Imprisoned? We can do it all, you know. Of course, the chance of being charged with treason does up the cost."

"Mercy is the most powerful Regalian to have ever been born. How exactly do you plan to take her down?" I asked.

Jules smiled. "We have an idea."

"What are we talking about?" I asked.

Creeky grew serious. "There is a land of torture and despair, between heaven and earth. A place where she won't exist mentally or physically for us."

I shook my head, confused. "She will disappear?"

Thu Dang responded. "Can that be done?"

"There isn't anything we can't do," Jules spat. "Don't doubt us, Mr. Dang. We won't hear of it."

"But this isn't normal Regalian power, is it? You pull from forbidden magic. You and your sister go against everything we were taught. Isn't that right?" I asked.

Creeky shrugged, nodding her head in agreement. "Pretty much, yes. Normal is boring, sweet girl. If you want something, you gotta play dirty." She smiled as if pleased about something. "And you do want something—or someone. Isn't that right? Yes, the dragon is appealing." She whispered, "I, myself, like a bad boy."

Jules cackled. "Let's face it, you like them all."

"That's beside the point. Now, Marley, this isn't a difficult situation. We cast a spell on Creeky's special tea, and you slip it to your dear sister. Simple as that."

I raised one brow. "But you want something in return. Isn't that right?"

Jules wrinkled her nose. "Maybe a little something. Nothing you're going to miss, I promise."

"Quite right," Creeky agreed. "You're getting a bargain, sweetheart."

Thu Dang hissed, "Can we get on with this?"

Creekly pushed her breasts forward. "I like a man who takes charge." After batting her eyes for several awkward seconds, I cleared my throat.

"Anyway," Jules continued. "We'll get Mercy out of the way, you will slip into her shoes without hesitation. Of course, until someone stronger is called forth."

"Excuse me?" Marley asked.

Jules laughed. "The universe doesn't allow just anyone to lead Seregalo. A higher power will eventually be born, you must know that. We can put you there, but it's up to you to figure out how to keep it."

I honestly hadn't thought of that, but I wouldn't admit it. "And you want?"

Venom laced Creeky's voice as it shook with dark need. "The boy. We want the boy."

I tilted my head, confused. "What boy?"

Thu Dang replied. "The boy from the dungeon. Ren. He's always seemed quite . . . different."

"Yes. Different," she responded. Creekly fought to hide the gleam in her eyes, but I could see the desire to possess the child. "Do we have a deal?"

"I take over as the leader of Seregalo. In return, I hand the boy over to you?"

Jules nodded.

"What do you want with him?" I asked.

"He has powers we don't see very often." Jules clasped her hands in front of her chest, and smiled. "That's all."

It didn't reassure me—at all.

"You don't think we would ever harm a child, do you?" She glanced toward Creeky who began shaking her head. "Never . . ."

I took a deep breath. Was there another option? I didn't see one. If I wanted Mercy out of my way—if I planned to take back my life, I had to do this. My shaky voice called out, "I agree to your terms."

Jules and Creeky stood, slightly off kilter, and grinned. Then they bowed, ungracefully. "All hail, Queen Marley."

CHAPTER
FIVE
DRAKE

"Mercy is shielding herself," I mumbled to myself. It was the only explanation. I swear I'd been through every single room of the Domicile, and every time I sense her, she disappears once again.

My body tensed with anxiety at the thought of something looming over our wedding day.

I found myself once again in the old library on the second floor. I loved the scent of the old leather-bound books, filled with Regalian history and family trees. On more than one occasion, I sat in this very room when I couldn't sleep, reading about my family history—searching for guidance so hopefully I wouldn't lose my sanity to the dragon within.

Just like my grandfather had done . . .

Looking back, I think my father knew all along. There were times when my temper had gotten out of hand, and he would take me for long walks to cool off. My mother would watch me with sympathetic eyes, as if she could sense it. They all knew I was different.

Maybe that's why Asher hated me.

I wanted to hate him. There were times I wish I had killed him myself, especially when it concerned Mercy. But at the end of the day, the memory of us playing baseball together as children drifted back and I missed the bond we had before everything went to hell—before Aadya had my parents killed.

I missed them so much. Especially now, in this crucial time in my life when I felt as though a wrong decision could cause me to spiral out of control. Mercy grounded me, she kept me calm, which is why I needed to see her.

"Drake? What are you doing in here?"

I turned at the sweet voice, calling out from the doorway. Nora smiled, the pink flush of her cheeks permanent since Caleb's presence in her life. "I've been looking for Mercy, but I found myself wandering in here. Something about this room always seems to call out to me when I'm struggling."

"Struggling?" Her brows furrowed as she walked into the room. "With what?"

I tilted my head back and exhaled. "Nothing. Everything."

She sat in the small armchair by the window, obviously not in any hurry to rush out of the room. This was Nora's way of telling me she had time for me, something she did often when she wanted to help.

She told me once that emotional interference was the weakest gift a Regalian could possess, and she yearned to feel useful, as if she had a purpose in the midst of such powerful friends. She had no idea how much we needed her. Her need to feel helpful is what pushed me to open up.

"I want to be there for Mercy, but I don't know how. Regalians are terrified of me, and if I'm being honest—"

She leaned forward, her eyes full of pity I never wanted. "What? Tell me."

"I'm scared, too. I don't blame them. Turning my control over to something that strong and dominating is terrifying. What if I somehow lose myself and never return? What if I kill someone else?"

She shook her head. "You won't."

"How do you know? I have before."

"To save our lives! Plus, it's one of the rarest gifts in the world, Drake. I can't see anyone carrying this power that isn't completely in control over it. It was given to you for a reason."

"How do I trust that? There is nothing the dragon wants more than to be free, Nora. It's there everyday, every hour, reminding me that my body is not my own."

"It's not. I think once you accept that, and learn to coexist, your life will get easier."

I took a deep breath, wishing it was that easy.

"You are not your grandfather, Drake."

I glanced up, shocked. How did she know?

"You aren't the only one who reads, you know. Maybe part of his unstable history is because he drove himself mad trying to control it. Sound familiar?"

I chuckled. "Giving it to me straight today, aren't you?"

She asked, "What else is on your mind?"

I cut my eyes toward her direction. "What isn't?"

"You are marrying the love of your life today, it sounds as though you need some perspective," she teased.

"As long as I can keep her sister out of my bed," I mumbled to myself.

"What was that?"

I sat down in the chair beside her. "Nothing. Just grumbling, I guess. Have you seen Mercy today?"

"No, I haven't. But you aren't supposed to see her before the ceremony anyway. It's bad luck, remember?"

"I'll take my chances, Nora. I might relax if I could just talk to her."

"Wanna go to the pub? A beer might make you feel better."

I chuckled, shaking my head. "You don't even like beer."

"I'm trying to help and Colton isn't here. I'd do it for you," she admitted, completely serious.

"As much as I appreciate the thought, I think I'll pass."

She stood, wrapping her arms around me for a quick hug. Warmth from her embrace seeped into my chest, relaxing me from the inside out. I smiled.

"Who needs a beer when I have you?"

"I know, right?" She walked to the door, but stopped before leaving me to my thoughts. "You're stronger than you think you are."

"I hope you're right."

CHAPTER
SIX
MERCY

"Mercy? Drake is looking for you. I told him he couldn't see the bride before the wedding, but you know how he can be."

I didn't have to turn around to see who it was. Nora's sweet presence reached out, calming the hurt and anxiety in my heart. I remember the first time we met at Fremont, how a mere hug could evoke peace into my troubled mind. All at once, frail arms wrapped around me from behind and I grinned.

"You always know what I need," I mumbled.

"Drake can sense you—he'll find you eventually."

"That's why I keep moving," I replied. "I need to be alone. I've managed to avoid him for the past two days."

Nora took a deep breath. "Wanna talk about it?"

I shook my head. "I think I'd rather wallow in it for a bit longer." The mountainside loomed over the other side of the river, a tall rock formation creating a wall around the Domicile.

Nora stepped back and sighed. "I've never met anyone who loves to wallow more than you."

Her pale blonde hair framed her pretty face, light blue eyes sparkling. Her pink cheeks radiated a delightful glow I'd never noticed before. "Love looks good on you, Nora."

She smiled. "It feels nice to be loved. I've never had that before, you know. Caleb is kind and thoughtful, more than I deserve."

"Do you have a date set for the ceremony?"

She shook her head. "I wouldn't take away from your day, you know that. We'll plan it when things calm down."

"I'm happy for you." I tried to smile, but I knew it didn't reach my eyes.

"And you," she added. "You're getting married today, remember? We have to celebrate!"

I turned away from Nora, unable to share her enthusiasm. Her small hand gripped my arm, pulling me back around. "Talk."

"I caught Marley sneaking out of Drake's room in the middle of the night—in her nightgown."

Nora froze, as if unsure I said what she thought I said. "What?"

I cringed at the look on her face. I knew exactly what she must have felt in that moment. Disbelief. Confusion. Doubt. I knew it all too well, because I had sifted through every emotion within the last twenty-four hours. "Gotta be a misunderstanding, right?" I asked.

She bit the side of her lip, thinking. "Are you certain it was his room?"

I nodded. "She didn't seem upset about getting caught, but hopefully she saw the error of her ways."

"Meaning?"

I sighed. "I may have lost it . . . a little."

I jerked my head up when I heard her giggle.

"A little?"

"I lost my shit, Nora," I admitted. "I think you know that."

"He wouldn't do that to you, Mercy. You are his mate, and his body is biologically wired to only want you."

"I know that, but . . ."

"But what?" she asked.

"What if he's different? What if dragons have harems or something?"

She laughed. "Don't be ridiculous. I'm sure there is a perfectly reasonable explanation, but you'll never know until you ask."

"Ask if he needs more than one woman in his bed? Hardly . . ."

Nora grinned. "Why would he? He has said more than once that you are more than he can handle," She joked.

"He better remember that." I cut my eyes to the side and grinned. "I'm not sure I've ever been that angry before. I've been jealous, but I could have killed her. I might have if Neela hadn't walked out of her room."

"Don't be so hard on yourself. Drake would kill someone in a heartbeat if the shoe was on the other foot."

I nodded. "You're right, thanks for the reminder."

She pushed my hair from my face and smiled. "I'm always here, but you have to let me in. Stop making my job as your friend so damn difficult."

I laughed. "I'll do my best."

"Ms. Monroe?"

I turned toward the double doors of the Domicile where a Custos guard stood. "Yes?"

He shuffled from one foot to another, nervous. I could feel anxiety bubbling up inside of him, as if I would lash out at any moment. Did they not know me at all?

He nervously choked out, "You have a visitor."

"I'll be right in, thank you." My eyes met Nora's and I shook my head. "Poor guard. I thought he was going to wet his pants."

She laughed. "What are they scared of?"

I glanced out over the mountainside and sighed. "Change. They don't know me, Nora. They aren't sure what I'll do. I can sense their fear."

"They'll warm up, just give them time. Go relax, you have a big day ahead of you."

I turned toward the Domicile, "Meet me at the altar?" I asked.

Nora smiled, but I could sense her worry over my situation. "Wouldn't miss it for the world."

I turned, hating I didn't have more time for Nora and Neela. I knew they understood, but their support was vital, and I knew it would do me good to talk things out with them. Everyone needed someone, and my circle of trust was considerably small.

"Hey Mercy?" Nora called out.

I looked over my shoulder with raised brows.

"There's a lot of jealousy coming from Marley. I can feel it—daily. Don't let things cloud your judgment when it comes to Drake. You *know* him. Plus, he really needs you right now."

I nodded, knowing she was right, then hurried through the doors, my shoes clacking loudly on the sleek black tiles. Nora was right, but my own brand of jealousy refused to relent. Maybe if I had a few minutes to think, some quiet time to sort through my thoughts, things would make sense. I bounced from meeting to meeting, without a lull in the day.

I met most of my visitors in the small study on the main floor. Surrounding myself with family pictures and heirlooms brought comfort, almost a feeling of unconditional love and support. I froze in the hallway as a presence I knew all too well stepped behind me.

"You're a hard woman to track down."

I spun, meeting Drake's eyes. I wanted to jump into his arms and slap him at the same time. I knew I wasn't being reasonable, but my heart and mind were at odds. "I'm on my way to the study, can I catch up with you later?"

"Later?" He asked. "Like at the altar?"

The frustration Nora had relieved began to resurface. "I'm sorry, but I've just needed some space, Drake."

"What's going on with you?"

Me? What's going on with me?

"I have a lot on my mind. If you'll excuse me . . ." I spun as he gripped my arm, jerking me around to face him. I wanted to burn his hand, take the feeling from his limbs, anything to hurt him the way Marley did me. But I didn't. We all had to grow up eventually, right?

"Did you visit Ren? If the boy is having issues, I don't mind working with him. You know that." He continued, "I want to help if you'll let me."

"No—I mean, yes he's having issues, but that's not it." I couldn't think straight around this man. Since the day we met I have acted like a prepubescent, lovesick puppy. Could he smell my pheromones? Oh Jesus, I'd never thought of that.

"Talk to me," he pleaded.

The pull we'd grown accustomed to intensified by our proximity. He stepped forward and my gaze fell to his lips, inches from mine. "Why don't you talk to me about Marley?"

His brow furrowed in confusion. "Marley? I don't want to talk about her."

"You sure there's nothing you want to tell me?"

Drake glanced down the hallway to ensure we were alone, then pulled me to a dark corner out of the way. "What's going on?"

My eyes burned as I fought tears, and I hated how my bottom lip quivered. "I saw her coming out of your room."

Drake didn't budge. He didn't give anything away, as if blocking all emotion from me. "It isn't what it looked like."

"She made it look pretty bad."

He took a deep breath and looked away from my eyes.

The fact that he didn't want to talk about it angered me further. I turned to leave, frustrated.

His grip on my arm tightened. "I thought it was you, Mercy. She climbed into my bed and kissed me. I immediately realized it wasn't you, and kicked her out."

"You should have told me."

"You should have more faith in the man you're going to spend the rest of your life with."

Jealousy got the better of me. "Maybe I should." I couldn't even look him in the eyes when I said the words, because I knew none of it was true. I didn't doubt him at all.

Drake stepped forward and my back hit the wall. His lips hovered less than an inch from mine. He placed his hands on the wall, caging me in and the muscles in his arms flexed from his restraint. "Tell me you don't trust me."

He pressed against me, overwhelming me with his scent and warmth. I took a deep breath, trying to refrain from moving forward just enough to feel his lips on mine. My body craved him. I opened my mouth, then closed it, knowing I could never truthfully say the words. He knew I trusted him completely.

Drake leaned back. "That's what I thought."

I slammed my hands against his chest. "You should have told me," I snapped.

"You're trying to develop a relationship with her. I don't want to come between you."

I closed my eyes, attempting to process his words. "You swear you didn't go further?"

"I hate that you even have to ask me that."

"But you wanted to," I added. At that moment, I'd never felt more glutton for punishment. My heightened emotions were getting the better of me, and I chalked it up to hormones and wedding stress.

"I did when I thought it was you. Things quickly . . . declined after I realized who was in my bed." He placed his hands on my face, forcing me to look at him. "I love you. I'm marrying you. I don't know what Marley was thinking or what she's been through, but something is off. I get a sense of attachment from her, and I don't have a clue where it's coming from."

Emotions flooded my heart. Drake had never let me down before, but the woman I wanted to understand and love, my sister, crawled into my boyfriend's bed in the middle of the night. "I need to get going. I have an appointment." I turned away, trying not to cry over a situation I knew wasn't his fault.

Halfway down the hall, his dark voice rang out. "I'm going to marry you."

I paused before walking into the study, and looked over my shoulder. Exhaustion filled his dark eyes and a rare moment of vulnerability escaped. My body warmed and the fragrant scent of roses filled the hall. Drake knew what he was doing to me. "I have to go."

I opened the door to the study and quickly closed it behind me. I placed my palm on the heavy door, closing my eyes—fighting the need to run back to him. My emotions bounced from wanting to help Marley to jerking her red hair out by the root. I hated how much I cared for her.

"Those emotions are intense. Some things never change."

My head popped up. I slowly turned, not quite believing he was there. "You came."

"Did you think I'd miss the chance to walk you down the aisle?"

I bolted across the room into Fitz's arms. The familiar scent of aftershave and old leather books surrounded me, comforting me. All the emotion, the stress of portraying the confident woman I didn't feel, collapsed in his presence.

"You have no idea what this means to me."

"I promised your father I'd always be there for you, Mercy. It's an honor." He leaned back, studying my face. "Wanna tell me what that was about?"

"Nothing like a little wedding drama, right?"

He smiled, the wrinkles around his eyes showing his age. "You aren't a drama kind of girl—never have been."

I sighed, tight-lipped. "Apparently my sister is."

He frowned. "I was hoping that wasn't the case, but I'd be lying if I said I'm surprised. You forget how many years she's lived with Aadya."

My mouth fell open in shock. "As a hostage."

He tilted his head to the side, thoughtfully. "Was she?"

"Fitz, you didn't see her that day. She was desperate to get away from Aadya."

He pulled his pants leg up slightly before sitting on the sofa. "Don't let your emotions blind you. I know you crave this bond with her, but I wouldn't let my guard down if I were you," He sighed. "There's a lot at stake."

I sat beside him, my posture slumped and defeated. "I

just wanted to help her. I don't know what she's been through, but I'm trying to be understanding. Well, I was until she pushed me too far. I swear she craves attention."

"From your fiancé, I'm guessing?"

"As much as I appreciate these talks, let's not go there." I pursed my lips. "I have another favor to ask you."

He tilted his head. "You have my attention."

"There's a boy who needs help. I thought if he had the support of a nice family, a loving home, his life would be different. I thought he would thrive. I've never seen anything like it, Fitz. Something dark is inside of him, something sinister."

"What of his parents?"

I shook my head. "I have no idea. I found him locked in the dungeon on my first day at the Domicile. Josiah took him to the Hughes family, but recently they've grown nervous to be around him. Fitz, I swear he's aged years in a matter of months."

"Literally?"

I nodded.

Fitz leaned forward, resting his elbows on his knees, his hands clasped. He stared intently at the floor for several seconds, as if processing everything I'd said. "I'll take a look, see if I can come up with anything. He sounds extremely repressed, dangerously so."

"I'm afraid whatever damage Aadya has done is irreversible. What if we can't help him? I can't lock him back up. I won't."

"Have you spoken to anyone else about him?"

"Just Isolette. Ren was such a sweet kid, Fitz. I don't know what happened."

"Ren?"

I nodded. "After Ren saved my life, I named the boy after him."

"This is a lot to handle in your first few months, Mercy."

My eyes once again filled with tears. "Why do you think I called you?"

He wrapped his arms around me, kissing the top of my head. "Let's get you married first. How does that sound? One step at a time."

"You think I'm taking on too much?"

"Don't you always? You can't take care of everyone. Marley is an adult. You're doing the best you can with her, but she isn't your priority. As far as Ren goes, I'll visit him tomorrow and see what I can come up with. Focus on your ceremony this evening." Fitz stood to leave. "Go get your hair and nails done—things girls do on their wedding day."

I scowled. "It's like you don't know me at all."

. . .

I couldn't figure out why I had agreed to this. We could have eloped, just an intimate ceremony without an audience. That's what I really wanted, right? I sat on the end of my bed, a white silk robe wrapped tightly around my waist. My feet bounced against the tile floor, anxiously. I listened throughout the house, a rare action on my part.

I could hear Josiah and Fitz in the library, discussing the politics of Seregalo, the chef yelling at her staff over the lack of prep work the previous day, and Neela discussing the flower arrangements with the coordinator. It all seemed a bit over the top for someone who didn't want a big event.

I only needed Drake.

"I've seen that look before, hun." Hillie called out from the door. "You need a drink." She shut the door behind her, then sat her bag beside me on the bed. "Or something stronger. I keep brownies in here for emergencies."

My eyes widened. That's all I needed—to get high before I said my vows. "That's very thoughtful of you, but I think I'm good."

She unwrapped the cellophane from the square of chocolate and took a large bite. "Suit yourself."

"How's Quinn?" I asked.

"Sexy as ever. That man is a beast I tell you." Her eyes glazed over at the mention of her larger than average Irish mate. "He's out of town on business, but will be back next week." She shivered at the thought. "I can't wait to get ahold of him."

Like usual, it was more than I needed to know.

She nudged my arm. "What's going on with you, cuz? You aren't the glowing bride I thought you'd be."

I stood, pacing the room. "I don't know, Hillie. Something is off. It doesn't feel right. It has to be nerves, right?"

"Sugar, I told you to eat the brownie. It would've helped."

Groaning, I collapsed on the bed. "What is wrong with me? For the first time in my life, I have everything I could want. Why do I feel unsettled? Why can't my sister act normal instead of competing with me?"

I'd never seen Hillie's eyes darken at the mention of another before. She embraced everyone—loved everyone she came in contact with.

"What?" I asked. "Be honest."

"You know I'm not one to gossip, but I think you should watch that one, Mercy. She has the eyes of a snake."

"What do you mean?" I asked.

"Focused and sly. Determined to get what she wants, no matter the costs. You know I don't delve into the minds of others very often, but I tried with her. That wall was strategically placed, as if she were hiding something. If I pushed hard enough I could get through, but it takes a lot for me to violate someone that way."

"I get it. I'm not gonna lie, I'd considered raiding her thoughts as well. I don't know what to do about her, Hillie. My parents would expect me to take care of her. I'm not sure I have the patience."

"These things take time, and today is not the day to figure everything out. We do need to talk about your hair. Time is running out."

"What's wrong with it? Drake likes it down."

"That's how you plan on wearing it? All wild and wavy?"

I nodded, feeling close to tears. "Does it look bad?"

"Girl, we gotta get some class up in this joint. Some intricate braids and sparkle. Where's your eyeshadow? Your bling? Where is your village?"

"I asked Neela and Nora for some alone time."

"Am I interrupting?" Icy peaked her head through the crack in the door. "I can come back."

"See if you can talk some sense into this girl, Icy. I need to get dressed anyway." Hillie wrapped her arms around me and smiled. "See you down there."

After Hillie left, Icy stood on shaky legs, staring at me. I waited several seconds, but she stayed silent. "Are you here to lecture me on my lack of style?"

"I'm here to tell you that I'm proud of you. I'm honored to be your friend and thankful for our quiet moments together. I hope Drake knows he'll have to share you."

I laughed. "Don't worry, it's in my vows."

"You're not dressed," she observed.

"I know. I've been out of sorts today."

Icy hobbled forward on her cane, sitting beside me on the bed. She reached over, gripping my hand, her thumb swiping over the top of my mother's ring. "Will you wear the necklace also?"

"Necklace?"

"Your grandmother had a matching set. I believe she handed down the ring to Annabel and the necklace to Aadya. Do you have it?"

I remembered the glow of the emerald around Aadya's neck, then picking the stone up from the ground after her death. "As a matter of fact, I do." I walked across the room, opening the top drawer of my dresser. As I lifted the necklace, it brightened, intensified by my touch. The mysterious stones always captivated me, as if they had a significant purpose in my life.

"Seems a little strange wearing it though."

"It's a family heirloom, Mercy. Don't let her taint it."

I laid the necklace on the table in front of me, along with my ring, staring at the gems side by side. Icy reached for the jeweled comb she always wore, tucked securely in her salt and pepper hair. "Something borrowed." Icy pulled one side of my hair back, securing it with the emerald encrusted comb. "Now you're perfect."

I stood, looking into the mirror. "It's beautiful. Thank you so much."

"I'll never be able to repay what you've done for me, child, but I'll keep trying until the day I die."

After a long embrace, I walked Icy to the door where we bid farewell. Before closing the door, she whispered, "One day at a time, Mercy. When you feel lost—when you feel as though you can't make it another day, stay strong. Our hope lies with you."

Her words confused me, and I stood shocked at the seriousness in her tone. "I'll remember."

Icy patted the side of my face, and with tears in her eyes, she walked away.

Just as I reached to close the door behind her, a meek voice caught my attention. "Mercy? Can I talk to you?"

I glanced up into the green eyes of my sister. I had never wanted to hit someone so much in all of my life. "I don't have much time, Marley."

"This will only take a minute."

I waved goodbye to Icy as Marley followed me into my room. My patience wore thin and I reminded myself not to do something I would regret. "What is it?"

She stood in front of me, dressed in a pink chiffon gown, her bright red hair curled in ringlets. "I need to apologize."

"For?" *Like I didn't know.*

"I screwed up. I made a mistake. It could have destroyed our relationship, not to mention your wedding."

"You say that as if I still want a relationship with you." I hated how much I wanted us to be close.

"I don't know what I was thinking. You have to believe me, it will never happen again. I haven't slept for days, beating myself up over it. I'm just . . . messed up."

I glanced down at the floor, unable to meet her eyes. "I see."

"I've never received a lot of attention, Mercy. At your engagement party, Drake commented on how lovely I looked. I felt beautiful. I didn't think about my actions, I was so focused on the possibility of someone wanting me for the first time."

"And?"

Her shoulders fell from shame. "Then I snuck into his room, the night you saw me in the hall. It didn't go far, I swear. We kissed, but he stopped it before anything happened. I wanted you to know he loves you, Mercy. I'm so sorry for acting so selfish."

I nodded, contemplating her half-ass apology.

"And I'm sorry for what went down between us in the hall. It's hard to not be jealous of you. You have everything I've ever dreamt of. You're the sister that has everything."

I didn't know what to say. Her story matched Drake's, but I didn't feel any better about someone putting their hands or lips on my man. I also didn't have a clue what she had been through growing up and how it had affected her. I didn't want to be the reason Marley spiraled.

What if she did regret it? What if this time, she turns her life around?

"Thank you for telling me. I want us to be friends, Marley, but you can't cross a line like that again. Do you understand? It's unacceptable."

"I do, I promise. I want us to be close, but I don't know how. I've never been close to anyone before, but I want to try. Can we start over?"

I took a deep breath before answering, doubting every word that came out of her mouth. The only reason I considered it at all, was because I knew my parents would expect me to show her grace. "Sure."

She walked toward the small table beside the doorway, where she left a large gift bag. "I brought a wedding gift."

I sighed. "You didn't have to do that."

"It isn't much—just a peace offering." She pulled a tall bottle of dark liquid from the bag, along with two glasses.

"What is it?" I asked.

"Just a sip of wine. Something to calm the wedding jitters."

I eyed the bottle skeptically. "I may have a glass later, after the ceremony."

"You see, it's a family tradition to have a drink before. I thought it would be nice for us to do it together." She jiggled the bottle in front of me.

"Family tradition? Where did you get it?" I asked, raising one brow.

"Um. Um . . . Grandmother Monroe gave it to me."

"She did?"

"That's right. She said our parents celebrated with the exact same thing on their wedding day." Marley grinned, brightly.

The smile on her face brought more peace than I expected. If she was willing to start over, I could too. "That's sweet, Marley."

After carefully pouring two glasses, she held her drink high into the air. "To you and Drake."

I tapped my glass against hers and smiled. "To sisters."

A dark shadow crossed her face, as if taken aback. Her eyes drifted toward the emeralds on the table, then she nodded in agreement. I turned the goblet up against my lips, the dark liquid earthy and sweet. "Thank you, Marley. This means a lot to me."

She watched me, completely unemotional. "Me too. I'm going to make my way downstairs so you can finish getting ready." She sat her cup on the dresser and made her way toward the door abruptly.

I saw the way she looked at the necklace, and I knew she must feel somewhat resentful. Is that why she rushed out of the room? After all, she was Annabel's daughter also. Shouldn't she have something from our mother? I made the decision right then, after the wedding I would give the necklace to Marley. She deserved a family heirloom to hand down to her daughter one day.

I forced words I didn't feel, a peace offering that would mean more to her than myself. "Marley? Are you staying for the reception?"

"The reception?" she asked. "Of course. If you want me there."

I nodded. "I do. It would mean a lot."

Her smile spoke volumes. "I'll meet you down there." Her eyes sparkled as she left the bedroom, looking more at peace than she did when she arrived.

I turned toward the mirror on the wall and took a deep breath. I secured the necklace around my neck and slid the ring onto my finger. Finally, I let the excitement of the day sink in, relishing the fact I would soon vow to be with Drake for the rest of my life. My one true love. My Allegato match.

The dark red dress hung on the wardrobe, and reminded me of something from a fairy tale. I reapplied my lipstick, and combed through my hair before turning toward the gown I would walk down the aisle in.

I'm ready.

I stumbled back as the dress blurred in front of me. I pulled from my sensory gift to adjust my vision, but it did little to help. A slow burn built inside my throat, a heat I couldn't control as I clutched my neck for relief. I reached for the remaining tea, and curiosity flickered through my mind as I caught sight of Marley's cup, completely full.

Would she?

I replayed the conversation in my head. Her submissive nature, her loving spirit—it was all a lie. A ploy to get what she wanted.

What did she do to me?

I turned my wrist over and over, forcing the gift of time interference to the surface, but it was no use. A wave of fire flooded my veins, overpowering my gifts, and I could barely stand. As the scorching pain consumed my body, the flame that housed my power turned into a mere sizzle, and I fell to my knees, unable to cry out.

Drake. I had to get to Drake.

I reached out through our connection, desperate to feel his presence, but panic clouded all reason, and I couldn't focus enough to sense him.

I crawled across the cold tile floor toward the door, my silk robe catching underneath my knees. My nails clawed the porcelain, and I clenched my teeth as the muscles in my abdomen spasmed, feeling as though they were ripping to shreds. The heat around me dissipated into frigidity, a cold steam covering my olive skin, crawling into my pores. I collapsed, barely able to take a breath as pain shot through my chest.

I opened my mouth to scream, but there was nothing. I could feel the life pull away from my body as I laid my cheek on the floor, eyes struggling to focus on the crack under the door. I prayed for someone, anyone, to save me from the horrendous pain, but no one came.

The floor began to move beneath me, and my body dropped as if falling, right before my vision went black.

CHAPTER
SEVEN
MERCY

I woke abruptly, struggling to move—my body held down by an uncomfortable weight. My breaths came in short gasps, as the throbbing in my head intensified. Adrenaline rushed through my veins as the memory of my wedding day drifted back. I squinted, fighting to open my eyes. I blinked, wincing against what felt like dirt or debris.

My eyes burned from the grit, but I was unable to reach up to relieve them. Confusion clouded my mind as I attempted to get my bearings. I felt as though I was breathing through a dense filter, unable to get air through my nose or mouth.

Even wiggling my toes felt difficult, as if restricted.

Where am I?

I fought for my interference power. I could sense a small spark—barely a flicker of a depleted gift. Silence surrounded me, not a river or bird nearby. I focused on moving my hands, feeling for anything that might help me up. The pads of my fingers rubbed against something cold and coarse, something that felt like ground.

I maneuvered my hand around and felt the same thing above. I pushed one finger up, and smooth dirt gave way—I began to panic.

The bitch had buried me alive.

My hands began to shake from fear, and I found myself gasping against the earth, unable to calm myself. I bent my knees, but once again hit a heavy weight above. If I could just use my power, I could easily move the dirt, but I couldn't do anything.

Powerless.

I didn't train for this. My heart pounded as I felt all around me, unable to find a way out. There was a moment of pure panic, as I tried to determine which way was up. How far did it go? Would I survive? It had gotten harder to breathe and I knew the air wouldn't last. I pushed my fingers into the soil, clawing my way through dense ground. My fingernails bent against the onslaught as I dug, dirt drifting in and out of my nostrils with each breath.

I clawed a trail in front of me, digging to where I could reach my face. I rubbed my eyes and nose, but it didn't matter. Dirt continued to fall, blocking my airway. I halted, fighting the need to gasp. I tried to meditate, just as Ren's father had taught me, but the feel of something crawling up my leg and not being able to do anything about it kept me from focusing.

I visualized the predicament in my mind, running through each scenario, and the chance I would suffocate by the time I got myself out of there. I could already feel my chest burning from the lack of oxygen. If I could somehow get into an upright position, I could dig to the surface.

I closed my eyes and began wiggling my fingers into the soil overhead. Hard ground gave way to crumbling dirt as pieces began falling into my eyes and nose. I would pause, blow out my nose as hard as I could to free the airway, then attempt to take another breath before digging again.

Eventually, I was able to sit up as I continued wiggling my way through the earth. My chest heaved, and my pace quickened. I ignored thoughts of insects around me, focusing only on surviving. The silk robe I still wore bunched around my waist as I finally pushed to my knees. Raw and burning, my broken fingernails dug fiercely, giving it everything I had as my head spun from the effort.

I have to stay awake.

All at once, my fingers broke through the thick layer of soil above me into fresh air. I began to hyperventilate, my nose and mouth blocked by falling debris. With everything left inside of me, I pushed my hand through the surface, desperate for air.

As I pulled my arm down, light shined from the small hole above me, and I began to sob. Tears mixed with dirt, caked around my eyes as I took a few seconds to breathe. A little at a time, I continued to widen the small hole I'd created. I attempted to climb against the side of the hole, but my feet slid over and over, sinking into the dirt like quick sand. I took a deep breath and jumped, gripping a small root above my head to hold my weight.

I groaned as I pulled myself out, gasping and crying. The muddy robe barely covered my body as I coughed and spit the dirt from my mouth. The trickle of a small stream, mere feet from where I sat, ran through the middle of a forest. I crawled over, rinsing my eyes and mouth so I could see better.

Leaves and grass surrounded the hole I had crawled out of, the remaining ground completely untouched. I focused on what should have been a freshly dug grave. How did she get me in there? Tall pine trees towered over me as the dim light of sun shone through the canopy. For miles, I could only see forest, as if nothing else existed.

A gruff voice broke through the eerie silence. "Better off climbing back down, girl."

I spun, scampering to my feet. "Who's there?"

"Trust me. That hole is the nicest place you'll see around here." A figure in a brown, ratty trench coat sat up, as if waking from a nap. "Not many get out of the ground—just stay there for the rest of their existence. Not sure what's worse." He scratched his beard. "Not sure at all."

"Stay there? That's not possible. I'd die."

He threw his head back, cackling. I stared, not in the mood for a homeless man's hysterics. I used to live in New York—he didn't phase me.

He finally composed himself, then nodded. "In your dreams, girl. No dying here. Just suffering." He shook his head. "Nah. Nobody gets off that easily."

I glanced from one side to another, crossing my arms over my chest. "Where am I?"

He stared, blank-faced at the ground. "Don't matter much, does it? You ain't goin' anywhere."

I needed him to answer one question, just one. "Is there somewhere I can go? I need food and clothes. I need . . . help."

"Most just fight for them. Take em' off someone else's back."

"Fight for them?" I asked.

"That's right. Best be ready to fight, or climb back in that hole where you started." He met my eyes. "Your choice."

"Fight who? I don't understand."

"Everyone." He sat up straight, narrowing his eyes on

the trees in the distance. "Better get on, now. They're coming."

I turned, but didn't see anyone in the woods. "Who?"

"Raiders. You don't want to be found by them. They can be . . . unpleasant."

My mind went a million different ways. How crazy could this guy be? I had to be close to home, maybe Ireland? "Well, thank you for your help. I'll be on my way."

I walked about fifteen feet before I heard his shaky whisper, "Don't walk. Run."

I looked over my shoulder, my brows raised. "I'm sorry, what?"

Intensity filled his eyes as he called out, "Run."

I looked up, and in the distance a group of men, maybe five or six that I could see, stood perfectly still, watching me. Most were stoic and emotionless, except the large, brawny man standing in front. His pale blonde hair had been slicked back, his skin tan from being out in the sun. When my eyes met his, he winked.

I didn't give it another thought. I turned, bolting through the forest on bare feet. I didn't have a clue what awaited, but a deep, dark feeling warned me to keep going. The sharp edges of pine cones bit into the soles of my feet as brush and vines scraped the sides of my legs, as if attempting to trip me.

I gasped for air, weaving through the tall pines and rocks. The rhythmic crunch of leaves under their boots echoed around me, making it difficult to pinpoint their location. The crunching became louder—closer. I caught sight of a thick canopied tree up ahead with low branches. I jumped as high as I could, gripping the lowest branch with both hands.

I took a deep breath, then pulled up to my elbows. I

never realized how much I had grown to depend upon my Regalian power instead of physical strength. I had always kept myself in shape, but even I wasn't ready for this.

A deep voice rumbled somewhere behind me, and I knew they were close. I clawed my way through the branches, wrapping my arms around the trunk of the tree. I lost footing, and slid a few inches down the bark, scraping the skin off my arms and legs.

A deep voice rumbled from the ground. "Shh. Did you hear that?"

They were directly below me. I stayed perfectly still, praying for the strength to hold on. Every move I made, I feared it would capture their attention, like a beacon directing them toward my hidden branch in the tree. So I held tight with my arms and thighs, staying perfectly still.

"I don't hear anything. I bet she ran toward the river." He scoffed. "Didn't look like she had anything with her we'd want anyway."

"She has something I want," another murmured, causing another man to cackle.

"Keep your eyes open. I want her found."

I waited for them to leave, then refused to move for several minutes after they had disappeared into the forest. Slowly, I released my hold on the trunk and climbed to a thicker, more stable branch. Leaning my head against the bark, tears filled my eyes. I silently cried, feeling more help-less than I ever had in my entire life.

What could I possibly have done to make Marley hate me this much? What did she have planned in my absence? I couldn't feel my connection to Drake any longer and that alone weakened my willpower like nothing else.

I *needed* him.

I wasn't sure what to expect from this land. I didn't

know how to survive without my power. What I did know, something I was absolutely certain of, is that this hell had a life of its own—one that didn't want me to survive.

My vision blurred as my body began to slump against the tree trunk. The scrapes and gashes along my arms and legs burned, as the mix of blood and dirt caked the sides of my feet. I pulled the shredded robe tighter, watching as the sun quickly set, and the moon rose up behind it. I squinted, confused, and seconds later I collapsed against the rough bark, giving in to the darkness.

. . .

I PULLED my legs against my chest, shivering. My fingertips numb, I lost my grip on the branch and jolted upright, the remnants of sleep evaporating like a fog. Sheets of snow and ice layered the forest, a blizzard like I'd never seen.

I couldn't have been asleep for more than a few hours.

I listened for movement or voices, but I was completely alone. I wasn't sure if I would be able to find shelter, but if I stayed in the tree, I would freeze to death for sure. I climbed down from the icy branch, but about halfway down, I lost my balance and slipped, landing on my back on the snow-covered ground.

I winced, partly from the impact, but mostly from the cold. My entire body shook, as my teeth chattered against the bitter wind. I walked for what felt like miles. By the time I reached the frozen river, I had completely lost feeling in my extremities, stumbling around uneven terrain on shaky legs. A loud piercing scream filled the air from the woods behind me, and the chills that ran up my spine had little to do with the snow.

Small beads of ice pelted me in the face as I squinted against the storm. Again, a terror-filled sob reverberated off the trees, spurring me on. Running wasn't an option, every time I picked up speed, my legs would buckle. A tall rock formation in the distance caught my attention and I stumbled my way toward the mountainside, searching for anything to block the wind and snow.

I placed my hands on the rock, feeling for a crevice or opening, but paused when the blue hue of my hands caught my attention. I flipped my hand over, and the tips of my fingers had turned black.

I'm going to die out here.

I smelled it before I saw it. The smoky scent of dead wood over flames. I spun, searching for any sign of what could possibly save my life. I walked the expanse of the rock, then turned, backtracking. There in the smallest crevice, a trickle of smoke escaped the confines of the stone. I turned sideways, attempting to slide into the narrow opening of what appeared to be a cave.

I turned my head, pushing my body through the crack, my mind vaguely wandering if I would even fit. Doubt pushed aside, I took a deep breath, inching my way inside, desperate for warmth. All at once, the crevice gave way and I fell forward on my side against hard stone. Heat from the fire surrounded me, and I gave into the exhaustion, laying my head against the ground. Flickering flames danced in front of me, and I closed my eyes to relish the feel.

I didn't care where it came from or who else was there —I was in survival mode. I couldn't be sure how long I laid there, drifting in and out of consciousness, but my fingertips and toes began to sting, as blood returned to my hands and feet. The slightest movement intensified the pain, but gradually heat spread throughout my body, and I relaxed.

My throat ached, dry and raw, as I tried to swallow. A shadow flickered behind the flames, followed by a frightened moan. I pushed myself up, squinting toward the corner of the cave where someone hid underneath a small scrap of a blanket.

"Hello?"

Silence.

"Is someone there? I don't mean any harm."

The stranger shifted, then hesitantly pulled the blanket away from their face. A petite young girl, no more than six or seven, eyed me suspiciously. Her dark brown hair fell around a pink headband, and wide blue eyes met mine through the firelight. Her sweet spirit reminded me of Nora.

"I'm Mercy."

Silence.

"Do you have a name?"

She nodded, but didn't speak, whether terrified or strong-willed, I didn't know.

My gaze traveled around the cave walls, where flint engravings marked the days spent, and what looked like coal and blood diagrams of gruesome deaths from years past. How many have died in this horrible place? How long had this child been here? Why her?

"I won't hurt you."

She bent her knees to her chest and buried her head, rocking back and forth. I pushed to my feet, shuffling toward the cave wall toward the drawings. Brutal images of torture . . . throats slit, hanging by tree branches, eaten by large pythons, things I never wanted to imagine had been drawn out before me. I looked over at the small child in the corner.

"You've been here for a while?"

She took a deep breath, then nodded.

I sat down beside the fire, contemplating my options. "Do you know anyone that has gotten out?"

Her blue eyes squinted as she shook her head.

"What do you eat?"

She nodded toward the floor, where a pile of berries and shelled walnuts had been collected. I had a feeling she didn't leave the cave often, but it was smart on her part. Not many people could fit through the opening to attack.

I sat quietly by the fire, unsure how to have a one-sided conversation. Maybe if she got to know me, she would open up. "I'm Mercy Monroe, the leader of Seregalo."

Her eyes widened and she swallowed as if nervous.

"Are you a Regalian?"

She quickly nodded.

"Can you use your gift here?"

She glanced toward the floor, shaking her head.

Something about the mysterious land suppressed our magic, but I wasn't sure how. Could it be a spell, similar to Aadya's dungeon? How close were we to Seregalo? Ireland? I had so many questions.

I closed my eyes, focusing on my source of power, but it was as if I'd taken a wrong turn, unable to find the path. I breathed in my nose and out my mouth, searching for the spark I knew was hidden behind malevolence.

All at once, the young girl screamed, staring wide-eyed at the empty space in front of her. My heart pounded as her scratchy voice cried for pity, begging for her life. I searched the cave, but didn't see a threat. Her small frame shook all over as she backed further into the corner. I crawled toward her, doing anything I could to not only comfort her, but quiet her screams before we were discovered.

"Shh. It's okay. There's no one here. See? No one except us."

She shook her head over and over, pushing me away. She pointed across the room and sobbed, unable to catch her breath.

"What is it? Tell me what you see."

I attempted to hold her, make her feel secure, but it was no use. Once again, she fought my embrace, staring at the cave wall as if someone stood before her.

I didn't know what to do. Right as I leaned forward, a hot breath blew across the back of my neck, and a dark chuckle echoed around the cave that I knew all too well. I closed my eyes, hoping it was only a nightmare. A bad dream I never expected to relive.

I slowly turned, and my heart dropped at the sight of the dark, evil eyes I hoped to never look into again. Bile rose up my throat, and I fought to swallow it down.

"Hey there, gorgeous. I've missed you."

My chin quivered as I whispered, "Asher."

CHAPTER
EIGHT
MARLEY

"Where is Mercy?" Drake asked.

Neela glanced over her shoulder nervously, widening her eyes at Nora. "I'm sure she's just taking her time. You know how brides can be." She grinned, attempting to soothe him.

He stepped forward, his eyes intense and unsettled. "No, I don't. Mercy isn't like that and you know it. Where is she, Neela?"

The wedding guests shifted in their seats, eyeing each other as if witnessing a scandal. Even from where I stood, the red tinge of his eyes shined brightly as he grew angry. I knew this wouldn't be easy. The transition, the acceptance that Mercy was, in fact, gone. Drake would grieve, he would mourn the woman he thought he loved, then he would move on.

I know he will.

Fitz stood at the end of the aisle, shaking his head at Drake.

I moved forward, reaching for his arm. "Give her a few more minutes. I'm sure she wants everything to be perfect."

Neela's eyes drifted to where I held Drake's arm, then she smiled, obviously hiding her dislike for me. "Of course. I'll see if she needs any help."

Neela turned for the Domicile, but Drake stopped her in her tracks. "I'll go."

Neela, Nora and myself followed him toward Mercy's room, barely able to keep up. I fought hard to play the ever-worried sister, only wanting the best for Mercy on her wedding day. If they knew the truth, if they found out what I had done, it would be over for me.

He took the stairs two at a time, reaching Mercy's door within minutes. He knocked, but there was no answer. "Mercy? It's me, babe. Everything okay?"

Watching him wait, so unsure of himself was the hardest part.

He turned the knob and the door swung open. Drake walked inside the empty room, turning to inspect every corner, as if she were hiding behind the bed or dresser. "Mercy?"

Silence.

Neela's eyes were filled with worry as she headed toward the bathroom, then returned, shaking her head. Nora wrung her hands, unsure how to help.

"Where could she be?" I asked. "She was just here before I came down."

Fitz stood in the doorway, thoughtful. "How did she seem?"

"Fine," I replied. "A little anxious about what happened earlier in the week, but otherwise okay."

"Wait," Neela interrupted. "What exactly are we talking about?"

I attempted to look ashamed. "You know, about me and Drake."

Nora spoke up, "She has been out of sorts about that." She turned toward Drake, as if embarrassed for him. "I spoke to her earlier today."

Drake closed his eyes, tilting his head back as if frustrated. "Nothing happened."

"Can someone please tell me what is going on?" Neela shouted.

"Well," Nora began. "Mercy caught Marley coming out of Drake's room in the middle of the night . . . half naked."

Neela turned her evil eyes toward Drake. "I can't believe you!" Then she stepped toward me, gritting her teeth. "And you! That is your sister!"

"Nothing happened!" Drake replied, his voice filled with annoyance as he balled his fists. "I swear!"

"Is this why I woke to Mercy kicking Marley's ass in the hallway?" Neela asked.

"What?" Drake and Nora asked together.

I bowed my head, an effort to look ashamed. "She was rather violent."

"I can't believe this," Drake growled. "She should know me better than this."

Neela threw one hip to the side and glared. "I thought I knew you, too."

Drake snatched a glass candle from the top of Mercy's dresser and threw it across the room, shattering it against the far wall. "I didn't do anything with Marley!"

"Marley? What about Marley?" A high-pitched, angry voice belted from the doorway.

"Apparently," Neela shouted. "Something happened between those two!" She pointed toward Drake and I, just as I imagined her tattling on someone in grade school.

"Drake is telling the truth. I told Mercy it was a stupid

mistake on my part," I confessed. "He didn't do anything wrong."

"Says you," Hillie spat.

"That's enough," Fitz exclaimed. "Let's split up and search the grounds. She couldn't have gone far."

Neela, Nora and Hillie hesitantly left to find Mercy. Drake walked toward the windows, watching the wedding guests, fidgeting in their chairs below. Fitz put his arm around him, gripping his shoulder.

"Send them home," Drake mumbled.

"But . . ."

"This isn't the way I want to marry her."

Fitz nodded with sad eyes. "We'll find her. Then we can plan the perfect ceremony. I promise." He turned to leave but halted when he saw me standing there. I couldn't read his thoughts, the protective wall he'd created must have taken years, but I sensed doubt and suspicion.

I nodded, smiling sweetly. "I'll be right down."

Fitz left without another word.

As soon as everyone had gone, I lifted the girls higher into the dress, and sashayed toward the window beside Drake. "I remember standing at a window exactly like this, watching Mercy and Felix's ceremony."

"That wasn't much of a ceremony," he replied. "Aadya forced her."

"I don't remember what she looked like that day, or what Felix wore. I recall you, chained and helpless as the woman you love almost married someone else. The look in your eyes, the desire. I've always wanted that from you, Drake."

He frowned. "It will happen one day, Marley. Someday, someone will come along that sees you and only you, as if there were no brighter stars in the sky. They will adore you above all others, just as you deserve. It's just not me." He spun and left the room, leaving me humiliated.

I clenched my teeth in frustration. I wanted to lay down on the floor and kick and scream like a petulant child. It's my turn. Drake was supposed to fall in love with me. I had planned to be his world.

He just didn't remember.

. . .

MARLEY- SIX YEARS OLD

"Marley? Can you come in here?"

I gripped the Barbie doll in my tiny fist, upset for being interrupted. How many times do I have to tell her? "I'm busy!"

"Young lady, I won't ask again!"

Throwing the doll across the room, I stomped toward the living room, where I knew Aunt Isla would be waiting, along with her useless husband, Cliff. This is how our family meetings always began. I would do something that someone had a problem with, and now I would be forced to endure a family therapy session so it didn't happen again.

Last week, her seven-year-old daughter, Allie, complained I was giving her dolls haircuts. It was completely absurd, everyone knew I was in an Indian phase and only wanted to scalp something. I've never claimed to be a beautician, but whatever.

Allie's brother, Ben, didn't tattle very often. At ten-years-old, Ben was somewhat more mature than his little sister, allowing me to hang out in his room while he murdered innocent bystanders on his video game. Those days were the best.

The bright blue walls of the hallway blinded me as I shuffled across thick carpet, grumbling the entire way. Family pictures hung along the wall, the perfect family of four and myself, standing awkwardly beside them. I had to give her credit, Aunt Isla did make an effort to include me, but I had no intention of sticking around here for long.

I stepped into the cozy living space, filled by the large brown sectional and television. Cliff sat on the reclining end of the sofa, still wearing the navy blue uniform of the plumbing company he worked for during the day. He and Aunt Isla sat tense, staring at the two strangers on the other end of the sofa.

"Yes?" I snapped.

A man turned, looking over his shoulder. His gaze traveled from my red hair to the toes of my pink socks. He grinned, shaking his head. I took in his dark brown wavy hair, olive skin and the whitest teeth I had ever seen. He didn't frighten me, but his affectionate gaze made me uncomfortable.

Then, a boy peeked his head around the man. The spitting image of who I assumed was his father, except the eyes. They weren't just brown.

They were black.

He pursed his full lips as if scrutinizing me, just as curious as I was.

"You look just like your mother," the gentleman said fondly.

I scowled. "I wouldn't know."

His eyes softened, but I didn't want his pity.

"My name is Dorian, and this is my son, Drake. I'm a friend of your parent's, and I promised I would check on you. They miss you very much."

I hated how he talked to me, as if I were some young, ignorant child who would buy into every word he said, waiting for the day Mommy and Daddy would come back for me.

Screw them. Screw all of them.

"Marley is a very intelligent young lady—the top of her class," Aunt Isla called out. "Annabel should be proud."

"Why?" I asked. "What did she have to do with it?"

Silence filled the room.

Dorian leaned forward. "I know it's hard to understand, but one day you will. I promise they are doing what's best for you, Marley." He reached toward me and I backed away, refusing his touch.

He narrowed his eyes, as if analyzing my reaction.

Good Luck.

Ignoring the man, I brushed past him toward the boy. Surprisingly, he intrigued me—few people piqued my interest enough to speak to. His dark eyes met mine, but didn't submit like most. Drake stood taller, completely unafraid. There was fire in his soul that matched the darkness in mine. I couldn't put my finger on it, but he was different.

Is this what love feels like?

Smiling brightly, I stuck my hand out in front of me. "I'm Marley."

He hesitantly shook my hand, cutting his eyes toward his father as if unsure about the bold girl standing before him. "I'm Drake."

"Drake, we're gonna be good friends. I just know it."

...

MARLEY- PRESENT DAY

For the first time, I sat at the long conference table surrounded by Elders. I'd never been invited before, and a thrill coursed through me at the thought of taking my first step in ruling Seregalo. The inner Marley smirked at the circumstance she had created, but on the outside, I tried to appear exhausted—unable to sleep now that my dear twin sister had vanished.

"Marley, please know we are doing everything we can to find your sister," an older gentleman I wasn't familiar with spoke up, his voice gentle and kind. "I know this must be difficult."

I nodded, teary eyed. "We only just found each other, you know?" I sniffed. "I'm not sure what we're going to do without her."

"Drake has been out day and night searching for her." The Elder named Gwendolyn shook her head. "There is no sign of her leaving Seregalo, I don't understand."

"It's only been forty-eight hours. I don't think we need to assume she is gone forever," Josiah snapped.

"Do you have any information, Josiah? Because it isn't looking good from where we're sitting," Gwendolyn replied. "We need to have a plan in place. Word has gotten out and our people are getting restless."

"There has to be a representative for Regalians. They need someone they can look to as a leader or chaos will ensue," Thu Dang added. "You don't want to cause disruption, do you Josiah?"

Josiah glared. "Who do you recommend? Her fiancé, Drake? At least he is strong and respected," he offered.

"Don't be ridiculous," Thu Dang snapped. "A respectable amount of fear is different than completely terrified. Plus, they haven't had an official Allegato ceremony so he has no claim."

"I'm confused," I lied. "I thought Seregalo chose the next leader by way of power."

"That's right," Josiah answered. "But until that happens —until we have a sign, we have to hold Seregalo together."

"I think the choice is obvious," Thu Dang mumbled.

Elder Isolette leaned back in her chair, listening to the banter around the room. She never commented, but I could only imagine what she wanted to say. As one of Mercy's biggest supporters, no one would be able to take her place in Isolette's eyes.

"Do we have to decide today?" Josiah asked. "As monumental as this is, I don't feel as though it needs to be rushed."

Thu Dang stood, angry. "I feel like you . . ."

All at once the double doors swung open, slamming against the frame. Drake stomped into the conference room, followed by Colton, Fitz, and Neela. "You have got to be joking!"

Thu Dang slowly slid into his seat, mouth closed.

"Mercy has been missing for less than forty-eight hours and you're just going to give up on her? Have you forgotten that she was chosen for this position? No one else. Her!"

"Drake, that isn't what we're doing," Josiah stated, calmly.

"That's exactly what it looks like. It took years of hiding her, people dying, including my parents, to get her on this council!"

"And we're supposed to do what? Let Seregalo fall

because she got cold feet?" Thu Dang smirked, and I couldn't help but be impressed by his courage.

Drake leaned over the table, his fist holding his weight on the cold marble. "She did not get cold feet."

Thu Dang's mouth fell open as he feigned innocence. "You'll have to excuse me. I was under the impression that an argument took place over a matter of infidelity. Am I wrong?"

Several members of the council glanced around the room, in shock.

Drake's voice lowered, "She did not get cold feet."

Gwendolyn cleared her throat. "We all know how Mercy feels about you, and no one here believes the rumors. I don't know what happened, but we have to appoint a temporary replacement until we get this sorted. There must be a face of Seregalo, someone to lead our people."

"Where is my Granddaughter?" A shaky voice shouted from the door.

We all turned to find Grandmother Monroe, red faced and angry.

"Where is she? Someone has to know something, people don't vanish into thin air!"

Josiah stood, as if ready to catch the feeble woman when she fell. "Mrs. Monroe, please calm down. We're doing everything we can."

"Don't talk to me like that, little Joe. I changed your diapers when you were only a babe!"

Josiah eased down into his chair, lowering his eyes.

"I want to see my Granddaughter, right now!"

I smiled, attempting to appear hurt. "I guess you aren't referring to me."

Grandmother Monroe met my eyes for a split second

before turning her attention to the Elders once again. "What exactly is your plan?"

Thu Dang sat up, as if needing the extra confidence to go up against the feisty old woman. "Neela has put together multiple Custos units who are stationed throughout Seregalo and Ireland. Stonedell has been completely sealed off until we determine what's happening. We're doing all we can."

She glared. "I'm sure."

Gwendolyn cleared her throat. "Mrs. Monroe, we must have a back-up in place for the sake of Seregalo. Mercy has been chosen to lead our people for a reason. We aren't turning our back on her, just assigning someone, temporarily."

Drake's gaze fell on Josiah, his eyes red from exhaustion and anger. "Fine. Then it needs to be someone Mercy trusts wholeheartedly. Someone in the bloodline."

I grinned, sitting up a little straighter. I knew he would come to his senses.

He continued. "I would like to nominate a candidate for consideration, as the mate of the current leader, I feel as though I should have a say."

"You weren't officially mated," Thu Dang mumbled.

"Our Allegato marks make it official," he spat.

Josiah nodded. "We will take it into consideration, Drake. Who do you nominate?"

"Hillie McDonnell, cousin of Mercy Monroe."

A hush swept over the room as sympathetic gazes turned my direction. Mercy didn't trust me, and Drake knew it. I couldn't deny the pain in my chest. I wanted him to believe in me.

"I second the nomination," Grandma Monroe called out.

Thu Dang laughed. "She doesn't even live in Seregalo."

"She did at one time," Drake replied. "Besides Grandmother Monroe, Hillie lived here longer than anyone else from Mercy's family. She left when Aadya destroyed her home."

My eyes traveled around the room, anticipating everyone's reaction. I kept quiet, hoping to maintain a neutral stance. For a split second, Thu Dang's angry gaze met mine.

Josiah nodded. "Do we have any other nominations?"

After several seconds, Thu Dang spoke up. "I'd like to nominate Marley Monroe."

Drake's head jerked back as if he'd been slapped. "On what grounds?"

I forced a tight smile. "This is uncomfortable."

"As if being the twin sister of our leader isn't enough," he replied. "Marley is strong. She cares for our citizens and would uphold Mercy's vision for Seregalo."

Gwendolyn cleared her throat, as if hesitant to speak. "Are we forgetting the reports we spoke of recently? The ones of her temperament?"

I gasped, as if shocked by the accusation. "I'm sorry, but this is the first I've heard of any reports. It sounds as though you are confusing me with my aunt. They need to understand that our red hair is the extent of our similarities. It wouldn't be fair to judge me based on how she treated others, now would it?"

Grandmother Monroe rolled her eyes.

Again, Elder Isolette sat with her arms crossed, studying the room.

Josiah spoke up, "Thank you both for your input on this situation. The council will deliberate over this, but please know we will not give up on finding Mercy. She is our priority."

Drake nodded, then turned to leave without another word. As the room cleared out, leaving the intimate circle of Elders to convene, I met Thu Dang's eyes and grinned.

CHAPTER
NINE
MERCY

Asher looked exactly like I remembered—cold, dark eyes and menacing glare. I always thought he looked like Drake, but not nearly as attractive. Evil radiated from his presence, and somehow he made the dimple in his right cheek appear sinister when he grinned. My stomach turned as his gaze traveled down my half naked body, barely protected by the robe.

"My brother taking care of you?" He stepped forward, "Because you know I will."

The little girl rocked back and forth in the corner, covering her ears. She closed her eyes, mumbling something that sounded like a prayer. This was hard enough on me, I couldn't imagine what she had been through. My heart hurt for the innocent soul trapped in this hell.

"Leave her alone, Asher. The child has no part in this."

His brow furrowed in confusion. "Child? I don't care about a child. It's you." His jaw clenched tight as he stepped forward once again. "It's always been you."

I didn't know what to do. The only thing I knew for sure is that I refused to go down without a fight. I inched back toward the cave door, preparing to run. "You're dead. I saw Aadya murder you in the dungeon."

"Did you?" He threw his head back, the evil cackle echoing inside the small cave.

"Drake had to watch his brother crumble to the floor, lifeless. He loved you. Did you know that? Through the betrayals and lies, he would have given anything to have you back."

Asher didn't flinch. "Not you. He wouldn't give you up. I guess it doesn't matter now, I'll have you one way or the other."

I spun, dashing toward the small crevice I had entered through. The rough stone wall scraped the skin of my cheek as I took a deep breath, shoving myself through the cramped space. The cold mist of snow hit my right hand as Asher jerked my other arm painfully, dragging me back into the cave.

I bent my leg, using my knee as an anchor in the cave wall. Asher painfully twisted my wrist and an intense streak of pain ran up my arm as it snapped in his grasp. I cried out in agony, and he chuckled, pleased with himself.

"Let me go!" I jerked, ignoring the pain. I fell from the cave entrance onto the snow covered ground. I glanced over my shoulder at Asher's thick shoulders inching through the opening. I didn't have time to wonder how he ever made it inside the cave—I ran.

My bare feet sunk into snow as I strained against the cold and wind. My heart pounded and already, my toes began to sting from the frigid temperature. I didn't stop to look behind me, but I could hear the crunch of snow under his boots—his heavy breathing as he closed the distance between us.

I scanned the trees and mountainside, desperate for

shelter from Drake's demented brother. I slid, falling on my stomach as Asher's weight came down on top of me, pinning me to the ice. My injured wrist screamed against the pressure, begging for relief. The bare skin of my legs and stomach hit the cold surface as his hot breath blew across my ear.

"Tell me, is this how you always wanted it?" He chuckled. "It's ironically close to my fantasy."

"Get off me!" I threw my head back, nailing him in the face.

"Damn it, Mercy!"

As soon as he reached for his nose, I crawled forward on my hands and knees. He gripped my ankle, running his hands up my legs to where the edge of the robe covered my backside. He crawled up my body, pushing his weight into my back. He ran his thick fingers up my thigh and whispered, "You know what happens next, don't you?"

A splintering crack, quick and sharp, startled me. I thought I had imagined it, but the crackling became stronger and faster, and we both froze. My breath caught in my throat as I realized we were laying on top of an icy river. I didn't even have a chance to take a breath.

The ice gave way, and the rush of frigid water swallowed us whole. I opened my eyes, fighting against the current of the river, but there was nothing but darkness. I pounded against the layer of ice overhead, my lungs burning for air. I spun, searching for a way out but halted at the sight of Asher only feet away.

My arms and feet flailed, as if I could swim away, but it was futile. His strong hand circled my neck, squeezing painfully, as he grinned in the depths of the frozen river. Black spots danced across my vision and my body begged to let go—to be free of the agony. My father's voice, low and calm, whispered, "You are so much more than your gift."

I opened my eyes, focusing on Asher's malicious grin. I refused to die this way. I would not become some sad, weak woman who's fight left her the moment she became powerless. This would not be my story. Reaching forward, I wrapped my hands around Asher's neck in return, squeezing as hard as I could, shaking from the effort. My broken wrist shot streaks of pain up my arm, and my vision grew hazy from the agony.

His eyes widened, and we both squeezed harder, determined to strangle the other. The harder I fought, the weaker he became, and I watched as Asher's form dissipated in front of me until he was no more. I couldn't wrap my mind around what had happened.

The current washed me downstream, and I began pounding on the ice, desperate to find a way out. Pain shot through my shoulder as I slammed into a large rock, pinning me between the bank and boulder. I clawed against the surface over and over, but it refused to give. I raised my fist for one final effort, but paused at the shadow overhead.

A tall figure with dark hair stood over me, looking down with eyes so black, his gaze stared into my soul even through the frozen river. My body began to let go from the lack of air as he pounded the top of the ice with a sharp object. Barely conscious, the ice finally relented and he lifted me, dragging me onto lush, green grass under a summer sun.

I gasped, the air filled with the scent of honeysuckle and thyme. Lifting my head, I blinked, confused and delirious. "Drake?" I couldn't have imagined that. Someone was here. Someone saved my life.

Chirping birds overhead and croaking from a nearby frog were the only replies.

After several seconds, I pushed myself to a sitting position and looked around. The rush of fresh water churned briskly over smooth stones, no ice in sight. Trees surrounded me with greenery, as a squirrel sat several feet away, collecting nuts.

I blinked, trying to make sense of my surroundings. What happened to the snow?

Crawling toward the river, I scooped water into my mouth, relishing the crisp, cool liquid on my dry throat. I paused at the sight of a small burlap sack, sitting on the opposite side of the bank, and I stared as if it would disappear into thin air.

Who left it? Why did they run away?

I pushed myself to a standing position, but quickly realized how much weight I'd put on my injured wrist. Holding my hand out in front of me, there wasn't a mark on the skin at all. The swelling and pain had completely disappeared as if it never happened.

I think I'm losing my mind.

One shaky leg after another, I crossed the river carefully toward the small bag. I peeked inside and breathed a sigh of relief at the sight of jeans and a cotton t-shirt folded on top of boots and a few apples. The jeans looked large enough to fit Drake, but I didn't care. I slid into them, rolling down the waist until they fit tight along my hips. The boots were tight, but better than nothing.

As I dropped the thread-bare robe from my shoulders, the gold of the emerald necklace hit my skin, reminding me it was still around my neck. I looked down at my hand, where the matching ring glowed brightly. Power radiated between the two, an invisible connection I didn't understand. Even powerless, I could feel the missing link—an intricate piece of an unsolved puzzle, as if it wanted to be of use.

The cotton shirt hung to my thighs, so I knotted the front to keep it from hindering me. The antique, jeweled comb Isolette had given me had tangled in the back of my long dark hair, and I gently pulled it free. I knotted my hair on top of my head, securing it with the silk belt of the robe, then placed the comb back into my hair so I wouldn't lose it.

I threw the sack over my shoulder, and carefully made my way toward the shelter of the cave. Just the thought of sliding through the small crevice once again caused horrible anxiety, but worry over the girl overpowered any fears I had for myself.

I should have been exhausted. My body should have ached from head to toe, but instead renewed energy coursed through me as adrenaline took over. My eyes darted from tree to tree, alert and on guard. I wasn't sure how far the river had taken me, but after several minutes the gray slate of the cave wall peeked through the trees.

The mountainside loomed over me as I slid my palm over the rock, searching for the entrance. I walked for miles circling the cave, but couldn't find the narrow crevice where I had entered earlier.

It couldn't have disappeared. Right?

I begin to panic, worrying over the young girl as if she were my own. I made another loop around the stone, but too afraid to call out for her on the chance someone else would hear—someone I didn't want to attract.

All at once, I froze at the sight of a soft pink headband,

caught in a patch of thorns up ahead. The filthy fabric was torn and dirty, as if it had been stuck in the brush for a long time. But it hadn't—I had seen the young girl wearing it that morning. I tightened my hold on the headband, determined to find her.

The sun shined overhead, a punishing heat that refused to relent. Sweat poured down the back of my neck as I hiked through the woods, searching for any sign of her. I scoured every inch of ground in front of me for a sign, my gaze traveling to the treetops for a glimpse of her hiding.

Had someone taken her? If so, how did I hope to find her?

A soft humming stopped me in my tracks. Kneeling beside a large oak, I scanned the forest for a threat. Several minutes passed, but there was nothing except the gentle melody of a sad tune.

A few feet at a time, I crept through the woods, following the soft hum. Behind a thick trunk of a tree up ahead, the sway of long blonde hair appeared from behind a tree, as if someone rocked back and forth.

I wasn't close enough to determine if the figure was a child or young woman. I took a few steps, then paused, slowly closing in on the stranger. Shaking and pale, I didn't feel threatened by her obviously weakened state, but kept my guard up just in case.

"Hello?" I called out.

The sunlight dimmed without warning, no beautiful orange glow or relaxing transition into night. A bone-deep cold replaced the warmth of the sun and chills trailed down the skin of my arms as paranoia trickled in. I stared at the huddled form, sitting cross-legged on the ground.

I tried once again. "Are you alright?"

She lifted her head, her straight blonde hair parting to reveal dim blue eyes, shadowed by black rings. With dry cracked lips, she muttered, "Do I look alright?"

I stumbled back, my hands shaking from disbelief and heartache. "It can't be. You're dead. I saw you die!"

"Yes, you did." She rocked forward, gritting her teeth. "And who's fault was that?"

I stuttered, unable to form a coherent thought, "I, but, we . . ."

Cassie glared. "You took him away from me. You took everything!"

I shook my head, frantically. "No! No, I didn't mean for it to happen. If I had known Dr. Lee was going to . . ."

"Stop blaming everyone else! That's all you do, isn't it? Blame others for all the terrible shit that happens when you are the reason it happens in the first place! You!" Blood began to trickle from her ears and nose, just as it did the night Dr. Lee took her life at Fremont with subconscious interference.

I fell to my knees, sobbing. The memory of her face, scared and vulnerable, stared at me in my nightmares too often. "I will never forgive myself. I'm so sorry," I cried.

Cassie blinked, bloody tears filling her eyes as she stared off in the distance, as if suddenly transported to a different time. She whispered, "My parents didn't come to my funeral. Did you know that? They sent flowers, pink roses that draped across a white casket. Pink roses were my favorite."

"I—I didn't know." Nothing I could say would take her pain away. No words would give Cassie her life back, and it felt callous to even consider speaking. She didn't want to hear from me. Why would she?

"I never realized how much my parents didn't care. I guess I hoped they'd be heartbroken, or at least sad. I'm ridiculous, aren't I? A stupid, ridiculous girl who didn't know how little she meant to the world. Drake didn't want me, he worshiped you. No friends. My own family didn't love me." Cassie broke down sobbing, unable to continue.

I crawled toward her, taking her cold hands in mine. "That's not true."

"It is!" She nodded. "My life was completely pointless!"

"No! You didn't get a chance to live. You didn't get the opportunity to figure out your purpose like everyone else." I pleaded, "It doesn't mean you didn't have one."

Streaks of blood ran down her face as she began to gasp for air. "You're lying. You know I'm worthless! That's why you let me die!"

"I should have protected you that night! I should have done more. I'm so sorry." I sobbed, covering my face with my hands. "Please, forgive me!"

After several seconds of silence, I once again whispered, "Forgive me."

When I looked up, Cassie had disappeared. I didn't bother glancing from side to side, searching within the trees. I knew she wasn't there, just like Asher wasn't there earlier.

It was the worst kind of torture, for someone to take your biggest regrets in life and shove them down your throat, as if your own guilt wasn't enough. It was a reminder of my inability to save those around me, a whisper of self-doubt and weakness.

I didn't need someone to show me how I had messed up. The vision of a life I'd ruined wasn't necessary. I lived with these reminders everyday. When I woke in the early morning, or closed my eyes at night, I saw the blood running down Cassie's face, the terror in Ren's eyes as he took his last breath, and sometimes on good nights, I would hear the pride in my father's voice as he told me he loved me.

"What do you want from me?" I screamed, sobbing in the forest alone.

CHAPTER
TEN
MERCY

I remember crying on the ground of the forest, begging for forgiveness. The image of Cassie's bloody face forever burned into my mind. My body frozen in grief, I laid on the brush and pine straw, unable to move.

I closed my eyes and prayed that when I opened them, I would be back in my bedroom, preparing for my wedding day—planning the rest of my life with Drake. Taking a deep, relaxing breath, I opened my eyes and focused on a woman, pacing in front of me. My stomach dropped at the sight of her long red hair, shielding her face in the dark. Her thin, white nightgown swept the dirt as she paced, staining the hem of the fabric.

She mumbled over and over, the sad, anxiety-ridden soul wringing her hands as she spoke. "She's coming. I know she's coming. I can feel the bitterness seeping from her pores as if she's fueled by it. They're close. I have to protect him."

"Who?" I asked. "I don't know what you're talking about."

The woman paused, slowly turning her head toward me. "Do you feel it?"

I blew out a shocked breath, meeting the bright green eyes of my mother. I pushed my hair from my face, as leaves and pine needles fell from the tangles. When I inhaled, my lip quivered and tears filled my eyes.

I watched her die. This woman, brave and strong, risked everything, so that her daughters could live. "You're here," I whispered. "I can't believe you're here."

She bit her top lip, as if trying not to cry. "Sweet girl, you know I'd never be far." She fell to her knees in front of me, pulling me into her embrace.

I gripped her nightgown, afraid to let her go, as if she'd vanish, leaving me to die in the woods alone. Sobs wracked my body as I let her hold my weight, physically and emotionally. "I can't do this."

"You can, Mercy. I know it's hard, but you can't give up." She kissed the top of my head.

"Is Dad here?" A strange combination of hope and worry filled my chest. I didn't want him in this world of pain and despair, but I needed him.

"Not here. Not in this place." She shook her head. "This world is . . . unique. Powerful. The Oblivion only takes from the ones who have something it wants."

My chest tightened at her words. *Oblivion*. My conversation with Icy came drifting back and I fought to take a breath. "You talk as though it's alive."

Her eyes widened, as she slowly nodded. "It uses everything it can to break you. Your fears. Your guilt. It will suck the will to live completely out of you."

"How do I get home? I have to get back to Seregalo!"

Her shoulders slumped, as she wiped the tears from my

cheek. "I'm so sorry. They will never let you leave." She paused, closing her eyes. "They're coming. I can feel it."

She glanced around the forest, her eyes full of paranoia. "Who? Who's coming?" I asked.

She whispered, "Raiders. They always come."

"What do they want?"

"Everything. They're scavengers, living off the weak, trapped in anguish."

I fell into her arms, desperate for her strength. She never raised me. My mother didn't teach me to put on makeup or walk in heels, but it never severed the bond between us. I needed her support—the unconditional love that we all crave from our parents. I needed to know that even if I failed, someone would be there that didn't love me any less.

"Please don't leave me. I can't do this."

Her fingers ran through the back of my matted hair, over and over. She gently rocked, attempting to soothe me as if I were a child. "You have to protect him. He needs you."

"Protect who? What do you want me to do?" I sobbed.

"It's time to run, Mercy. Don't stop."

I froze at the sight of her long red nails grazing the side of my arm. Her embrace turned cold and hard, not the comfort I had taken solace in moments before.

"Shh," she whispered. "I got you."

I jumped back, eager to put distance between myself and the familiar voice, dripping with disdain. A thin red dress replaced my mother's white nightgown, and the soothing smile transformed into an evil sneer.

I shook my head in disbelief. "You aren't here. This isn't real." My eyes traveled around the forest, attempting to decipher reality from illusion. "You aren't here!"

Aadya threw her head back, cackling. I covered my ears

as the echo of her laughter reverberated off the trees. She stayed seated on the ground, her legs crossed in front of her. "Oh, Mommy! Don't leave me, Mommy!" Once again, she broke out in fits of laughter, but halted abruptly. "Oh, I forgot," she whispered, sadly. "Your mother is dead!"

"Shut up! Shut up!" I couldn't take it. I didn't have a chance to catch my breath before the punishing memories suffocated me once again. I closed my eyes, willing the vision to disappear.

"Look at me, Mercy. I want you to remember the lives you've taken, you power hungry bitch! That's all you want, isn't it? You wanted my power so much, you were willing to murder me! To allow your freak of a boyfriend to rip my head off in front of my own people." Her voice turned frantic as she screeched, "Look at me!"

I hesitantly opened my eyes to find her standing inches in front of me. I gasped as my gaze went to her headless body and her pale, slender fingers clutching the hair of her decapitated head. Blood dripped from the corner of her mouth as she continued to taunt me.

"Something wrong?" Aadya smirked.

I couldn't shake it. The terror of my aunt standing in front of me overwhelmed all rational thought, and I knew as long as I focused on her, the longer I would be left to endure it. Her hollow, dead eyes blinked, as if waiting for my response.

"You deserved it all," I spat. "I'd do it all over again."

Aadya scowled. A look of annoyance crossed her pale face as a rustling in the distance pulled my attention toward the trees. Her frown immediately altered into a satisfying grin. "Here they come."

At once I realized, the Oblivion used the visions from my past to distract me, to stall me while Raiders closed in.

It wanted nothing more than to see me suffer. Without a second to lose, I did exactly like my mother said. I ran.

Before I ever learned about my lineage, before I could control my gifts of Interference, I kept myself in excellent shape. I could run for hours on my weakest days. But something about this place drained the energy out of me, and I found myself faltering after minutes on my feet.

The small sliver of moonlight did little to guide the way through the dense forest. Besides the crunch of twigs under the sole of my boot, not a noise could be heard. There were no voices, or shuffling of shoes, but I knew they were there. I had nothing to give, but it didn't matter. Something inside of me, a dark and chilling voice, whispered they would take anything I had left, including my motivation to survive.

My legs burned, but I pushed forward. Thorny bushes swiped across my arms as shallow roots caught the toe of my boot, almost tripping me. Clouds slowly drifted in front of the moon, blocking the sliver of light illuminating my path. I put my hands out in front of me, fearful of trees, but it didn't matter.

I didn't get very far.

Something hard slammed against my face, throwing me back several feet. My cheek underneath my left eye exploded in pain, and I cried out, turning on my side and cupping my cheek. I attempted to blink, but the entire side of my face had gone numb, and I knew the impact had shattered my cheekbone.

"Gotcha," a gruff voice called out.

I tried to look up, but struggled to focus through my good eye. The blonde raider from before stood over me with a large limb in hand. He smirked as if he'd won a prize.

"What do you want?" I choked out, holding the side of my face.

He kneeled down in front of me, looking around as if it were a secret. Then he whispered, "Everything."

"Maybe you're not here at all. You could be a vision, too."

He chuckled, glancing behind me as if meeting another's gaze. His head was larger than normal, with short blonde hair and dark eyes. His shoulders were broad, and his white teeth gleamed in the darkness. I imagined him with a wide gold necklace and fake orange tan in the summer—one of those guys who appeared to be in love with himself.

"Wanna know if it's real, pretty girl?" He grinned. "Does this feel real?"

He gripped my hair in his fist and dragged me backward through the forest. Sticks and rocks scraped my back and shoulders as he continued into the woods, but I couldn't reach anything to help me get to my feet.

I screamed, clawing at the legs of my attacker, refusing to give up without a fight. His dark chuckle joined several others, and my heart pounded from fear. My vision blurred from the throbbing in my face, but just as the sole of his boot kicked up beside my head, I grabbed his foot. I yanked as hard as I could, knocking him off balance enough to release his grip on my hair.

"You bitch!" He screamed.

He scrambled to his feet, but before he could get a hold on me once again, I swung my legs up, kicking him across the face. As soon as I jumped to my feet, someone grabbed me from behind, holding my arms behind my back.

Blondie stood, blood dripping from the corner of his lip. He smiled as if enjoying the sight of me restrained at his mercy. He painfully gripped my face with one hand, standing only inches in front of me. "Something is off with this one," he mumbled to the man behind me. "She's different."

I raised one brow, throwing attitude I didn't feel.

"Where did you get those clothes? If memory serves, you were running through the forest half naked the last time I saw you."

"Left an impression, didn't I?" I tried to grin, but I knew I looked ridiculous.

He stepped forward, one side of his upper lip pulling up in a snarl. "I won't ask you again."

"They were a gift."

His laughter echoed through the trees. "People don't give away anything. Not here. Just so happens we got things missing. You stole these."

I shook my head, denying it. "I didn't." I jerked away from his hold, scowling, but he tightened his grip.

"There's fire in her, that's for sure."

"Fire, huh?" An older man with a gruff voice called out from the trees. He leaned against a tall pine with his arms crossed, spitting into the darkness. "Doesn't look like much from where I'm standing." He pushed off the bark of the tree, stepping forward to get a closer look. He stood a foot taller than me, and his black beard and eyes would have been menacing if it weren't for a hint of warmth shining through. Something told me he hadn't always been so cold.

"Who are you?" he asked.

"Why does it matter?" I swallowed from nervousness, but tried to appear calm.

One side of his mouth pulled up in a smirk, then he leisurely walked around me, circling me as if I were his prey. "Who are you?"

I didn't think it would matter if I told him. I thought about what Icy had said about time—it didn't exist here.

These people more than likely had either been here a long time, or had arrived years after me. It didn't matter. Here, in this hell, we existed together.

"Mercy Monroe."

He scoffed. "Monroe, huh? I don't know any Monroes."

I exhaled, somewhat relieved. "What do you want from me?" I asked.

He smiled. "From where I'm standing, you don't have anything I want. No food. No supplies. That's a pretty necklace, though."

I jerked away from his touch.

"She's got something I want," Blondie called out, amusement gleaming from his too white smile.

"Shut it, Jacobs."

"But Reynolds—"

"You heard me," he grumbled.

I stared between the two men, my patience wearing thin. "Can we get on with this?" I shouted. "Before another natural disaster occurs?"

Reynolds didn't answer, just studied me as if I interested him.

I sighed. "I mean, I'm not on a time limit or anything, but if you're gonna kill me, let's do this."

He turned his head to the side to spit, then stared at my necklace. "Get her back to camp."

. . .

I FOLLOWED the men through the woods, one of them staying close behind. All of the trees and paths appeared identical, and I wondered how they even knew where to go. The terrain changed so often, along with the weather. The balmy summer day transitioned to a cool evening breeze, quickly turning into a heavy gust that swayed thick branches overhead.

I swear I could *feel* a storm coming.

After what felt like an hour, we walked up to a small campsite, where several men guarded bags of supplies. A small fire fought to stay lit as a couple of men slept on the ground beneath the trees. Reynolds led me toward the center of camp, and I fought to ignore the curious stares and angry whispers.

"Hey, D," Reynolds called out. "Need you to watch her while I speak to the guys."

My steps faltered when a tall, dark-haired man turned, shadowed by the tall trees above. His shoulders were wider than the average man. I could barely make out the cut of his strong jaw, but I would know him anywhere.

It was *Drake*.

The guard pushed me forward, as if annoyed by my sudden lack of urgency. As I shuffled further into the camp, he stepped into the fire light and paused. His eyes shifted from me to the man holding me. His angry expression hid the dimple in his cheek that I knew was there. The muscle in his jaw clenched tight as he met my eyes. I gasped.

It *wasn't* Drake.

"I got it from here," he rumbled.

"You sure, D?"

He nodded and the guard released my hands, hurrying across the camp toward food and water. He pointed toward the large tree stump beside the fire. "Sit."

I didn't know who he was, but my curiosity was strong enough to stick around and find out. He and Drake could have been brothers. I sat down without a word, watching his every move. The sway of his hips, the slight slump of his right shoulder, his biceps straining against the sleeve of his shirt. The striking resemblance caused a deep ache inside of me to cry out for Drake, as if a vital part of me had vanished.

He held out a small canteen, rusty from age. "Drink."

Thunder rumbled overhead as the wind whipped my hair across my face. I didn't ask questions, his tone warned me otherwise. Besides, I couldn't think of anything worse than what I'd already been through. Tipping the canteen against my lips, I swallowed. I honestly couldn't think of anything more satisfying in that moment than the warm, metallic-tasting water that hit my tongue. My parched throat begged for it.

"Easy there," he mumbled, kneeling in front of me. "Don't make yourself sick."

I lowered the water, but kept it close by. I refused to give it up anytime soon. "What is this place?" I asked.

He shrugged, looking around at the men standing about. "Survival."

"You and your friends survive off the weak," I spat.

"They are not my friends," he replied, anger dripping from his voice. "And I don't survive off anyone."

"Then why are you here?" I pressed. I tilted my head back as the lightest of raindrops began to fall. "Why do you stay?"

He lowered his head, scratching the back of his neck, then raised his head to meet my eyes. "Because there's safety in numbers. They may be useful."

"Useful?" I laughed. "I doubt it."

He smirked. "Where do you think you got those clothes?"

I had a feeling, but I needed him to say it. "I knew it was you. But, why? Why did you help me?"

He stood, taking a deep breath. "Seemed like the right thing to do."

I don't know why, but I had a feeling he was lying. Something in the way he lowered his voice, and he refused to meet my gaze. "That's a lie."

He jerked his head in my direction, but he didn't reply. I swear his eyes were filled with humor.

"Who are you?" I asked.

"They call me D."

"That isn't what I asked." I fought to maintain my fierce, determined look.

He laughed. "You are full of attitude, aren't you?" He reached out to graze the side of my face that continued to swell.

I didn't reply, but backed away from his hand.

Time stood still for just a few seconds as we studied one another, curious about the person standing before us. His features—his warmth—reached out to me on a deep level. A level of affection I didn't expect. But how?

He leaned forward, asking, "Are you hungry?"

"You have food?"

He turned, picking up a thick burlap sack, sitting beside a tree. "Mainly fruit and nuts. Fish when we can catch them." He handed me the bag, then sat down a few feet away.

"What are they going to do with me?" I asked, around a mouthful of blueberries and pine nuts.

He shook his head. "I'm not sure what they're thinking. I've never seen a woman in their camp."

Reynolds spoke quietly in the corner with a few other men, who frequently glared in my direction. I couldn't be sure what they wanted, but I didn't intend on finding out. "I really appreciate your help, but I think it's time for me to go."

He chuckled. "You're gonna just walk out of camp? As if no one will notice?"

The rain had gotten heavier, but the sensation of cool water relieved some of the ache on the side of my face. I leaned forward, whispering, "I've seen what this place can do. I'm not waiting around for the next disaster, thank you very much."

He froze, his eyes cutting from side to side, as if something had caught his attention. He stood, on guard.

"What..." I started.

"Shh. Do you feel that?" He held up one finger, as if the single digit would help him focus.

I didn't feel anything at first. But then, a low rumble built in intensity and the tree trunk beneath me began to shake. "What is happening?" I jumped from the stump as trees all around me began to fall, pulling up their thick roots from underneath the soil.

A bolt of lightning struck the tall pine behind me and he jerked me out of the way, tucking me safely into his side. "We gotta get out of here." He pulled me toward the tree line, but I hesitated, unsure of what to do. He met my eyes in the dark and asked, "Do you trust me?"

It honestly didn't matter if I did or not, I didn't have another option. But the truth was, I did trust him. I didn't doubt him at all.

"I trust you."

CHAPTER
ELEVEN
MARLEY

"Look again," I demanded.

Thu Dang paced the small family room, one hand behind his back while the other fidgeted at his waist. "We've looked everywhere. I can't find a single trace of the ring or necklace. Are you certain Mercy kept them in her room?"

"They were laying on the table by the window, both of them! They couldn't have disappeared!" I shouted.

"Maybe she put them on? Or someone came into the room after you left? Can you think of anyone that might have stolen them?"

"If I thought that, would I be wasting my time with you?"

One eye widened, as if surprised. "I had almost forgotten you were Aadya's niece, that is, until right at this moment." He smirked as if my attitude pleased him.

"Find the jewelry. Now."

He nodded, then cleared his throat. "It's my top priority."

"Is there anything else?" I asked, fidgeting with the white shell necklace I'd had since I was a child.

He quickly changed the subject as if it would improve my mood. "I've received word that Regalians have somewhat settled since you were named temporary member of the Elders.

"And Drake? How is he taking it?"

He looked down, unable to look me in the eyes. "Appears disheartened, but he will learn as everyone will in time."

"And what is that exactly?" I raised one brow, the slightest movement filled with sass and attitude.

"Who their leader truly is."

I turned away from his beady eyes, glancing out the window toward the courtyard. I didn't feel like a leader. A petulant child trying to prove herself in a world that wanted little from her, that's what I felt like. I stood at this window days ago, admiring the blooms on the magnolia tree. Now, the white silk flowers seemed to whither before my eyes.

"And the boy?" I asked, still staring out the window.

"I've sent an Elder to the Hughes home, explaining we would like to work with Ren, teach him to control his gift. Mrs. Hughes is frightened, but also has fond feelings for the child. I'm not sure how she will cope with us taking him away."

"Put him in the dungeon when he arrives," I demanded. "Don't waste any time."

"You think that's wise? The sisters will want him immediately. They will not take your bargain lightly, Marley."

"I'm not stupid. I know the deal, but if they want him, he has to be more powerful than we know. I'm not taking any chances."

"Of course." Thu Dang continued, "The recent reports are on your desk, minor affairs that need your attention."

"My attention?"

"Food shortages, wildlife management, legalities."

"Don't we have people to handle that?"

He smirked. "That would be us."

I spun, glaring at his degrading tone. "We are the most powerful land in the universe. How could we have food or wildlife issues?"

He grinned. "Surprisingly, not everything can be fixed with magic. Especially when it comes to citizen disputes."

I threw my hands up in disgust. "I don't have time to babysit these insufferable fools. We have more important things to deal with than petty complaints from spoiled citizens. This isn't what I signed up for."

"What did you expect? Look at you. You are exactly where you've always wanted to be—leader of Seregalo. Show them you are the one true ruler by making their concerns your priority. Take your place on the throne Aadya left behind. My dear, people are watching."

"Let them!" I shouted, but took a deep breath, quickly composing myself. "I will do right by my people, but I'm not done reclaiming what Mercy took from me."

He bowed his head, as if trying to find words that didn't upset me. "You do realize they are matched—practically bonded. That won't be easy to overcome."

I swallowed, a feeble attempt to keep my voice strong. "It doesn't mean anything."

"Doesn't it?"

"Is there anything else?" I quickly glanced away, unable to face him. I didn't need anyone to remind me of what I had lost to my sister. He didn't need to lecture me on the power of the Allegato. It meant nothing to me.

He turned to leave, but looked over his shoulder before walking out the door. "I'll make sure the boy is here by this afternoon." Then he vanished.

I balled my fists, needing to hit something. My head pounded from the intense drive to delve into someone's subconscious and assault their hopes and dreams. Sometimes, my gift acted as if it had a life of its own—desiring nothing more than to feed off another. It was almost addictive.

The small frame on the antique desk caught my attention out of the corner of my eye. I reached forward, running my fingers over the intricate, bronze design over a cherry wood frame. The oval picture inside struck me more than I expected, and I pulled my hand back as if it had burned me.

My mother and father, close to my age, sat together underneath a tree on a bright sunny day. Her head tilted back from laughter, and he stared at her as if she were the only person on the planet. I had no idea where the picture came from—I don't remember it from before. I wish I knew what had gone through my parent's minds. I yearned to know how they truly felt about me.

"You wanted to see me?"

I jolted from the deep voice at the doorway. Drake stood with his arms behind his back, refusing to look at me in the eyes.

"I've never seen this before," I explained, pointing to the picture. "They look so happy together."

He cut his eyes in my direction. "Mercy found it packed away. It's her favorite."

I nodded, then smiled sadly. "Any news on my sister?"

He took a deep breath, then shook his head. "You wanted to see me," he repeated.

I noticed how he refused to meet my gaze. "Yes, thank you. I wanted to speak with you about the boy. Ren."

"What about him?"

I hated the short and snappy replies, as if being in my presence was torture for him. "There are reports he is dangerous, and the Elders feel it is in our best interest to bring him back to the dungeon."

His entire body tensed. "What? They can't do that to him."

I stepped forward, attempting to comfort him. "I agree, but I'm afraid they outvoted me. I'm worried about him, Drake. He's just a child, and Mercy wouldn't want this."

"You don't know anything about her. Stop acting like you do," he demanded.

"I know she would protect Ren. Would she not?"

He walked toward the window, sighing in defeat. "What do you want from me?"

"Until we can figure out what is going on, I want you to keep an eye on him. Let me know if he needs anything. If they're going to lock him up, at least put a bed down there and make it comfortable. He isn't a prisoner, and I refuse to treat him that way."

"Mercy seemed concerned about him last week, but I don't think this is what she had in mind. Fitz is still here, I'll get him to talk to him also. Maybe he can help."

Wonderful. Dr. Fitzgerald to the rescue.

"That is brilliant. If anyone can help, it will be him," I agreed. "Can you meet me after dinner for daily reports? I want to keep a close check on him."

He turned to face me. "Everyday?" he asked. "Seems a little much, don't you think?"

I shook my head. "Oh, no. He needs us, Drake. We need to make him a priority."

He scratched the back of his head while focusing on the floor. "I'll make him a priority, Marley, but dinner with you is not."

I smiled, fighting tears of disappointment. "It brings me so much comfort to know I have you in my corner. I know Mercy will be proud to hear how much you supported me in her absence."

I thought at first he might laugh, but he cleared his throat and nodded somewhat composed. "Of course she would."

I focused on his thoughts, pushing everything I had to crawl into the smallest crevices where memories lay hidden. They had to be there. He had to remember. My hands shook from the effort, every inch of his mind locked tight.

He waited, watching me as if I'd gone off the rails. "Was there anything else?"

I met his eyes, realizing I had zoned out. "That's all for now. Thank you."

Drake didn't move, just stood awkwardly in the center of the room.

"What? What's on your mind?" I asked.

"You can't replace her. No one can. I don't know what happened, but I don't believe she ran away. Mercy has never run away from anything in her life."

Ouch.

"I'm not trying to replace her, Drake. I'm trying to help until she comes home. I'm not the monster you think I am."

He scowled. "I didn't say you were a monster."

"You didn't have to," I whispered.

He took a step back. "I'll come to the Domicile to check on Ren everyday—you have my word."

"What do you mean, come to the Domicile? Are you

moving out?" My heart pounded at the thought of him putting distance between us. That wouldn't help my cause.

"I am, until I find Mercy, anyway. It's not the same without her. It doesn't feel right."

"Maybe you should stay in case she comes back. You would want to be here, right?"

"She knows where to find me." Drake turned toward the door to leave.

"Catch you on the flip side," I called out, hating the high-pitched strain in my voice.

He froze, his hand gripping the knob. He looked over his shoulder, his eyebrows pulled together as if concentrating. "What did you say?"

I shrugged, nonchalant. "Catch you on the flip side. You know, see ya later."

He nodded slowly, but I could tell the phrase affected him. Drake reluctantly opened the door to leave and I grinned, satisfied with his reaction.

He remembered.

. . .

MARLEY- 10 YEARS OLD

"WHAT DO you think they're talking about?" Drake asked.

I pushed back and forth on my toes in the swing, not quite putting forth any effort. I stared through the window where Aunt Isla and Mr. Moreno sat at the kitchen table chatting over coffee. No doubt, talking about my latest issues at school. I couldn't figure out why he cared. "Me. Aren't they always talking about me?"

He scoffed, rolling his eyes. "It's not always about you."

I grinned, loving it when he teased me. "I'm glad you came—it's been a while."

He chuckled. "We were here last month, it hasn't been that long."

"It feels like it," I whispered dramatically. "What have you been up to?"

"School. Lessons. You know, stuff."

"Lessons? Lessons in what? Like baseball or something?"

He looked away, as if unsure how much he could say. "Yeah, something like that."

"You're a horrible liar. Did you know that?"

He smiled. "I know." Drake stood, backing up to gain traction on his swing before picking up his feet and flying through the air. "How much do you know about your parents? I'm just curious."

The last thing I wanted to do was talk about them. "They abandoned me as a baby. I know your family is friends with them, and your father promised to watch over me, but that's about it. I don't care. There is no excuse for what they did."

"But Isla and Cliff treat you good, right?"

I shrugged one shoulder. "I guess. They're simple, you know. Not like us."

"What do you mean?"

"They go to work, cook supper, pay bills while we do homework, everyone gets a bath, we say our prayers, then we get tucked into bed. Ridiculous. Every night is the same."

He laughed. "Sounds awful. What would you prefer?"

"Excitement and adventure." I threw my hands into the air. "Darkness around every corner with an adrenaline rush.

I want passion." I wagged my brows, causing him to turn away from my intense stare.

"You're very dramatic. Did you know that?"

I nodded. "So I've been told. What's it like at your house?"

"Mom stays busy with Asher. He's always whining about something or getting into trouble. She says his emotions are too much for him to handle, whatever that means. I'm homeschooled because we travel a lot. It wasn't always that way, but I like spending so much time with my dad."

"It sounds wonderful."

"Most days it is. We play games together, especially when we are on a road trip. My favorite is Dungeon and Dragons. Have you played?"

I shook my head, loving how his eyes lit up when talking about something he loved.

"I'll teach you how sometime. You'll love it, I know you will."

"If you love it, so will I." I smiled, brightly. I loved everything about him. "Tell me more about your parents."

"Dad loves to grill out, but he isn't very good at it. Don't tell him I said that. Everything is always burned." He wrinkled his nose.

I threw my hand over my mouth, giggling at Drake's scandalous confession. "I won't tell him, I swear."

He nodded before he continued. "Mom gets sad a lot. I think she misses where she grew up, but Dad says it isn't safe anymore. She takes me to Central Park on the weekends to play baseball with other kids."

"Tell me about New York."

"New York is sweet. Food carts are on every corner, and

Dad takes me to Yankees games all the time. You would love it."

"I'm not sure I'd like baseball. But I'd go for you."

"You never know, you might love it. What do you like to do? You're always tucked inside your room or hanging out in the backyard when we stop by."

"I like to pretend I'm in a faraway land, full of magic and never ending possibilities! Wouldn't it be amazing? We could go together."

His eyes brightened. "What would we do in this world?"

"Swim, stay up all night, play Dungeons and Dragons . . . anything we want!"

"Sounds like a date," he replied.

I froze. "A date?" *Did he really just say what I think he said?*

"Yeah. You know, a plan."

I nodded, unable to get the word *date* out of my head. Was that what he meant? It had to be, right? I didn't care that I was only ten years old. I would be with this boy for the rest of my life. No one could change that. "What do you want to do when you get older?" I asked.

"Play baseball for the Yankees."

"I guess I have to learn to love baseball now. You'll have to teach me."

A proud grin spread across his handsome face. "Deal."

"Drake! It's time to go," Mr. Moreno shouted.

I slumped into the swing. "But you only just got here."

He elbowed me, playfully. "I'll be back soon."

"Drake!"

"Coming, Dad!" Drake stood, and guilt flooded his eyes at the sight of me pouting. "I'll be right back." He bolted toward the car, and several seconds later he ran back with a baseball in hand. "Here."

I turned it around in my small hands, staring as if it would explode. His Initials, DM, were scrawled with blue ink on the side of the ball.

"Keep it. When I visit, I'll teach you how to catch."

I'd been given gifts from Aunt Isla before, but there wasn't a doll in the world that could compare to the ball in my hand. I'd never been athletic in the least, but I didn't care. I would cherish it as long as I lived. "I don't know what to say."

"You don't have to say anything." He backed up a couple of steps and smiled. "Catch you on the flip side."

CHAPTER
TWELVE
DRAKE

I stomped down the corridor of the domicile, eager to leave the desolate building behind. I couldn't feel the floor beneath my feet—I didn't feel anything. My sensory gift had blocked my anxiousness, along with the gaping hole in my chest. Without Mercy, there was nothing here for me.

I wasn't sure where to go, but I knew I couldn't stay there. I found myself walking around the town for hours, hoping I didn't run into someone I knew. The last thing I wanted was to face sympathy-filled gazes from people who didn't even know me. I could stay with Colton, but I remembered Fitz asking to bunk at his place, and the cottage would be crowded. No, I needed to go somewhere I could find peace.

Talk to someone who *wasn't* afraid to give it to me straight.

That's how I found myself on the steps of Mrs. Monroe's front door. I knocked, waited a few seconds, then knocked again. Finally, she opened the door, squinting. White smudges of flour smeared her forehead as she held her coated hands up to keep from touching anything else. I glanced from the dusty apron to her face and raised my brows in surprise.

"When I'm stressed, I bake," she muttered. "Might as well come on in. Nobody else is here to eat all this."

I followed Mercy's grandmother inside, past the old brown and yellow sofa to the bright yellow kitchen straight ahead. She didn't care how outdated her house was compared to everyone else. To her, it was home, and I loved that about her.

After washing her hands, she turned, holding a crumble-topped blueberry muffin closer to my face than I'd like.

"Oh. Um, no thank you, Mrs. Monroe." I mumbled, peering at her over the muffin.

"Ms. . . Not Mrs. Don't you forget it." She shoved it forward once again and glared. "I told you to call me Grandmother, but you already know that." She sighed, eyeing me suspiciously. "When's the last time you ate something?"

"Is this a dragon joke? Because that isn't funny," I mumbled.

She grinned. "You look thin, Drake. Have you been eating?"

I shrugged, sitting on a barstool beside the counter. "I don't have much of an appetite."

She nodded. "Thought as much. I have some tomato soup in the fridge. Let me heat some up for you."

"You don't have . . ."

She waved me off, refusing to listen. "That or a few muffins. I'm gonna see some food in you either way."

I didn't argue, I knew there wasn't a point. Ms. Monroe turned on the gas stove, heating the leftover soup in a shallow copper pot while I sat quietly, content with the silence. My gaze traveled over the dining table, where pictures of her, Noah and Annabel lined the far wall. Even one of me and Mercy sat framed on the kitchen counter, taken shortly after moving to Seregalo.

But I never saw one of her husband, or ex-husband, I should say.

I'd heard the stories from Mercy about the infidelity, but never wanted to ask. I'm not sure what gave me the courage that day. "Tell me about Noah's father."

She stood in front of the stove, stirring the soup with an old wooden spoon. The stillness of her hand was the only indication she'd heard me. After several seconds, she muttered, "Not much to tell."

"When did he leave?" I asked, curious.

"As soon as he got that girl pregnant, he left with her. He tried to move to Seregalo, but his child with her had been born ungifted, so the Elders refused her. He went back to the states with his new family, while Noah and I stayed here."

"So you weren't . . ."

"Mated? No. He never wore a mark, and I guess that should have been an indication of his inability to remain faithful."

"But you had a mark?"

She nodded, tearful. "I thought there was no way on earth there could ever be another man for me. We moved from Seregalo so my mate wouldn't come along some day. I got pregnant with Noah, then years later found out about his affairs."

I shook my head, unable to comprehend how someone could do such a thing. "I'm guessing his daughter is the one who raised Mercy."

She scowled. "Shame it is. That wretched woman didn't

deserve to breathe the same air as my granddaughter. I understand why Noah did it, but I still don't like it."

"I met him, did you know that?" I asked. "Noah saved my life."

"Mercy told me what happened, Drake. My boy would have walked through fire for his family, and you are one of us." She shook her head. "The agony he and Annabel went through breaks my heart." She sat a bowl of piping hot soup in front of me. "I remember your parents, you know."

I glanced up, surprised. "You do?"

"They were so in love, matched in every way possible. Your mother fell head over heels when she met Dorian. He moved here from Spain, with that silky black hair and olive skin, so much like yours. He had all the girls in town praying for a sensory tattoo to pop up on their shoulder. It didn't matter, he only ever had eyes for her."

I chuckled, but quickly grew quiet. "I know the feeling."

She reached for my hand and squeezed. "Have you slept?"

I sat in a daze, staring at nothing in particular. "I can't. I tried last night, but I ended up searching the woods behind the Domicile."

"Would you like to stay here? It might help."

I shook my head. "I'm not sure what I need. I've never felt so lost in my life. Considering I grew up on the streets, that's saying something."

She smiled. "I know just the place."

. . .

I FOLLOWED Ms. Monroe into the woods, and found myself quite impressed by her quick pace and spunky energy. Now, I knew exactly who Mercy got it from. She led me in the opposite direction of the Domicile, past the village where Neela's family lived.

A small stone cottage sat isolated by the river, and looked as though it had been untouched for years. Mrs. Monroe carefully picked up old flower pots along the front walk, complete with dried sticks from what used to be plants. She looked under each one, searching for what I assumed was a key.

When she lifted the last one, a brilliant yellow and teal design with a pink painted flower on the front, she chuckled to herself as if amused. "Couldn't remember which one it was under. Should've known."

She pulled the key free and shuffled toward the door. After fighting with the lock for several minutes, I carefully peered over her shoulder, impatiently. "Can I help?"

She scoffed, but eventually turned the keys over to me. The lock clicked free, but it took a shove to budge the oval, solid wood door. Dust blew into the air around me as I turned away, giving it time to settle.

When I walked into the cottage, I froze at the sight of the sheet covered furniture and dusty pictures hanging on the wall. There was no telling how long the home had sat empty. "What is this place?"

"It was Noah and Annabel's home. I wanted to give it to you and Mercy, but I didn't know if either of you would want it since the Domicile is so nice."

I could only imagine how Mercy's eyes would light up at the sight of the cottage. She would cherish every detail, big and small. "I couldn't imagine us living anywhere else."

She swallowed, the small movement full of emotion I

completely understood. "Well, then, you better get it fixed up for your bride. When Mercy gets back, she'll want to see it." She turned toward the door.

"I can't feel her."

She turned back to face me with sad eyes.

"I've always been able to feel her," I gasped. "I can't feel anything."

She palmed the side of my face and met my eyes with fierceness. "She's out there, Drake. Don't allow doubt to tell you any different."

"I'm trying," I whispered.

"Try harder. I won't allow you to waste away, pining for my granddaughter. So tell me, what exactly are you going to do about it?"

. . .

LONG AFTER SHE LEFT, I continued pacing from one end of the cottage to the other. Something about the cozy home did make me feel closer to Mercy, and for that small gift, I was thankful. But she was right, I had to start thinking outside the box and get Mercy home.

I washed a glass in the kitchen, sipping on enough water to keep me hydrated. I ignored the parched burn of my throat when I swallowed, and the turning of my stomach as my body greedily absorbed anything I would offer. My mind ran through every possible explanation, inside or outside of Seregalo. The only thing I knew for sure, is that no one had left through Stonedell that day.

No one.

At times like this, I pictured the worst. My thoughts grew hazy and dark as I imagined her suffering, being tortured in the worst possible way. I had already scoured every inch of the mountainside, but the dragon within sensed the proximity of the cave and begged to be released.

As many lives as Aadya had ruined, the memory of ripping her head from her body would haunt me for the rest of my life. Since that day, the dragon had never gained control again, but my weakened and highly emotional state wasn't helping anything. On more than one occasion, it begged to be released—to fly above the forest of Seregalo to search for Mercy.

My hands shook from anger and I threw the glass to the floor, shattering it at my feet. I stomped out of the cottage, desperate to figure out a way to reach her. I wouldn't give up.

I refused.

THIRTEEN

MARLEY

"What do you mean Ren's refusing to eat?" I walked out of the bathroom, raising one brow at the sight of Thu Dang sitting on the side of my bed. "Comfortable?"

He sighed, then stood with his arms crossed as if I were being ridiculous. "He's completely shut down. Transporting the boy to the Domicile wasn't easy. The Hughes are demanding answers, and I had to use subconscious interference to block him from draining everyone he came in contact with. I've never seen anything like it."

"I don't understand. What do you mean, draining?"

"He is out of control. As if he thrives off the energy of those around him. By the time we locked him up, I could barely stand." Thu Dang stepped forward and whispered. "This is more than we can deal with right now. I say we hand him over to the sisters and be done with it."

I paced in front of the window, going over my options. Dark magic wasn't something I wanted to get involved with. I wasn't exactly a nun, but there were things I didn't know enough about. As long as we held up our end of the deal, the creepy sisters would more than likely slither back into their hole, as if we'd never met.

But . . . What if there was more I needed to know? Could the boy be that powerful? Did I need him by my side? I had to know what we were dealing with before I put him in the hands of those psychotics—bargain or no bargain.

"Send Fitz to the dungeon. Report back as soon as possible," I decided, looking over my shoulder.

"Fitzgerald, Ma'am?" Thu Dang sneered at the name.

"Mercy asked him to work with the child. Let him follow through, see what he comes up with." I met Thu Dang's eyes. "Tell Creeky and Jules we're easing the child into their care. Hold them off."

He chuckled. "You've met them. There isn't a lie they can't see through, Marley."

"Then I guess you need to make it believable." I glared, daring him to argue. "Also, I want Neela and Nora out of the Domicile. I don't need someone looking over my shoulder every time I turn around."

"I can do that." He grinned, but didn't budge.

"Is there something else?"

His thumb brushed back and forth across his chin, as if contemplating his next words. "You should consider visiting him."

"Who?"

Thu Dang rolled his eyes. "The boy, of course."

"Are you mad? Why would I do that?"

"Drake arrived just as I left. Might be a good time to play the doting leader." He smirked. "Show him how much you care."

I stood up straight, tossing my hair over my shoulder. "Why didn't you say so? When did he arrive?"

"Maybe twenty minutes ago. He looked as though he'd been up all night."

"That will be all for now." I shooed him out the door, not caring if it offended him.

He bowed before me, then backed out of the room without another word.

I ran into the bathroom, spraying perfume and applying lipstick. My jeans fit tight and my white tank gave the girls a lift, so I felt good about my outfit. I bolted out the door, running down the stairs as fast as I could. I shouldered past a servant, knocking her to the side as she dropped her load of laundry, apologizing over and over. I ignored her like I did the rest, never bothering to acknowledge those beneath me.

I wanted them to *fear* me.

As I drew closer, something began to happen inside of me. The stone steps leading downstairs blurred as the air around me thickened. Pausing halfway down the steps, I leaned against the concrete wall for balance, gasping for air. I continued taking small steps, easing my way through the magical barricades of the dungeon.

By the time I reached the cells, sweat beaded along the back of my neck and heat rose up my chest. The spells Aadya had put into place to block the use of gifts lingered, but there was something deeper. Something alive that pulled at my mind, as if greedily searching for more.

Always more.

Drake's silhouette sat unmoving at the end of the row, facing the right side of the room. I walked by empty cells, one at a time, until I stood in front of Ren's prison, where Drake focused without blinking.

The boy sat on the floor beside his small bed, his eyes dim and vacant of life. Reaching out subconsciously, my power was not only blocked by the spell, but it ricocheted, causing me to stumble backward. My eyes went to Drake, who's color had drained from his face, and his heavy eyelids hovered as he watched Ren.

"I can ask the Elders to remove the spell," I offered.

Drake shook his head. "No."

"You can't do this everyday. I can barely stay down here right now."

"The spell keeps us from using our gift. I remember from being locked up before. That isn't what this is."

I cut my eyes toward the boy. "You think it's him? But how if the dungeon blocks power?"

"I think the spell is minimizing his power."

"So it could be worse?" I asked, shocked.

"Much worse." He met Ren's eyes and frowned. "I can't imagine what he's feeling."

I kneeled on the cold stone floor next to Drake, shivering as cold air hit my sweaty skin. Drake watched Ren, curiously, and I fought to stay silent, battling between demanding my own answers and silently supporting Drake.

"Ren?" Drake asked. "Do you remember me?"

Ren didn't so much as blink.

"We only want to help you," I lied. "Whatever you need." The air around me turned colder, and the lights above us flickered.

Drake sighed, frustrated. He shook his head, as if shaking off the suffocating cloak of magic. He tried once again. "I'm a friend of Mercy's."

All at once, Ren's eyes cut toward Drake and the intensity of his power subsided. "Mercy?"

I nodded. "That's right. Mercy is my sister."

He never looked in my direction, only focused on Drake. "Mercy's lost."

Drake didn't respond at first, and I wondered what went through his mind. "She'll be back, Ren. Mercy will be back, and she'll help you."

"I can't find her," he replied.

Drake leaned forward. "You have to talk to me—tell me what's happening. Are you in pain?"

"Pain is never ending. Your pain. Her pain. It's a cycle of hurt. I can feel you dying inside without her."

My throat tightened. "So what do we do? How can we help?" I asked.

"You want to help?" Ren scoffed. "Really?"

"What do you want from us?" Drake asked.

Ren shook his head. "You're the one who brought me here. Are you going to kill me?"

I gasped, unsure what he had just asked us to do. "What? No. Ren, I would never harm you. I swear!"

"Is that right?" Ren raised one brow, as if surprised.

I honestly didn't know what to say, so I lied. "Mercy will be back soon. I promise."

Ren tilted his head back, closing his eyes. "Tell me, can you feel her?"

After several seconds, Drake cursed under his breath and glanced away from Ren. "No. No, I can't."

I feigned shock and innocence. "What? What does that mean? Where is my sister?"

The boy began to rock, and his brows lowered as if concentrating. "So much love, but darkness is all around, smothering you." He met Drake's eyes. "But you don't know, do you? How would you? They took everything away."

"Know what? I don't understand," Drake mumbled.

"It's the magic," I whispered, nervously. "He doesn't know what he's saying."

Ren closed his eyes. "The remnants of first love linger, but deception is strong. Sandcastles on the coastline, baseball in the backyard, a first kiss beside the swing . . ." Ren scowled. "Shame that such fond memories are so corrupted."

Drake replied, "I don't know what you're talking about, that doesn't sound like Mercy and I at all. Plus, there is nothing corrupt about our relationship." He rolled his shoulders as if agitated.

Ren grinned, sadistically. "I didn't say it was Mercy."

. . .

MARLEY- TWELVE YEARS OLD

"GOOD CATCH, MARLEY!"

I grinned at his praise, running down the beach to where he stood. "Thanks. I've been practicing with Ben."

Drake pursed his lips.

"What?" I asked.

"Nothing. It's just, well Ben can't really help you like I can."

I grinned at his jealousy. "You know the tide is going to ruin our sand castle."

He glanced toward the shoreline, where the waves inched forward a little at a time. "I told you it isn't a castle, Marley. That is a Domicile."

I laughed at the unfamiliar word. "What is a Domicile?"

Drake chuckled. "I don't really know, but I hear my Dad talking about it."

"Well I think it's lovely."

"Domiciles aren't lovely, Marley. They're fierce." Drake turned to pick up his shirt.

Something dark caught my attention, and I reached out to touch his shoulder. "What is that?" I asked.

He looked over at me, narrowing his eyes. "What?"

"On your shoulder. I've never seen it before."

Drake froze, and when his eyes met mine, I could have sworn they were tinted red. "It's nothing."

I stepped closer, inspecting the black speckle of dots collecting along his shoulder. "Is it a tattoo? I mean, it's cool if it is."

He swallowed, then mumbled. "Yeah, something like that."

I nodded, trying to look mature. I didn't want him to think I couldn't hang. "Cool." The sight of Aunt Isla sitting in the sand with Mr. Moreno caught my attention. "What do you think they're talking about this time?"

The change of subject seemed to help his mood. "Same thing they always talk about. You," he replied, laughing.

I tilted my head, watching my aunt wring her hands like she did when worried. "Something is different. I don't know, maybe she's upset because I got suspended again." I shrugged.

His mouth fell open in shock. "Suspended? For what?"

"Cutting Lizzy Barker's hair in class. I warned her not to mess with me, and she told Jacob not to ask me to the Spring Fling dance because I had cooties."

Drake fought to hold back his laughter. "Well, do you have cooties?"

"Come and find out!"

I bolted toward the water, gasping as my legs splashed

through the icy sea. I could hear Drake running behind me, cackling.

"You are insane!" he shouted.

I had planned to stop before the cold water hit my waist, but Drake grabbed me from behind and tossed me into the air. As my head went under, I opened my eyes from the shock of the plunge, squinting past strands of seaweed and murky water.

Drake's blurry face drifted closer as he swam toward me, until he hovered inches away. He grinned, amused at our erratic behavior, but all I could do is think about our life together. I wanted him forever, just like this.

I leaned forward, pressing my mouth against his underwater. He stiffened, as if unsure how to respond. Not giving him a chance to pull away, I wrapped my arms around his neck and pulled him closer. His arms relaxed, and it thrilled me that he didn't pull away.

We came up for air, and just stood in the water, staring at each other. I didn't know what came over me, but I didn't regret it. I grinned, but it quickly vanished at the sight of regret filling his dark gaze.

"I'm so sorry, Marley. I really am," he murmured.

"What—"

"Marley!" Mr. Moreno called out. "Can you come here for a second?"

I turned back toward Drake, wanting to hear what he was going to say, but he dove into the water, swimming toward the shore. I waded through the ocean, crossing my arms in front of my chest, shivering. Drake rested by the edge of the water, looking out over the waves, deep in thought.

I trudged toward the dune where Mr. Moreno sat with my aunt. They both appeared grim, and I wondered what he wanted to speak with me about. No one ever wanted to talk to me, no one except Drake, anyway.

"Marley, Mr. Moreno would like to chat with you. I expect you to be on your best behavior and listen."

I smiled, sweetly. "Don't I always?"

She sighed, then turned toward him. "She's all yours."

He chuckled, and it surprised me how much it sounded like Drake. "Have a seat, Marley."

I kneeled beside him, and he reached for a towel tucked inside a bright yellow beach bag. "Here you go. I always bring towels, never know when Drake decides he wants to take a swim. He is so much like me at that age."

"But your other son, Asher, isn't?" Part of me was curious about Asher. The other, more hateful, part wanted to remind him that he had another son.

"Not quite, no. Asher isn't quite as carefree. He seems to always be searching for something greater, not enjoying the little things in life."

"Which are?" I asked.

He smiled, what I imagined a warm, fatherly grin would look like. My eyes drifted away from his face, uncomfortable under his dark scrutiny. "Family. Friends. Those moments of pure, unrestrained bliss where nothing in the world matters except the person in front of you. That's why I have to apologize for taking it away."

I sat up straight, not quite sure I understood. "What?"

"I know how close you are to Drake, but we have to leave, Marley. There are things happening you do not understand, and I think we may be putting you in danger by visiting. Especially right now when you may be coming into your . . . maturity."

"You aren't coming back?" I asked. "Never?"

"I hope we see you again one day, I really do. But right now, we are needed in New York."

"But . . . Drake."

He frowned. "I know you think a lot of Drake. You've been close for many years, but I have to put the safety of both of you ahead of friendship right now."

I gripped the sleeve of his cotton shirt, desperate for him to change his mind. "Please. Please don't do this to me. He's all I have."

Mr. Moreno's face fell, then he placed his hand over mine. All at once, warmth seeped into my joints and muscles, relaxing me. I whispered once again, "He's all I have. I don't care if I'm in danger."

"You may not care about yourself, but I know you would never want to put Drake in danger."

His words hit me hard. Pain shot through my chest at the thought of what I had to do. I looked up into his eyes as tears ran down my cheek. "I have to let him go?"

He nodded. "I'm afraid so."

"But he'll come back for me, right? When the danger is over?"

He leaned closer, his eyes full of a strange combination of warmth and regret. "After we leave today, Drake will have no memory of his time with you."

My mouth fell open in shock. "What? How is that possible?"

"Can I tell you a secret?"

I nodded, hanging on his every word.

"I have friends with special gifts, people that can make him forget."

My shoulders sagged and my chin trembled at the thought.

"I know you are young and confused, but please try to

understand. If someone tried to force Drake into confessing about you, I'd rather for those memories to be gone."

More tears began to fall. Everything in my life had been taken from me, starting the day I was born. Drake had been my only friend and one true love. How would I ever let him go? It wasn't fair and part of my heart hardened a little more that day.

I fought the tremble in my chin—the burning in my eyes. "Protect him. That's all I care about," I whispered.

He brushed my red hair from my face and smiled, sadly. "You'll meet again one day, Marley. I just know it."

I glanced toward the shoreline where Drake picked up a smooth white shell, turning it over in his palm. "Marley! I found one for you!"

FOURTEEN

MERCY

We ran through the forest, as wind whipped around my body, knocking me off balance into a tree. The guy they referred to as 'D' stayed close by my side, pulling me up and encouraging me to keep running. Although I trusted him, part of me continued to worry about his plan.

Why did he want to help me?

I pushed forward, my heart pounding from the sound of falling trees behind us. The pitch black forest in front of me gave way to an unknown abyss, and I couldn't help but wonder if we were being pushed into a trap. Multiple sets of bright yellow eyes hovered high in the trees, as if eagerly awaiting to see what happened next. The toe of my boot caught the edge of a rock, sending me flying forward, slamming into the stranger who rescued me.

We rolled down a steep hill covered in brush and thorns, finally coming to stop against a large tree trunk blocking our path. He landed on his back, with me on his chest, his arms wrapped protectively around me.

"Are you alright?" he asked.

I met his eyes in the dark, the mysterious connection evident with every look—every single time we touched. I didn't understand it. "I'm okay." I rolled off of him, attempting to regain my balance. "I think it's gone—whatever it was."

All at once, the ground beneath my feet began to shake.

"I think it's just getting started," he replied, hurrying to his feet. "Let's go."

I followed him through the dense forest, running as fast as my legs would carry me.

A low rumble drowned out everything around me as the sky turned deep orange, burning across the sky. A crack in the ground formed between us, spreading wider and wider. I jumped across to keep from being separated from him, reaching for his hand out of fear. Crevices in the ground began to appear all around us as we searched for a way through the never ending canyons.

"Don't stop!" he shouted.

Had he lost his mind? Of course I wasn't going to stop. The ground continued to shake, knocking me off my feet. I tumbled downhill, clawing at twigs and branches to regain control. Dirt began to split beneath me, and I crawled forward as rocks painfully dug into my palm. I glanced at where he'd stopped, trying to find a way back to him, but all at once, the chaos subsided. I tilted my head to the side, breathing slowly, as I took in the sudden stillness around me.

The mountains and valleys settled, leaving only dust and debris, as he sagged in relief. "I think it's really over." D stepped forward and immediately the crack in the ground between us widened. He froze once again, meeting my eyes.

"Aftershocks?" I asked.

His nervous gaze traveled around the forest, sharp and

focused. It was moments like that he reminded me of Drake. "Can you stand?" he asked.

I pushed up to my feet, and the ground trembled. I threw my hands out to help balance, and breathed a sigh of relief as it stilled once more. I decided to keep moving forward, but my next step was the catalyst. It only took one step—one small, insignificant shuffle—for the ground to open beneath me, as if desperate to swallow me whole.

Sharp edges of rock scraped against my arms and legs as I slid into the crevice. I gripped a thick tree root, dangling with one hand, the other pulling and clawing up the cliff-side. My shoulder burned from the effort of holding my weight. So many things had gone through my mind in the past couple of days, but I'd never taken a few seconds to actually accept I might not make it. What would happen to my friends and family? Regalians?

I tried not to think that way, but now, dangling over the high cliffside, it crossed my mind.

"Mercy! Can you hear me?"

"Yes," I choked out. "I'm here!"

A swift breeze blew by, carrying the terrified scream of a small young girl, one I knew too well. I stilled, wondering if I had lost my mind. But again, a tortured cry of help echoed through the canyon where I dangled helplessly.

"D! You have to find her. She needs us!"

"I'm not leaving you!"

"Please. I'll be okay. I think I see a way out of here," I lied. "Go help her and I'll find you by the river." I closed my eyes, tightening my grip on the tree root. "Please!"

"Damn it," he mumbled. "Hold on. Don't try to move. I'll be right back, I swear it!"

I listened to the sound of his boots crunching against brush and fallen limbs, the noise drifting further and further away. The high-pitched scream of the young girl reverberated off the canyon once again, and my heart clenched at how terrified she had to be. The orange tinted sky cast a hazy glow around me, and I searched the side of the cliff for something else to cling to. Dirt crumbled underneath my fingertips as I clawed, desperate to fight my way to the top. I couldn't see it, but my left toe caught on something that felt like rock, only a couple of feet away.

I swung to my left, but I wasn't close enough to use it for support. Bowing my back, I surged to my left once more, this time snapping one side of the root above, dropping me several more inches toward the dark abyss. My toe caught the edge of the rock and I slowly put weight on it, testing for stability.

It wasn't large enough to stand on, but would hopefully provide enough leverage for me to get a better grip on the tree root. I pushed up on the small stone ledge, and repositioned my hand on the root. The sweat from my palm made it difficult to maintain my grip so I pushed up on the ledge to adjust my hand.

I fell.

I gasped as the rock gave way and the root slipped from my fingers. The cliffside rushed by me in a blur. My mind raced and I couldn't think, overwhelmed with panic.

I am going to die.

Air slipped through my fingers as my arms and legs flailed. My elbow slammed against something hard, and for a moment I could think of nothing except the agony of my bone cracking. I couldn't raise my right arm at all, but continued reaching out with my left hand, feeling absolutely nothing.

Everything I had experienced up to that point, didn't hold a candle to the physical pain that came next. My back slammed against a jagged shard of rock on the side of the cliff, the anguish of a twisted spine blurring my vision as I arched my body, my screams echoing along the crevice of hell. Stabbing pain burned from the middle of my spine toward my neck as my broken body violently plunged toward the canyon floor. Nausea rolled through me, and I hoped I would black out before I hit the ground.

I prayed for death.

All at once, the back pain subsided, as did the flailing of my legs. The injury had taken away my ability to feel anything from the waist down—the realization bittersweet as the ground below me came into view.

I took in a deep breath and closed my eyes, bracing for the impact I knew would come. Ironically, I didn't think of Drake. Images of my friends and family didn't appear, as I would have thought. The pale skin and bright red hair of my sister entered my mind as I fell. What could I possibly have done for her to sentence me to this hell? For my life to end with so little meaning, alone and afraid.

How much did she hate me?

If by some chance I survived. If I ever walked again, I swore to hunt her down and make her pay for everything she had done. Then, she would know the agony I felt.

Then, she would be the one praying for death.

The impact of the ground shook me so hard, I felt every rib break, collapsing my lungs. Every few seconds, I wheezed, gasping for air, the copper taste of blood dripping from my mouth.

The chosen one.

My head hung twisted to the side as my crumpled body lay on the rocks.

The powerful one.

I glanced down at the emerald ring on my finger as black spots danced across my vision.

The strong one.

I'd never felt weaker—more vulnerable as I lay there suffering alone, waiting to die.

. . .

ANGUISH STIRRED ME, pulling me from the blackness. Pressure built in my chest as I swayed back and forth over something hard and uncomfortable. I couldn't be sure how long it went on, but I groaned when I didn't think I could go any further.

"Shh. I got you."

"I—I can't . . ." I groaned, painfully.

"Almost there. Just a little longer. Stay with me. I won't lose you," a deep voice muttered, out of breath.

He continued walking, the patter of little feet shuffling behind us. Sweat rolled down my face and neck. It could have been blood, I honestly didn't have a clue. Every time I attempted to open my eyes, I became nauseated.

"Here. Lay it right here. That's it, now get my bag —hurry."

Strong hands laid me gently on the ground, the delicate action shooting pain through my chest and head. I turned my head, vomiting on the ground, choking on the sour taste of bile and blood in my throat.

"Damn it, M—" He paused, as if frustrated. "We've got to get some water in her. Here, hold her head."

Tiny, timid hands held the side of my face while trickles of warm water dripped down my lips. I opened my mouth, the gashes in my lips stinging as they split wider. I managed to drink several drops before choking, and I winced as every cough brought more discomfort.

"I can't," I mumbled. "Sleep."

A rough hand brushed across my forehead. "Rest. We'll watch over you."

. . .

I STRUGGLED TO WAKE, tormented by visions I couldn't escape. My worst nightmares flashed before my eyes like one second images, one after the other. Me, crawling on the ground while dragging my numb legs behind me, searching for a way out of the Oblivion, Drake comforted by my treacherous sister in my very own bed, and even my cousin, Hillie, hung for treason in the streets of Seregalo while Custos forced her husband to watch.

Thu Dang held Neela's head under water as she fought to breathe, Nora being passed around the Custos guard as if she were worthless property, and even Ren sitting in a dark room alone, praying for death to take him from the misery life had offered.

I thrashed, as if I could fight my way out of the mental anguish, but I couldn't. The Oblivion wasn't done with me. Laying there at that moment, I began to fear it never would be.

"Shh. Shh."

Something soft and sweet pulled me from madness, and I fought to open my eyes. Water trickled around my mouth and I eased my split lips open, hoping the kind soul would offer a few more drops. Once again, water dripped into my mouth and I fought to swallow.

I had been thirsty before, or so I had thought. No, true thirst is something most people will never experience. It's a wilted plant left uncared for, drooping on the ground, limp and discolored. It's a baby bird knocked from its nest, lost and alone, while gasping for anything it can get its mouth on before it takes its last breath.

True thirst.

After several drops of water, I sighed in relief. I blinked, the bright stars overhead shining as if all were right in the world. This version of hell was anything but bright and shiny.

Pushing up on my elbows, my fingers slid through coarse sand. Tears filled my eyes at the sight of my wiggling toes, the pain in my back easing to a dull throb. I didn't understand how I could recover from those injuries—how I survived the fall at all. Then I realized, the Oblivion would never give me the satisfaction of dying.

It *wanted* to torture me.

I pushed up, and on the other side of a small fire, familiar blue eyes met mine. I sighed in relief at the sight of the small young girl from the cave. The memory of her screams, as I held on to the side of the ledge, terrified me more than my own death. She was only a child.

Her tiny hands clutched a small canteen and I grinned.

"Thank you for the water," I choked out, my voice scratchy and hoarse.

She nodded, just enough to let me know she heard.

My eyes traveled around, but little could be seen in the darkness. Cactus plants surrounded us and sand stretched as far as the eye could see. "Did he bring us here?"

Once again, she nodded, her small frame shaking from

either the cold night air or fear—could have been both. I didn't see D, the kind stranger, anywhere and I wondered where he could have gone.

"Will he be back?"

She glanced over her shoulder as if looking for him, her dark hair fell around her shoulders in tangles. She shrugged, the only answer I'd receive.

I'd never been in a desert, let alone at night, and the brisk cold breeze surprised me. My clothes were covered in dry blood, but almost all of the scrapes and gashes had begun to heal. I took a deep breath, grateful when my lungs expanded, filling with fresh air.

"Look who's awake," a deep voice called out.

I jolted, searching for the familiar voice in the darkness. Finally, black boots stepped into the sand in front of me. He stood tall, wearing worn jeans, his wavy dark hair curling against the collar of a brown jacket. His broad shoulders that should have been menacing, comforted me.

I nodded toward the young girl. "Thank you for saving her."

He shook his head, as if I were a petulant child. "Almost lost you in the process."

Tears filled my eyes at the memory of falling into the canyon. "I'd do it all over again if it means she's safe."

He cursed, unable to look me in the eyes. "Damn Monroe blood," he mumbled, more to himself than me.

I sat up straight, not sure I heard him correctly. "What did you say?"

He stalled, as if trying to figure out a way to explain. Finally, he sighed and met my curious gaze. "It's the Monroe blood. It tends to make you impulsive."

"How do you know who I am?" One brow raised higher than the other.

He grinned, but I maintained my fierce determination to learn the truth, and his cute smile wouldn't get him out of talking.

"Let's just say I know your family. We'll leave it there." He turned toward the young girl, but I didn't plan on letting him get off that easily.

I rose up on my knees, struggling to get to my feet. I was ashamed to admit how grateful I felt for having his back to me. I didn't need him to witness my struggle. My ribs ached, and the throb in the back of my head intensified as I stood up straight.

Finally, I found my balance and hobbled to where he stood in front of the fire. "Oh, no you don't! You don't get to know all about me, but keep your little secrets. That isn't fair! I don't even know who you are!"

He tilted his head to the side, just enough to meet my determined gaze. "My name is Dorian Moreno."

CHAPTER
FIFTEEN
MERCY

"What did you say?"

He smiled, sadly. "I would have told you earlier, but I didn't know how you'd take it. I didn't want to make things more complicated than they already were."

The dark hair and dimpled smirk—a connection I didn't understand . . . now it all made sense. His all too familiar eyes stared at me patiently, as if waiting for me to accept the truth of his words. Eyes I'd looked into so many times before, a gaze I would know from anywhere.

Dorian had been a loyal friend to my parents. Alongside his wife, he lost his life fighting the battle against Aadya along with several others. I realized then, he probably recognized me as Mercy Monroe, daughter of Noah and Annabel—not his future daughter-in-law.

"I don't know what to say," I admitted.

It was all I could do to maintain eye contact, and I found myself looking away from his intense scrutiny. If I was being honest, it hurt my heart to look at him. Everything about him reminded me of Drake, and the need to be near him rose to the surface, overpowering everything else in that moment.

He kneeled before me, clasping my hands in his own. "Do you know who I am?"

I nodded. "You grew up with my parents. They loved you very much."

He glanced away, clenching his jaw. "I, um, well . . ."

"It's quite surreal to meet you, even under these circumstances."

He sighed. "I knew I shouldn't approach you, I worried it would make things harder for you, but I feared you'd drown in the river if I didn't."

Then it hit me. I would have drowned because his son, Asher, tried to kill me. Did he even have a clue? Did he even know he had two sons? "Did you see anyone else that day? In the river, I mean?"

He shook his head. "Was someone else with you?"

My shoulders relaxed. "Just a vision, I guess. It felt so real."

"It is real," he replied. "To us, anyway. I swear this damn place is hell bent on testing us mentally and physically. It's like it's trying to drive us mad."

I slid my foot through the sand, mesmerized by the coarseness of something that didn't even exist. "Maybe that's what it wants."

He peered out into the distance, lost in his thoughts. "My mother used to tell me stories as a child, how the dark magical land seeped into your soul, toying with your spirit while it determined your worth." He chuckled. "I thought she was full of shit."

"She's right," I sighed. "But why some and not others? I mean, I've put together a reasonable explanation of who's to blame for my Oblivion holiday, but why others? Why that sweet little girl over there? Why you?"

"Maybe we hover between light and dark. It doesn't know what to do with us." He grinned. "Maybe we're the stubborn ones who refuse to die."

I raised my brows in surprise. "That's about the most logical explanation I've heard so far."

His throaty chuckle, so full of life, filled me with joy for the first time in days. "Tell me about yourself. Where are you right now? What is it like where you live?" I asked.

He sat on the ground beside me, resting his elbows on bent knees. "I live in Seregalo, but my heart is in Astriawell. Something about the country speaks to me—it brings me peace."

"Astriawell? My cousin Hillie lives there with her husband."

He smiled, nodding. "That's right. I'd love to have a place like that one day. Somewhere surrounded by pasture and wildlife, to raise a family away from it all."

"Sounds wonderful, especially right now," I replied, my gaze traveling around the desert.

He nodded, then continued, "My true love and Allegato match is a beautiful and smart woman named Analise. I'm not sure I remember a moment in my life when she wasn't present, even as a child. I adore her wit and ability to see through my bullshit." He chuckled, then grew serious. "All I want is to grow old with her. It's all I've ever wanted since I laid eyes on her."

"How did you end up here?" I asked.

"It happened on my way home one night. I remember someone whispering my name." Dorian relaxed one leg, keeping the other bent to his chest. "It was pitch black outside, and it became eerily silent. I reached out, but my power hit a wall, as if blocking me." He clenched his teeth. "I didn't hear anyone behind me, but before I knew it, something cracked me in the back of the head."

"And you woke up here?" I asked.

He nodded. "What about you?" he asked while sifting through the sand beside him.

I had a feeling he already knew. Something about the way he said the words, were spoken as if they were meaningless, small talk to fill the silence.

"I'm lucky enough to have a sister who hates me."

He chuckled, but didn't respond.

"We only just met, but are struggling to see eye to eye." I straightened my shoulders at the mature, level-headed interpretation of our relationship.

He smirked. "Meaning?"

"Meaning she is a raging psychotic bitch who tried to kill me on my wedding day." I shrugged.

I can't always be mature.

His eyes widened, but not over my sister's deviousness. No, he was taken aback by my bluntness. I could tell by the humor in his eyes and the dimple in his cheek. I knew that dimple all too well.

"Siblings . . ." he muttered.

"Do you have any? I've never heard much about your family."

He smiled, the adoration evident in the twinkling in his eyes. "I do. Two younger brothers—twins."

My mouth fell open in shock. "That's amazing. I didn't know that."

"They are a handful, that's for sure. My poor mother never expected to raise a herd of rowdy Moreno boys, but here we are."

Drake has two uncles? Did he even know? He was small

when they left Seregalo, so he may not even remember his extended family. A dark shroud covered me, drowning my excitement over telling him. Would I ever find a way back home?

His tone grew serious. "We're gonna get you home. I promise."

I tilted my head to the side, pursing my lips in thought. "How do you know what I'm thinking? Subconscious interferer?"

"Wouldn't matter. Couldn't use it here anyway, right?" he replied.

"That's true. Plus, I feel like I remember someone saying you are a sensory interferer."

He nodded. "Sensory and Subconscious, actually. Although I don't use my subconscious power unless it's life threatening."

"Two gifts? That's rare."

He chuckled, a deep rumble rolling through his chest. "Not as rare as six."

I shrugged, not quite as confident as someone with six gifts should be. "Not helping me much right now, is it?" I glanced across the fire pit, where the young girl began to inch her way toward us. She moved forward on her backside, then stopped, glancing around the desert as if trying to seem inconspicuous.

"Do you know anything about her?" I asked.

He sighed, his gaze resting on the shy child. "She hasn't spoken, but I know she has a set of lungs on her. I can't get the sound of her terrified screams out of my head."

"What happened?"

He swallowed, his throat no doubt as dry as my own. "Same as you—caught in a crevice during the earthquake, or whatever it was. I found her clinging to a rock halfway down, screaming. I made it down to her, then eased my way down the canyon with her on my back. We walked for what felt like an hour before finding you."

His eyes filled with tears. "I've seen a lot of shit. Never felt as though I'd puke until I saw you twisted and broken in a heap on the rocks. I just knew I'd lost you. You should have died, and it would have been my fault for leaving you."

I shook my head, thoughtfully. "None of this is your fault. But you are right about one thing—I should have died."

He laid back in the sand, staring at the stars shining above us. "The Oblivion isn't done with you yet."

The emerald stones of my ring glowed brightly, lighting up the night sky. "That's what I'm afraid of."

. . .

THE DREAM STARTED AS A BLUR—BARELY perceptible as I struggled to focus on the obscure scene before me. I could feel overwhelming fear and angst radiating from a small figure, one undoubtedly too small to understand the significance of the intruders that day.

I wanted to reach out, help them in some way, but I could only make out the outline of multiple figures standing close together, tense and guarded. I blinked, attempting to focus, but it was no use.

The *Oblivion* wouldn't allow it.

If I couldn't see, I'd listen. I closed my eyes, putting forth every ounce of energy I had into distinguishing the voices. They were familiar, but something kept me from fully grasping their identity. As if a memory I longed to reach had been blocked.

"Don't touch him," a tortured cry shouted.

"Well, well. Who's this? What's your name, little one?"

The small child, maybe three years old, hid behind his mother, unable to look the strange woman in the eyes. He shook from head to toe, clutching the back of her sweater.

"He means nothing to you. Let him be. This is between me and you."

"Interesting. How old are you little one?"

He buried his head, hiding from the terrifying woman standing in front of him.

She smirked, as if enjoying his discomfort. *"Maybe I should take a look . . . just a peek."*

"No! Leave him alone!" Desperate pleas from the mother echoed through the trees as men pulled her away from her son. *"Please! He is nothing to you!"*

The hateful woman jerked the child toward her, gripping his arm. He cried out in pain, but mostly fear, as he struggled to escape. The crack of a slap halted everyone as the child lay on the ground, his small palms covering the side of his face.

"You will do as I say." She glanced toward one of the men at her side. *"Pick him up."*

The man gripped the child by the back of his neck, lifting and shoving him toward her. She stepped forward, somehow full of grace and menace at the same time. She placed her hand on his forehead and his little body bowed from the contact.

"Stop! You're hurting him!"

After several more seconds, the strange woman lifted her hand, watching the child fall to the ground. *"Interesting."* She turned toward the mother, who hung weak and sobbing in the guard's grasp. *"We're taking him with us."*

The mother began fighting, clawing her way toward her son.

All at once, her body convulsed and she rose to her feet, shaking from pain. The strange woman held one hand out, as if controlling her. A man picked up the small boy from the ground, and disappeared into the forest.

"You know why I'm here." She grinned. "Let's make this easy, shall we?"

"Go to hell," the mother spat.

"MERCY. MERCY, WAKE UP!"

I jolted from the nightmare, turning from side to side as if they would be standing close by. It felt so real. "Dorian?"

He sighed in relief. "I've been trying to wake you for over an hour. What the hell is going on? You've been screaming, 'Don't take him' over and over."

"I have?" The memory of the young mother crumpling to the ground brought chills across my skin. It nagged at me —the inability to think clearly. I needed to know what happened. I had to understand the vision, because I felt as though it had significance on my life, whether in the past or future, I didn't know. "I'm sorry. It was only a nightmare."

He sat back on his heels, and exhaled. "Sounded like more than just a nightmare. Are you sure you're alright? You scared us."

I glanced at the pale blue eyes focused on me, filled with worry. The last thing I wanted was to frighten the poor girl further. I tried to relax, taking a deep breath and laying back on the sand. "I'm sure."

"Are you hungry? I have a few things I stashed away."

"I don't think I can eat," I admitted. "I'm so tired."

He nodded. "You've been through a lot, plus being separated from D—I mean, your mate won't help." He glanced away, unable to meet my eyes. "It takes a toll on you."

I jolted, shocked by how much he knew. "How did you know . . ."

"I know the feeling. The emptiness. It's a need that food will never replace."

My heart clenched at the thought. "I'm going to try to rest."

I closed my eyes, but the image of the young boy tormented me, his mother's screams echoing in my head. I shivered, unable to shake the feeling of impending doom. I'd never be able to sleep.

Then a warmth, small but comforting, snuggled against my side, clinging to my filthy clothes just as the boy did to his mother.

The young girl wrapped her arms around me, clutching me as if she feared I'd disappear at any moment. I looked up at Dorian, smiling at the sight of her seeking comfort in my arms. But his smile also held a hint of despair—as if he knew the solace would be short-lived.

CHAPTER
SIXTEEN
MARLEY

After the tenth time yelling at someone to go away, the door to my office swung in with force. I turned, fueled by frustration, ready to rip someone's head off. I jerked the door open, realizing that particular someone happened to be the love of my life, and my mood improved drastically.

"Drake! Please come in. You know you don't have to knock." I beamed, giving extra effort in batting my eyes and tossing my hair over one shoulder. "What brings you here?"

He looked over his shoulder and nodded for someone else to join him. An unwanted guest, a third wheel I had no patience for. Either way, I smiled because any friend of Drake's was a friend of mine.

Right?

Colton entered first, then Fitz shuffled in with his arms crossed, completely unemotional. It didn't matter that we didn't know each other, he'd made up his mind about me after talking to Mercy. I knew she'd filled his head with lies, making herself out to be the innocent orphan, when she's the one with blood on her hands. How many had died for my sake?

Exactly.

"Colton. Fitz. What brings you here?" I asked, politely.

"I hope we aren't interrupting," Fitz replied.

"Not at all. I always have time for friends."

Yeah, right.

I threw the stack of papers on the desk—I'd considered burning them minutes before. That's how I fixed the problems of spoiled Regalians. More and more, crops and fruit trees began to die. Rumors of a rebellion rustled among the farmers, convinced it was Seregalo's way of being left without a true leader. Especially since the land had thrived under Mercy's reign.

Fitz cleared his throat, obviously trying to hold his tongue. "Yes, well, I spent some time with Ren this morning. Do you have any idea how long he's been here?"

I shook my head. "I don't. I've been here for over five years, but never went to the dungeon. I'm sorry I can't be more helpful."

He raised his brows. "Wow. You were quite the fortunate prisoner."

Colton snickered.

I tilted my head, glaring in his direction. "Fortunate is not how I would describe my life, Fitz. Not all of us have been so lucky to be trained and taken care of at Fremont."

Drake stepped forward. "Look, I think it's best if we stay focused. We have some concerns about Ren. Fitz went to visit him with me this morning and he has an idea."

I jerked my head toward Fitz. "Well?"

He sighed, then sat in a lounge chair by the window. "It's unlike anything I've ever seen. The shielding spell in the dungeon set him back years, but it isn't just that. I expect him to be around nine or ten years old—still too young for a Regalian to come into his power. I can feel the magical vibrations even through the spell."

"So you're saying he's too young to be this powerful?"

He nodded. "Maybe that's why Aadya locked him up. She's always been terrified of someone having more power than her. If she couldn't control him, the next logical thing would be to detain him."

I bristled at his tone. They didn't like my aunt because they didn't understand her. "I think we're getting ahead of ourselves."

"He brought up Mercy again," Drake muttered while staring out the window. "He said she's lost, and we have to find her. We have to help her find the way."

I walked to where he stood, his black eyes completely lifeless. He'd lost more weight, and the circles under his eyes had darkened. If he would let me in, I would make him forget all about her. He'd never feel lost again. I gripped his forearm, refraining from wrapping my arms around him.

"Drake, I miss Mercy just as much as anyone. I don't know what she's thinking, but I'm not sure if a small child is the answer. You are her mate. If you don't know where she is, how can he?"

He turned to face me, the muscle in his jaw clenching over and over. "It doesn't hurt to try. Right?"

I didn't have a choice. If I refused to help, I would once again be the unfeeling sister who everyone despised. No, I needed them to see that I cared. Whether I truly did or not, they didn't have to know. "Tell me what to do."

Fitz leaned forward, resting his hands on his knees. "We've got to get him out of the dungeon."

My eyes widened. "Are you crazy? You can barely stand

to be around him with the spell dampening his power. What if he goes crazy? What if he kills someone?"

Colton spoke up, "I think you're being a bit hasty. Ren would never go that far. I mean he hasn't yet."

"What if he does?" I pressed.

"We won't let that happen," Fitz answered. "We'll have backup."

"Backup?" I laughed at his lame plan, knowing it won't be enough if the boy gets angry. I felt the vibrations coursing from his cell in the dungeon. I knew the destruction he could cause if provoked. "Please tell me you know what you're doing."

Drake shrugged. "We're figuring it out along the way."

"I can get him out without being seen by the guards. No one will know you had a part in it, Marley, if that's what you're afraid of," Colton added.

I shook my head, turning toward the large glass window behind my desk. Biting my thumbnail, I ran through the possible scenarios of how this could affect me. I didn't care about Mercy or Ren, they weren't high on my list of priorities. Let's be honest, they weren't on there at all. But how Drake saw me, that was important. I wanted him to look at me the way he did when we were kids. To do that, he needed to see me as his friend. He had to be sure I was on his side.

I turned, Drake's intense gaze waiting for me to respond while Fitz watched me, suspiciously. "Okay, I'll do it."

Drake stepped forward and hugged me, obviously relieved. I took a few seconds, relishing his arms around me, pretending it was for a different reason. He pulled back, and I grinned, bashfully.

"You have to find someone who can control him. And, we can't do it at the Domicile. I'm sorry, but I'm responsible for this place while Mercy is away. I'd like for her to come back to it in one piece."

Fitz nodded. "We can do that. We need a couple of subconscious interferers to help with his mental stability. I'll be there for his emotions. Will you come?"

I started to say *yeah right*, but unfortunately it came out, "Of course, I will."

"This means so much to me, Marley." Drake reached for my hands, squeezing them between his warm palms. "Mercy will forever be grateful, and so will I."

I didn't reply, I couldn't. Somehow this twisted game had been reversed and I felt backed into a corner, unable to make a move.

"Anything for my sister."

. . .

"I'M SO glad I amuse you."

Thu Dang stood in my bedroom that evening, holding his too-thin belly, doubled over from laughter. "I'm so sorry, truly I am, but this is quite the predicament. You're telling me you're holding the child hostage in the dungeon, with the psycho sisters breathing down your neck, and you've agreed to let him roam free so that he can hopefully bring back the sister you so deviously sent to the Oblivion. Does that cover it?"

"You're enjoying this," I spat while pacing the room.

"On the contrary, I'm slightly concerned. Let's not forget I stuck my neck out for you with that bargain. You think they'll just let it go? Forget about the boy?"

Anger and frustration built over the situation I'd found myself in. "I don't think that!" I yelled. Taking a deep breath, I attempted to regain composure before someone heard us fighting. "We don't even know if the boy can help them. What if he's crazy? Fitz himself said Ren was too young to harbor natural Regalian power."

"He isn't too young," Thu Dang mumbled.

"What?"

"The child was born with gifts, they never waited to manifest," he explained. "That's why she locked him up. Aadya feared what his lack of control would do to Seregalo."

"You mean she feared he'd take control."

He shrugged, fighting a smirk. "Same difference."

"His powers . . . what gift does he hold?" I asked, although I wasn't sure if I wanted to know.

"Maybe subconscious? That's just a guess. I never spent much time in the dungeon with him."

I shook my head, backing up. "There's something else. I've never felt that way in all my life like I did with him. Exhaustion flooded my body, and I couldn't think straight. There has to be something else."

He shrugged. "The problem is that we don't know for sure. Considering who his paren—" Thu Dang paused, catching himself.

"What?" I asked. "You know where he came from?"

He fumbled over his words. "No, I just mean, considering we don't know who his parents are, it will be hard to know what the future holds for him."

I met his eyes. "The sisters have to know, or else they wouldn't want him."

"What do you want me to tell them?" he asked. "It

better be clever. Last time they threatened to cut my testicle off and steep it in tea."

I raised one brow. "Testicle? As in one?" Did I want to know? Better yet, did I want to know why they knew he only had one?

Nevermind.

He glanced away from my curious gaze and cleared his throat. "I'll call on them immediately."

"Tell them they'll have the boy by the end of the week. That should hold them off."

Thu Dang bowed, then left me to my thoughts.

I began to worry how powerful the boy could really be. Can he help Mercy get home? What then? Would she know I was the one who sent her there? Will I be cast out of Sere-galo? Where would I go? I laid in bed that night, tossing and turning over things I could do nothing about.

Whatever happened, Drake needed to see the good inside of me. Once he got to know me again, he would remember our connection. I ran the pad of my fingertips across my lips, remembering our first kiss in the ocean—the last day we spent together.

I sat up in bed, more determined than ever. Slipping into my robe, I padded out the door, down the stairs toward the dungeon. The staff had long ago retired, and dim light from the hallway lit the path in front of me. I didn't think or plan it out, but I needed to speak to the boy alone, and this would be my chance before all hell broke loose.

The chill from downstairs swept across my skin like an icy whisper, seeping into my pores. Just like the time before, it became hard to breathe, and I found myself gasping for air. Sweat beaded along the back of my neck and I shook as cold air hit the perspiration on my skin.

For several seconds, I stood in front of his cell, watching

him sleep on the small bed. He laid on his side with his eyes closed, without so much as a blanket to keep the chill away. I wasn't sure if I should speak or not, I didn't want to startle him. Honestly, the thought of being alone with him frightened me.

"You're not Mercy," he whispered. His eyes remained closed, but he knew I was there.

"No. I'm not."

"You have similarities, did you know that?" He squinted his eyes tighter. "But very different people."

"I have red hair like my mother, and her hair is brown."

He shook his head. "Don't compare yourself to her. You are nothing alike."

I bristled. "You're the one who brought it up."

"Where's Aly? I want to go home."

"Aly?" I asked.

"The Hughes. I want to go back to my room."

"Did you like it there?" I asked, curiously.

"They were good to me."

"They are scared of you, Ren," I admitted.

"I would never hurt anyone on purpose. I want to go home."

I nodded, remembering what it was like to be an orphan, clinging to anyone who showed me the slightest bit of attention. "Soon, alright?"

"What are you doing here?" he asked. "Sneaking down here in the middle of the night, alone. What are you keeping from the others?"

I tilted my head to the side, thinking. "How do you know so much? Are you a subconscious interferer? Can you read my mind?"

He scoffed. "I don't know what I am, I never had the chance to learn."

"Drake thinks you can help us find Mercy. Can you?"

"Does that worry you?" he asked.

I shifted from foot to foot, nervously. "Why would I be worried?"

He finally opened his eyes, pushing up from the small bed. "I can feel you, even with the shield you have in place. I can't imagine how strong your emotions would be without the dungeon's spell. The bitterness and jealousy. The need to prove yourself. The desire to be loved."

I glanced around the concrete prison, nodding at his observation. "Did you know that Drake and I were close as children? He doesn't remember it. His father made sure to hide the memories to protect us. I think he didn't want him getting close to me."

"What do you want, Marley? Why are you here?"

"Do you know where she is?"

"I know you know more than you're letting on."

"How do you know that?" I asked.

"I've always been able to read people, intuitively. Sometimes I can hear your thoughts, feel your emotions, and I can't stop it. I feed off of your power."

"Feed off it, how? What do you mean?"

He took a deep breath, and I immediately lost my footing, feeling as though I would tumble to the ground. My vision blurred, and the silence in the dungeon began to hum, building and building until I clung to the bars for support.

His cheeks flushed, and his eyes brightened. "Like that. I feel energized and full of life. Not only that, but I can tap into your subconscious power, even if only for a time."

The fog cleared and I stood straight, clearing my head from his assault. I'd never felt anything like it, and now I knew how much he had been holding back. "Drake wants to get you out of here so you can help us find Mercy. You have to promise you won't hurt us, especially him."

"I would never purposely harm anyone, Marley. All I want is to find Mercy."

"Why? Why do you care what happens to my sister?"

"I can sense your nervousness. You're worried what will happen if I reach her. Aren't you?"

No matter how hard I fought it, my eyes filled with tears. "Does that make me a bad person?"

"What makes you a bad person is that you're crying for yourself, not your sister."

I pushed the emotion aside and clenched my teeth. "You are a child. What do you know about pain and suffering? How could you possibly understand what it's like to have the weight of Seregalo on your shoulders? You can't! Stop treating me as if I'm a petulant child!"

He smirked. "Stop acting like one."

CHAPTER
SEVENTEEN
MARLEY

I didn't sleep at all the night before. Visions of a dying Seregalo plagued me, trees rotting from the inside out and flowers nowhere to be seen. The Domicile cracked down the center, fissures branching out along the stairwells and rooms, before the building collapsed to the ground, devastated by Mercy's absence.

A dying Seregalo *terrified* me.

Drake, Colton and Fitz planned to meet me with their back-up crew the next day and I tossed and turned, worrying about what he had planned. I offered the services of my most trusted advisor, Thu Dang, but Fitz refused, saying he would feel more comfortable with someone who hadn't tried to kill Mercy in the past.

Whatever. I didn't see the issue.

After showering and changing into something more presentable, I sat on the edge of my bed, staring at the deep orange glow of the sunrise outside my bedroom window. Like flames, the sunlight spread across the horizon, licking the top of the mountainside with mesmerizing intensity.

For once, I didn't think about how much I hated my

family. The worry of Drake not returning my affection didn't exist. I watched the gift of the sunrise, completely focused on the burning glow of the new day.

A new opportunity.

I sat, thinking about the day Aadya found me—the moment that forever changed my life.

. . .

Something was happening to me. I sat at the dinner table across from Aunt Isla, just as I had for years. But something was different. The typically quiet woman had been making comments under her breath, as if unable to contain her opinion about those around her.

"Marley looks pale, but more hateful than normal, if that's possible."

"I wish Cliff would go to work tomorrow and not come back."

"What made Allie cut her hair? It looks awful and makes her face look too thin."

I couldn't take it any longer, I glanced up from my plate of mashed potatoes and peas, ready to scream at the top of my lungs. That's when it happened. I heard her voice yet again, but her mouth never moved. I froze, staring at the middle-aged woman who'd raised me, her salt and pepper bun pulled tight on top of her head.

"Sick of damn peas. I hate peas."

There it was again. My eyes traveled to her son Ben, sitting beside her. I tilted my head forward, listening intently. "What am I going to do? Could Beth really be pregnant? I think she's lying."

I choked on a mouthful of potatoes, shocked at hearing his scandalous confession.

"Marley, are you alright?"

I gulped the water in front of me, nodding. Slamming the glass on the table, I quickly refilled it with the plastic pitcher, and turned it up once again. Everyone at the table stared as if I'd lost my mind. No one said a word.

"What is wrong with her?"

"She's psycho. I wish Mother had never taken her in."

"Dinner just got more interesting."

I attempted to set the glass on the table with more grace than before. "Can I be excused?" I asked.

Aunt Isla eyed me curiously. "Are you sure you're okay?"

I nodded, more spastic than I intended. "I'm sure." I stood, turning from the table and ran out the back screen door.

I bolted for the tall willow tree in the corner, the wispy limbs creating a magical curtain of privacy from the world around me, or so I pretended. The past year had been difficult for me after Drake left. I'd asked Aunt Isla if she'd heard from Mr. Moreno, but the answer was always the same. Hurt turned into anger, a rage I couldn't control.

I hurried under the tree as if safe from everyone's thoughts around me. I didn't understand what happened at the dinner table, and there wasn't anyone who could explain it to me.

Or so I thought.

"Hello there," a soothing voice cooed. "Are you Marley?"

I stayed perfectly still, unsure whether to respond or stay silent.

"I'm a friend of your mother's—your real mother," she continued. "Can I sit with you?"

I eased forward on my knees, peeking through the limbs toward the back of the house. Aunt Isla wouldn't appreciate someone in her yard, and I knew I'd get into trouble for talking to a stranger.

The woman kneeled before me. "It's okay. It will be our little secret."

I felt connected to the woman with flaming red hair and bright green eyes, identical to myself. I nodded, sliding back under the tree to make room for her.

She crawled underneath, scowling at the dirty hem of her tight red dress. She sat upright, plastering on the fakest smile I'd ever seen. I could tell this wasn't exactly something she wanted to be doing. "Now, then. That's more like it."

I sat, watching her with interest. "What do you want?"

"I'm your Aunt Aadya. I'm here to bring you home."

"Home? I am home."

She shook her head, disagreeing as she glanced around. "No. You are meant for so much more, sweet girl. I'm going to show you."

"Show me what?"

"Who you're meant to be."

. . .

I opened my eyes, the memory of her confidence renewing my spirit. "You can still do this," I whispered to myself. "Aadya knew who you were meant to be. She could see your potential when everyone else couldn't."

"Talking to yourself again?" An amused voice called from the doorway.

I didn't turn to face his snarky expression. I couldn't. Yes, I trusted him, but that didn't mean I liked him. "What do you want?"

Thu Dang sighed, as if bored. "Your guests are here."

Guests? How long had I been sitting there? This time, I spun to face him, eager to know who they trusted enough to bring. "Who?"

"Drake, Colton, Fitz, and Hillie McDonnell." He pursed his lips as if the names left a bad taste in his mouth.

"Hillie McDonnell? You've got to be joking."

"I'm afraid not."

I stood, smoothing the front of my silky white blouse, then shouldered past the grinning fool in my doorway.

He stiffened as I walked by, and I could feel animosity radiating from him. "Anyone else you'd like to invite? You know, to undo everything we've worked so hard to build?"

I looked over my shoulder without meeting his eyes. "Watch yourself, Dang. I don't have time for your arrogant ass. You may just find yourself in the dungeon."

I walked away, heading toward my office. I had dressed sharp and business-like, hoping to show confidence. Hillie was not an ally of mine, and I would keep my guard up when she was near. She was a strong subconscious inter-ferer, but rarely used her gift. That was the problem with most of them—they were morally conscientious.

I felt her on multiple occasions, attempting to ease her way into my thoughts, but I had been trained by the best. No one could penetrate my wall. Aadya made sure of it.

I pushed the door open, taken aback by the scowl on Hillie's face. Fitz sat, unemotional and quiet, just like Colton. Drake grinned, a grateful smile just for me. His usually snug cotton shirt hung loose around the shoulders and his golden skin had turned dull.

My heart hurt to see him grieving his mate, and part of me wondered if he would survive it. I would never have the chance to show him how good it could be between us if he didn't pull through. I closed the door behind me and sat down at the desk to face them.

"Hillie, what a pleasant surprise," I began.

Her blue eyes appeared heavy and relaxed. "Just so you

202

know, I ate a brownie before I came, so you can't sour my mood." She grinned, as if ruining my day.

Her eyes were heavy and her grin relaxed. She truly did come to the meeting high. "I hope you brought enough for everyone—we may need it."

Drake stepped forward. "We stopped by to see Ren before coming to your office."

My brows raised in surprise. "You did what?"

Fitz nodded. "An experiment. Hillie is a powerful Regalian, but we wanted to see how she would react to Ren's energy. We think with her being . . . high, it actually shielded her from Ren's advances.

"Is this a joke?" I asked.

"No." Drake shook his head. "She didn't seem to be aware of the energy change, at least, not in the way we were. She wasn't phased at all. Even Colton vomited."

"Thanks, Drake." Colton mumbled, still pale.

"Powerful Regalian?" I asked, turning toward Hillie. "When's the last time you used your gift successfully? I didn't have a problem blocking you."

Hillie's lazy grin was my only answer.

My head filled with pressure and an unbearable ringing in my ears intensified. I forged the shield around my mind, throwing everything I had against the onslaught. Sweat beaded across my freckled nose from the effort and the image of Hillie grinning blurred in front of me. All at once, what started as a small fissure in my wall, began to widen more and more.

Panic set in, and I began to worry about her ability to see inside my mind. My power writhed, self-conscious and weak, under her invasion. I'd never felt this level of strength from another before, and it made me question everything I knew.

I shoved against her as hard as I could, then shouted, "This isn't the time or place!"

At least she had the decency to look surprised, as if she never meant to hurt me. "Oh. I'm so sorry. I thought you wanted me to prove myself."

Clearing my throat, I sat up straight. "I thought you didn't use your gift. What is it . . . unethical or something like that?"

"Only when it's life threatening."

I laughed. "You've used it on me, even before today." I tilted my head, fighting for my dignity after our showdown.

"Maybe I view you as a threat," she muttered.

"Maybe you should."

"Considering that demonstration, I don't feel as though I have anything to worry about." She relaxed back in the chair, twirling a curl of hair that had escaped her messy bun.

"That's enough," Drake called out. "The truth is, I'm doing this with or without any of you."

My mouth fell open in shock, but I couldn't find the words to chastise him.

"I know, Marley. You are our temporary leader and you outrank all of us. But this is my mate. My future wife. Nothing will stop me from getting her back, wherever she is. If you're going to help, you might as well learn to get along."

Everyone in the room nodded in agreement.

"Good. I think we should take Ren to the cave on the mountainside."

"Cave?" I asked.

He nodded. "An ancient Moreno hideaway. Mercy and I are the only ones alive today that know about it. We won't have to worry about anyone finding us while we try to reach her. It's on the mountainside across the river. We need to travel separately so we attract less attention."

"Drake," Colton replied. "Are you sure you can handle it? That cave . . ."

"I'll manage. It's the safest place."

I hated this. All of it. I despised how much he loved her. The thought of helping him get her back turned my stomach. Why did I agree to any of this? I should have just killed her myself. For a split second, I considered taking care of the boy. That would solve our problems, especially if Drake didn't suspect me. What about the sisters? I could turn him over to them, and claim he'd been kidnapped.

"When?" I asked.

"Sunrise tomorrow. We can't waste anymore time."

Fitz stood, quieter than normal. "I'll be there."

Hillie sat perfectly still, her bright eyes focused, as if studying me. "I'm in." She stood, taking a possessive stance close to Drake. "I'll do anything to have my cousin back."

I nodded in her direction. "Don't forget your brownies."

. . .

WE ALL HAVE REGRETS, but few of us are lucky enough to be able to rectify our mistakes. My biggest screw up in life thus far, is letting others affect my judgment, as I had Drake. I woke with clarity the next morning, determined to do what I had to for the sake of my future.

Drake would be part of that one day, no matter what happened.

But first—me.

I sent Thu Dang after the psycho sisters long before sunrise. By the time Drake arrived, Ren would be gone, me as surprised as everyone else. I couldn't allow him to reunite Drake and Mercy, even if there was only a small chance he would succeed.

I slipped into comfortable clothes, grabbing my flashlight and cell from the dresser. The staff had yet to stir, so I hurried downstairs before anyone saw me. I felt watched, as if the Domicile itself judged my every move, disappointed in my actions.

To hell with this place.

Adrenaline coursed through my veins as I fought to catch my breath. I hurried down the stone steps toward the dungeon where Thu Dang would meet me to hand off the boy to Jules and Creeky. I aimed the flashlight toward the steel bars, shuffling toward the last cell on my right.

The one that was open.

I froze, peeking inside as if Ren would jump out at any moment. Under the bed, beside the bedside chamber, even the other cells—I searched every corner of the dungeon, hoping for any sign of him.

Thu Dang hurried down the stairs with a flashlight of his own. "What's happened? Where is the boy?"

I clenched my teeth, painfully, until streaks of pain shot through my jaw. With everything inside of me, I threw the flashlight up against the cell wall, shattering it on impact. My chest heaved from rage. "He's gone."

CHAPTER
EIGHTEEN
MERCY

I don't know what startled me that morning. It wasn't another blizzard or earthquake, there were no raiders ambushing me, or a corpse waiting to taunt me. More of a whispered warning, one that stirred me from sleep, creeping up my spine like a spider.

I pushed up from the ground, but the lack of desert sand surprised me, and I jerked my hand back, startled. Droplets of water trickled over the rocks beside me, as a small stream made its way through dense jungle moss.

The young girl lay fast asleep, unphased by the change in scenery, as Dorian slept a few feet away under a low hanging tree covered in vines. A bird chirped in the distance, loud and cheerful, but somehow mocking me at the same time. Sometimes when the scenery or visions changed, it felt as though we were only there for entertainment.

Let's see what we can do to them today . . .

In the deepest, darkest part of the jungle, whimpering caught my attention. I froze, knowing the possibility of losing my mind was an option, and listened once again. It sounded like a child whimpering, not far from where I sat. I wasn't stupid, I knew the power this place had over my mind. I also knew there could be another child trapped, just like the young girl laying beside me, and that was enough to take the risk.

I stood quietly, stepping around small twigs and rocks, so I wouldn't wake my companions. After walking for several minutes, I paused to listen, searching for the pitiful cry tugging at my heart. Glancing over my shoulder, I could no longer see Dorian or the child, and prayed I would be able to find my way back to them.

"Pst. Pst, over here," a deep voice whispered.

I stopped, looking from side to side, my pulse quickening at the possibility of what I'd gotten myself into. A dark skinned man in a white shirt appeared between the trees on my right, waving in my direction.

"Mercy! I'll help you. Follow me!"

I knew that voice. I had found comfort in that voice not too long ago. I hurried through the trees, not quite believing my eyes. I stopped, needing a second to gather my thoughts. Was he real? Could he possibly be in the Oblivion? No—it wasn't real.

Stay strong, Mercy. You know he isn't really here. You know he's gone.

"Ren," I muttered. "You're not here."

He froze when I spoke, then slowly turned around. Blood covered the front of his shirt, and he scowled when I stood, unaffected. He wanted a reaction from me—that was his whole purpose for being there.

"You don't care at all, do you?" he asked.

"He isn't real. He isn't real," I whispered over and over.

"Do you ever think of me, Mercy? I gave my life for you,

for a woman who didn't love me. The least you could do is pretend you care."

It had to be another test. I muttered, "Ren isn't here. Stop trying to hurt me." In truth, the sight of him did hurt me—a reminder of another life lost on my account, another beloved friend who I would never see again.

When I opened my eyes, Ren was nowhere to be found, and the jungle darkened, transitioning to pine trees once again. Without so much as another thought, I spun, running in the opposite direction, needing as far away from that memory as possible.

Crying began to get louder, and the outline of a small child huddled beside a stream took form. His back to me, he stared out in front of him, crying and calling out to his mother. "Mommy! Don't leave me!" He reached forward, sobbing, as a man dressed in all black grabbed him by the arm, dragging the dark-haired boy behind him. "Mommy!"

Knowing the power of the Oblivion, the probability of it being another vision, rather than an actual child, was high. Either way, it was something the mysterious land wanted me to see, and I'm ashamed to say I was too curious to turn away.

I hurried toward the vision, but no matter how hard I ran, I could never reach him. Out of nowhere, a heart wrenching scream that sounded like a grown woman in pain, echoed from the trees. I turned from one direction to the next, unable to pinpoint where the cries were coming from. "They're playing with you, Mercy. Stop acting like a fool," I mumbled to myself.

"Alright there, lass?"

I jumped at the sudden presence, sitting beside the river bank. A woman with a chestnut braid across one shoulder, wearing a long, yellow dress and white apron, sat sharpening a silver handled knife on a sharp piece of flint.

"Did you see a boy come through here?"

"Seeing things, you are," she grumbled. "I've seen a lot here. Ignore most of it, that's how I stay alive."

I clenched my fist, frustrated at her words. "Is this what you call living?" I asked. "Pardon my bluntness, but this doesn't feel like much of a life. Don't you have family you want to return to?"

Her eyes filled with sadness, and I immediately regretted my words.

"How bout you let me borrow that, and I'll see to it." The wrinkles around her eyes deepened as she squinted against the bright sun. She nodded toward my neck where my mother's necklace laid against my skin.

"What?" I grasped the emerald in my palm, holding onto it for fear of it disappearing.

"Shame it is, for someone to have it and not understand its power."

Something in the way she spoke pissed me off, as if I weren't intelligent enough to possess the gem. "And I guess you know all about it?"

"A lifeline it is—get you home if you let it. You must be very important to someone."

I stepped forward, all of a sudden very interested in what the strange woman had to say. "What are you talking about?"

She grinned, her focus returning to the blade of the knife. She enjoyed the fact that she'd attracted my attention. "Only a few exist—most handed down by the oldest families in Seregalo. I grew up in Astriawell, so I've seen one before. My name's Marie."

I sat down beside her, completely absorbed in anything

and everything she could tell me. "My cousin Hillie lives in Astriawell. Tell me, what does it do? How can it help?"

"Where'd you get it?" She looked up from her task. "If you don't mind me asking."

Something about the way she said it, the humor in her tone, told me she already knew where it had come from, but I indulged her anyway.

"It was my mother's."

Marie nodded, as if she expected the answer. "Annabel," she smiled, lovingly. "Knew the twins, I did, although I never took a liking to Aadya. You don't look like them though." She wiped both sides of the blade on the skirt of her dress, then continued sharpening once again. "You look like your father though."

"So I've heard." I kneeled beside her. "Tell me, how can the necklace get me home?"

Marie leaned forward, whispering. "No power in the Oblivion, that gem there—nothing can take its power."

"So you're saying my necklace has its own power? Even here?"

She nodded. "That's right. Up to you how to use it." Her eyes traveled around the forest as if afraid of being overheard.

I glanced around, but didn't see anyone nearby. "How do I get out of here?"

Marie's throaty chuckle turned into a wet cough. "How do you get out of anywhere? Go through the door you came in."

I stood, frustrated at the woman as if she'd created the rules herself. "I came here through the damn dirt. Are you telling me I have to bury myself alive?"

"Buried underground, jumping from a cliff, drowning in the river . . . I've seen them arrive just about everywhere."

She leaned forward. "Woke up in shark infested waters myself." She shivered. "Don't want to do that again—almost lost my leg."

I stared at her, speechless.

"She's a lunatic, I tell you! Don't listen to a word she says!" A deep, gravely voice called out.

I turned toward the tree line where the old man I met when I arrived leaned against a tree. He softly blew into his harmonica while glaring at Marie like he wanted nothing more than to slit her throat.

"Ignore the old man. He thinks he's smarter than he is, I tell ya!" She replied, louder than necessary.

I closed my eyes, attempting to regain control. "If I hadn't crawled out of the grave, could I have used the necklace to go right back home?"

She paused, thinking it over, then began to laugh. "I reckon so. Ain't that something."

I spun on my heels, stomping away before I attacked either one of them. All this time, through all of the suffering and pain, I've had the answer around my neck. Not to mention the ring, which they never even noticed. I muttered over and over under my breath about the ridiculousness of the situation.

"Hey! Hey Annabel's daughter! Don't forget, you gotta channel the power or you won't make it. You gotta use it as your source!"

"I got your source," the old man muttered.

Marie growled. "Shove it up your . . ."

"Thank you!" I called out, still cursing under my breath.

"Use it like a damn back-up battery pack," I muttered. I was still pissed by the time I reached Dorian, pacing back and forth where the young girl rocked, as if soothing her own anxiety.

He stepped forward. "Mercy! Thank God!" "His dark eyes were filled with worry, but his lips were pulled tight as if angry. "Where have you been?"

"How did you get here?" I called out, urgently. "I need to know where you came in at."

"What? What are you talking about?" he asked.

"When you arrived, what's the first thing you remember?"

He looked down at the ground, silent. When he looked up with heavy eyes, I knew it wasn't good. "A cave." He sighed. "A cave of venomous snakes. Please don't tell me I have to go back."

I cringed. "That won't be pleasant." Being buried alive doesn't seem so bad anymore.

"What is this about?" he asked.

"I might have found a way to get us home." I spun toward the young girl, then kneeled in front of her. "I need you to tell me how you got here. Can you do that?"

She backed up, shaking her head as if afraid.

"You don't have to be scared. We're gonna get you out of here, but you have to trust me. Can you do that?"

Once again, she tightened her lips, completely silent.

"You have to tell me!" I shouted.

"Mercy, she's terrified," Dorian called out.

I spun to face him. "We're all terrified! And we're gonna be scared the rest of our life if we don't try to get home!"

Dorian's deep voice boomed, "Calm down!"

"Don't tell me to calm down! Look at us. Look at what we've been through, Dorian. We will live through this hell day after day if we don't try to get out of here! I'm not leaving without either of you, so you better find the courage you need to survive this." I screamed, "Both of you!"

Everyone halted, and we looked at each other for

several silent seconds as they seemed to process my words. I knew the possibility of getting us all home had thrown me into hysterics. I took a deep breath, trying to calm my nerves.

"The river," a timid voice whispered.

I met the young girl's eyes, and my world forever changed. "What did you say?"

She took a deep breath. "The river."

I fell in front of her, palming the side of her face. Her icy blue eyes sparkled and all at once, everything made sense. *The river.*

"So how did you survive?" I asked.

Icy smiled. "You wouldn't believe me if I told you."

"Isolette?" Tears fell down my cheeks. "Icy?"

She began to cry, her hair falling in front of her face as she nodded. "Daddy calls me Icy."

She fell into my arms, and I held her shaking body as she sobbed, the dam of fear and sadness breaking free. No matter what happened, I wouldn't give up until she made it back. She had stood by my side when others refused. I wouldn't have made it without her, and I owed her the chance to live.

Memories of our last day together drifted through my mind—the day of my wedding. I reached toward the top of my head, and pulled the emerald encrusted comb from my hair. I stared at it, angling it underneath the glimmer of sunlight as the stones lit up in my palm. I raised my hand, watching the emeralds on the ring light up in the same way. Then, her suggestion for me to wear the emerald necklace on my wedding day.

Icy's last words echoed in my mind. *"One day at a time, Mercy. When you feel lost, when you feel as though you can't make it another day, stay strong. Our hope lies with you."*

I glanced toward Dorian, where he stood watching us intently.

"Icy? I want you to listen to me." The child's eyes glistened from tears. "I know you're scared, but there's a way to get you home. I need you to be brave for me, alright?"

She nodded.

"We've got to get you to the river."

She backed away, as if terrified. I knew it had to be traumatizing. She was only a child and there was nothing pleasant about this place.

I turned toward Dorian. "We can use the jewels to get home. We can use them as our source and manifest our gifts."

"How do you know?" he asked.

"The Irish woman, Marie told me."

Dorian's brow furrowed, as if skeptical.

"I know how it sounds, but I think she could be right. There has to be something magical with these gems or she wouldn't have asked me to wear them that day."

He threw his arms up. "Who?"

I pointed at the young girl beside us, huddled on the ground. "Her!"

Icy gasped, cutting her eyes between me and Dorian. "Me?"

I leaned forward, desperate for her to understand. "Icy, one day you are going to be a powerful Elder in Seregalo—a respected leader and friend to me. You told me about this—this land and the power it held over you. I sat with you inside your house while you described drowning in the river."

She shook her head as if unsure of my sanity. The air around us pulsed with nervousness. I knew how I sounded. No one had to tell me I acted like a crazy person that day, but it didn't matter. Nothing mattered in that moment except making sure we all got home.

"You were fishing one Sunday morning and you lost your pole—the one your father gave you. Right?"

Her eyes traveled nervously between me and Dorian.

"We are going to get you home, I just know it. You have to trust me. I need you to be brave. Do you trust me?"

I wouldn't force her, this had to be a decision she made all on her own. I waited, shifting my weight from foot to foot, eager to put our time here behind us, desperate to get everyone home to their family.

She sat up straight and took a deep breath, her eyes filled with new resolve—a confidence that wasn't there before. That is the moment I knew Icy trusted me. "I'll do it."

I smiled, envisioning the strong woman she would become.

"So what are we supposed to do? Throw the child into the river and hope it works? I am not okay with this," Dorian snapped.

I shrugged. "Do you have a better idea? I'm not seeing another option and I'm tired of running for my life every-day, wondering if this is the day I won't come back."

"So we're what? Cheating the system? Hacking the Oblivion?"

My eyes traveled around the jungle, nervously, as if the magical land were listening. "Yeah, I guess so."

He lowered his head, massaging his forehead with his fingers. "I can't believe I'm considering going back to that cave. Damn Monroe blood. Moreno's aren't this reckless."

"Don't even get me started," I snapped.

He glared, as if testing me. "And if it doesn't work?"

I groaned, the entire conversation exhausting me. "Are we really worse off than we are now?"

His throaty chuckle surprised me, and he closed his eyes before speaking. "I don't guess so."

I stepped closer to where Icy couldn't hear me. "I don't know if it will work. But everything in our world has to do with power, and I don't think the Oblivion is any different. The first thing it does is take our magic when we arrive. We have to show dominance. If it respects our power and submits, maybe it will release us."

He stared, as if thinking through everything. He nodded. "Like you said, we won't be worse off than we already are."

We packed up our belongings, deciding to head into the forest toward the river. As often as the terrain and environment changed, we really weren't sure which way to go, but decided to walk in the same direction I had gone that morning.

We walked for hours, but the river was nowhere to be found.

"Do you think it knows we're trying to escape?" Dorian asked.

"I wouldn't doubt it. This place is a parasite, living off tortured souls."

I swiped at the vines in front of my face, clearing the path in front of me. When I didn't hear the shuffle of tiny footsteps behind me, I froze. Looking over my shoulder, I watched as Icy stood perfectly still about ten feet behind me. She stood with her head tilted back and eyes closed, as if listening for something.

"Icy?" Dorian called out. "Are you okay?"

"Do you hear it?" she whispered. "The water. Can you hear it?"

In the distance, a rush of water that almost sounded like static, flowed to our left. "You're right. I think that's it."

Dorian led the way through the trees and eventually, a river came into view, maybe twenty feet across in width.

Icy wiped her shaking hands down her pants, and fidgeted from side to side. Her small chest heaved from nervous breaths. "I'm scared," she whispered.

"We're right here with you," he replied.

"Do I have to go first?" she asked. "Can I watch one of you?"

I met Dorian's eyes and I knew he felt the same way I did. "Icy, we want to both be here in case you need us to get you out. You have two people that aren't going to let anything happen to you. Okay?"

Her little voice shook when she whispered, "Okay."

I kneeled beside her, hoping to sound confident in a plan I didn't even know would work. "Do you remember when you first found your elemental gift? Remember searching for your source of power and connecting with it?"

She thought for a few seconds and nodded.

I removed the comb from my hair once again and held it in front of her. "I want you to do the same thing with these stones. Use them to fuel your gift and control the water. No matter what happens, you are in control. Do not let the water have power over you."

"Then what?" she asked.

"We know the river is an entrance, so we can hope it is also an exit. Just maintain control until the Oblivion submits and releases you. Can you try it?"

She muttered so low, I almost didn't hear her. "What if it doesn't?"

I grinned, hoping it comforted her. "Then Dorian and I will be here to pull you out."

I secured the comb in the back of her hair, making sure it wouldn't slip out. Then I tipped her chin up and grinned. "Can you do me a favor? When you grow up, bring this back to me on my wedding day so we can do this all over again."

She cracked a smile. "I won't forget." Icy wrapped her arms around me, her tiny fist knotting in the back of my shirt.

"Thank you, Mercy."

Dorian and I watched as Icy stepped into the river, gently flowing downstream around her. She held onto the side of a large rock, easing herself into the water. It wasn't deep, only rising to her waist, but the unlevel terrain made it difficult to stand against the current.

She closed her eyes, as if concentrating on the gem. Dorian and I sat silently, watching her, anticipation thick in the air around us. After several minutes, I could have sworn the water rippled around her, as if avoiding her presence. The comb in her hair began to flicker, and hope welled within me.

Dorian reached down, gripping my hand in his. "She's doing it," he whispered.

I nodded, even though he couldn't see it. His eyes were locked on Icy, just as mine were. The spark of hope quickly dwindled at the sight of Icy's eyes widening in fear. A loud crash came out of nowhere, and my body jolted at the sight of an angry rush of water plunging toward the small child.

"Icy!" I shouted.

The wave knocked her backward and her little body immediately went under. Dorian and I ran down the riverbank, searching for any sign of her. "Do you see her?" I shouted.

He slid to a stop, pointing downstream. "There! I think I see her hair!"

My heart beat violently against my chest. What if something happened to her and the Oblivion decided it was done with her? I would never forgive myself. My legs burned as I pushed forward, desperate to keep sight of her. She broke through the surface of the water, gasping for breath and crying for help.

"Use the gem, Icy! Try to focus!" It seemed absurd to tell a child to focus while drowning, but it was her only chance. Her head disappeared under the rapids once again and Dorian dove into the water without hesitation. He swam in her direction, but it was no use. The waves tossed against the large boulders, blocking him from reaching her.

The Oblivion continued to toy with her, refusing to let her get the upper hand.

Her head came up once again, and I could have sworn she looked directly at me.

"Control the water!" I shouted.

When she went under once again, I dove into the river to help. I fought against the rapids with Dorian, and immediately understood how difficult it would be to focus on your power while fighting to breathe. Did any of us have a chance?

The water threw Dorian from side to side, and a cut on the top of his forehead bled down the front of his face. As soon as I yelled his name, a large wave pummeled me, and I choked on a mouthful of water, gurgling and fighting my way to the surface. I caught sight of Icy, struggling underwater, and for one final time, her icy blue gaze met mine, full of panic.

A green glow began to illuminate the water around us, as the thrashing of waves dissipated. The waves began to calm around us as I kicked to the surface, wrapping my arms around a rock on the side of the riverbank. The green glow intensified and the river stilled, completely unmoving. A bright flash of light broke through the valley and then evaporated into particles. Everything around us settled, silently.

Dorian and I began to panic.

"Icy! Icy, where are you?" I shouted.

He swam down the river, now gentle and complacent. We searched everywhere until he turned toward me and whispered. "Mercy, she isn't here."

My shoulders sagged in relief, and I began to sob.

. . .

"How do we know for sure?" he asked. "I know I shouldn't, but I can't help but wonder if something bad happened to her."

"I don't know, D. I don't want to think about what will happen if she didn't make it. I have a good feeling, if that helps."

"Do you think we have to leave the same way we came? I'll take the river over the snakes, anyday."

I grinned. "I don't know that either. Marie said to leave through the same door we came in. I'm assuming that's what it means, but I honestly don't know."

"How did you get here? I don't think you've ever said."

"Buried alive. How am I supposed to manage that?"

"Want me to bury you?" He grinned.

I raised one brow at the excitement in his tone. "The river is sounding better and better." I stood, taking one last glance at the water before turning away. "But I have a feeling this place won't accept it. It wants to push us to our limits, and I don't think it will give an inch." I pulled my wet hair back once again, wrapping it into a bun. "Do you have any idea where this cave is?"

"Past the river and the campsite where the raiders brought you, up the mountainside. Not sure if the Oblivion will change that location, but we'll see."

"Let's get to it," I said with enthusiasm I didn't feel.

"Mercy, why don't we get you home first. I don't like the idea of leaving you here alone. What if you don't make it back?"

"I'll make it home. I swear it."

"But . . ."

"Look, Dorian. I can't tell you anything about your future, but I need you to make it back. For your family's sake. For mine."

He tilted his head back and closed his eyes. "You are so stubborn."

I leaned forward and whispered, "I've heard that from a Moreno before."

He smiled. "I bet you have."

We continued walking, following the path of the river, in comfortable conversation. It felt easy with him, as if I'd known him my entire life. There was an air of hope hovering between us, a possibility of getting home we didn't know existed.

"If you could tell your younger self something, anything at all. What would it be?" I asked. "It's something I've been thinking about since I realized who Icy was."

He grunted. "I would say don't sneak out of the house at the age of sixteen because my father is not someone to piss off. Maybe try not to test my mother so much. And when Analise Parker declares her love, tell her how you feel. Don't make her work so hard for it," he chuckled.

I laughed. "Sounds like you have it figured out."

"What about you?"

"Don't trust people just because they're blood. That's the big one." I elbowed him, grinning. "Cherish every moment with those you love, because you never know when it will be your last. Show the love of your life how much they mean to you, everyday. Don't let them doubt it for a second." I cut my eyes toward him and raised my brows. "What do you think?"

"I think you have it figured out."

CHAPTER
NINETEEN

MARLEY

Thu Dang gripped me by the arm, jerking me to a stop. "Where do you think you're going? The sisters are on their way, and I will not be responsible for your foolishness!"

"You need to remember who you're speaking to." I pulled away from his grasp. "I'm going to find the boy before this blows up in my face. Stay here and make yourself useful," I spat.

I could feel the heat of his glare as I hurried out of the dungeon. I could only assume someone had slipped in and taken Ren to the cave earlier than expected, right under my nose.

Pissed was an understatement.

I bolted through the backdoor of the Domicile and closed my eyes, mentally reaching out for any clues I could find. It would be difficult if the culprit was Hillie—her gift could block mine easily, and I hated to admit she was more powerful. Drake had perfected his wall, but I wasn't sure about the boy. Although strong, he'd never actually been trained to do anything.

Screw it.

I knew the cave was on the side of the mountain, so there was no point in wasting anymore time. I walked to where old, fallen trees laid over the river, and carefully stepped to the other side. Surprisingly, I'd never explored this side of the Domicile and had no idea where I was going, but I continued through the trees, stomping through pine needles and leaves.

Why did they sneak him out? Had they gotten wind of my plan? Did they not trust me? Of course Hillie didn't trust me. Maybe I needed to remind her that she has more than one cousin. She hadn't even given me a chance.

Not that she would like me.

When the stone of the mountainside came into view, I held my hand above my eyes to block the sun, searching for something like Drake had described. I didn't see anything above me, but froze when the thoughts from another drifted into my mind.

"He's anxious, I can feel tension radiating from him. If we don't calm him down, he'll never be able to stay here."

Fitz. For some reason, he'd let his guard down and his thoughts drifted by me like a brisk breeze. I closed my eyes and eased forward with my hands on the rock, sensing his presence more and more the further I walked.

"He could go off the rails at any moment," Colton thought. *"I'm not sure about this."*

After fifty feet or so, I glanced up and saw a small ledge, one you would never suspect to be anything other than rock jutting out from the mountainside. But they were there —I knew it. Small dips throughout the stone, almost stair-like, made it climbable and I slowly made my way to the top. As I grew closer, my energy began to deplete, and my head pounded from pressure.

I heard Fitz before I saw him, speaking softly as if trying to calm Ren down. "Listen to me. You have to focus. Take deep breaths, okay? Over and over. That's it."

When I peeked above the ledge, my body jolted at the sight of Fitz standing over Drake. He wasn't trying to calm Ren down at all, he'd been talking to Drake. I hurried into the cave and Hillie smirked at my presence, obviously high as a kite.

"I guess I'm late," I announced.

Fitz frowned. "Hillie felt that we needed an earlier start."

I nodded. "Good idea. Let's follow the lead of the buzzed Regalian. Smart."

She smiled, as if her latest thought brought more joy than anything ever had. "I have an idea! Let's push Marley off the cliff. Wouldn't that be fun!" She clapped her hands in front of her, grinning from ear to ear. "I'll go first!" She stepped forward, but Fitz caught her by the arm.

"Let's focus, ladies." He kneeled in front of Drake, looking concerned. "Are you going to be alright? You don't have to stay."

Drake swallowed, as sweat ran down his pale skin. "I'm not going anywhere." He looked as though he'd lost another ten pounds. My heart squeezed painfully at the sight of him, weakened and obviously in pain.

"It might take time," Ren whispered from the corner. "Get some air—it will help."

I stepped toward the boy, watching him closely. He crossed his legs in front of him, closing his eyes in concentration. "How long have you been trying?" I asked.

Colton sighed. "A couple of hours." He placed one hand around Drake, helping him to the ledge of the cave. "Take a deep breath. Focus." He eased him toward the edge, encouraging him to breathe, then stood watching over the forest, as if keeping an eye out.

I watched as he fought to sit up straight, as though he would collapse at any moment. "What's wrong with him?" I asked.

"The dragon," Ren replied. "Being this close to the cave —it demands to be free."

"Not to mention he's grown weak from mourning his mate," Hillie spat. She sat in front of Ren, nibbling on a brownie in her hand. "Let's try again."

Ren shook his head. "I've used you too much already. You won't last." He looked around Hillie toward me. "Would you like to try?"

I took a deep breath. How would I ever get Ren back to the Domicile before the sisters arrived? Could Thu Dang hold them off a little longer?

"Unless you aren't interested in helping Mercy," Hillie muttered under her breath.

"She's my sister. Of course I'll help." I pushed her aside and took a seat in front of Ren.

She handed me a small bite of brownie. "It helps." Then she leaned forward to whisper, "You can trust me."

I snatched the brownie from her hand and focused on the boy in front of me. My vision blurred immediately and my words were stuck in my throat. I took a bite of the chocolate, attempting to calm myself down. Ren watched with interest, as if curious how I would react to him outside of the dungeon.

It felt as if someone were sucking the source from within me, invading the deepest, darkest corners of my mind and using me as fuel for a much hotter fire. I cringed, but began to feel the effects of the brownie. As bad as I hated to admit it, it did take the edge off.

"Is it working? What do you see?" I choked out.

"Darkness. Nothing but darkness right now," he answered. "There is no sound. No life."

Fitz turned from where he sat with Drake. "What does that mean? She is still alive, right?"

"She has to be," Drake muttered. "We have to find her."

I felt the pull, more intense than before, almost painful. Ren used my power to feed his own, attempting to connect with Mercy. My hands stiffened, my fingers splayed wide as if trying to stop his assault on my source. I turned my head away from him, my body doing anything it could to escape the boy in front of me.

All at once, my eyes met Hillie's across the cave and she smirked.

The bitch is enjoying this.

He released his hold and I fell backward, landing on the cold stone of the cave floor. It took several minutes for me to right myself, and I sat catching my breath, attempting to clear my thoughts. "That didn't take too long. Did you find anything?"

Ren's eyes widened. "We've been at it for over an hour. You are focusing, right? You have to help me, Marley."

My mouth fell open in shock. "Of course I am! It would help if you'd tell me what I'm looking for!"

He tilted his head, then one side of his mouth pulled up in a smirk. He leaned forward so that no one else would hear. "You are a smart one, aren't you? Too bad the intelligence is overpowered by bitterness."

I ground my teeth. "Stay out of my head."

"Are you going to tell him the truth?" he whispered. "Are you going to tell him how you fell in love with him as a boy? How you want Mercy out of your way?"

"This is not why we're here," I spat.

228

"No." He shook his head. "We're here because you made a deal with the devils. Don't you realize? I just spent an hour inside of your head."

I stumbled back, embarrassed that I didn't think of this before. I bared myself to this child—every fear, every desire. "I'm leaving."

He shrugged. "I thought you wanted to help your sister."

I exhaled, frustrated at being so careless. "Hillie, I believe it's your turn."

"Woo hoo! Let's get this party started!" She danced her way toward Ren, more stoned than I'd ever seen her.

"Marley?" Fitz called out. "Can you sit with Drake for a little while? I'm going to try and help stabilize their emotions while they focus. Colton, you keep watch."

Ren smiled, and I'd never wanted to slap a child more.

"Of course." I sat beside Drake and reached for his hand, but froze at the sight of his eyes, completely red. "Oh, Drake. What can I do?"

He shook his head. "Distract me. I'm not sure I'm strong enough to keep the dragon under control. I need to concentrate on something else."

I nodded, but then sat silently, struggling to come up with small talk. I thought of Mercy distracting him underneath the waterfall that day.

Now there's an idea.

"I sense something," Ren whispered. "I can feel her. Do you hear water? You're doing it, Hillie. Stay with me."

I ground my teeth, thinking how much I hated every one of them.

Drake gasped, clutching his abdomen. I leaned forward, placing my hand on his. "Do you remember the first time you met me? Right after you . . ."

"Bit Aadya's head off? Yeah, this isn't helping," he mumbled.

I watched him double over in pain, agony I knew that wasn't only caused by his gift, but his love for my sister. He would never abandon her. Drake was too loyal to walk away, unless he had a reason. Part of me swore I'd never bring it up for fear of what it would do to our relationship.

Now, sitting here beside him, I knew it was my only shot. I knew there was a chance Ren would tell him, and I couldn't let that happen. He needed to trust me. We needed a connection that no one else could take away from us. I decided to be honest with him.

"No. That wasn't the first time."

He raised his head, his forehead wrinkled from confusion. I knew it helped, his curiosity overpowered the dragon's voice in his head and his body stilled. "What?"

"I met your father when I was only six years old, do you remember?" I asked, hesitantly.

He looked away from me, as if the answer could be found in the treetops outside the cave entrance, then he shook his head. "No. Are you sure it was him?" He cringed, wrapping his arms around his waist. "Could have been someone else," he muttered through the pain.

I tried to be strong, but my shaky voice betrayed me. "I can show you, if you'll let me."

"Marley, I don't know what you're talking about." He looked over his shoulder at Ren, rocking back and forth. "You need to save your energy for Ren."

"Please, Drake. It won't take but a second."

He sighed, and his red-tinted eyes met mine. "Okay. But only a second."

"You have to let your guard down. Let me in and I'll

show you my memories." I watched the hesitation cross his face. "Please."

He shook his head, "I can't believe I'm doing this."

Drake closed his eyes, and I kneeled in front of him, and cupped his face in my hands. "Let me in. Remember. *Please remember*."

CHAPTER
TWENTY
MERCY

Dorian's hand covered my mouth, keeping me from speaking. "Shh," he whispered. He stood behind me, pulling me behind a large oak, out of sight. "Raiders." He slowly removed his palm, and pointed through the trees at two men walking in our direction. "If they discover the significance of your gems, we're done for."

I kept my voice low. "What if I can use the stones as a source right now? Then I would have my power to defend ourselves against them."

"You don't want to risk it. Save them for getting home," he replied.

I nodded, I knew he was right. We stayed perfectly still, hiding behind the old oak until they passed, looking for their next victim. "I think they're gone."

I crept forward, searching for anyone nearby. All at once, a huge limb swung toward me, striking me in the face. I flew back, slamming against a tree and sliding to the ground. Pain shot through my nose, and blood, warm and sticky, dripped down my lips. I blinked, trying to clear my vision, but it continued to get worse.

Large black boots stepped in front of my line of sight and a deep, throaty chuckle reverberated through the trees. "Look at what we have here. Been wondering where you two ran off."

I staggered to my feet, then came face to face with Reynolds, the same man who dragged me to their campsite. "Hello to you, too."

He grinned, his teeth black and breath sour. "I believe you have something I need."

"I don't believe I do."

Another guy I didn't recognize held a knife to Dorian's throat, keeping him immobile. My gaze traveled between the two, trying to figure out how to escape without getting Dorian hurt in the process. Yes, he could possibly survive anything the Oblivion threw at him. But what if he didn't? Not knowing what to expect was the worst part of it all.

Reynolds gripped my shirt in his fist, jerking me toward him. I cringed as the smell of his breath hit my face. "Heard the woman was talkin' to you down by the river. The necklace. I want it now."

"You wouldn't take a family heirloom from a young woman, would you?"

He nodded, matter of factly. "I would indeed."

Damn it.

I scowled as he tightened his grip. "What are you going to do? Kill me for a worthless piece of jewelry?"

He raised one brow, then briefly glanced over his shoulder at his partner. He glanced back at me and whispered, "What do you want me to do?"

I pulled away, but he refused to release me.

Dorian jerked forward, but the knife pressed into his skin, drawing a thin line of blood.

"There's something sexy about your strength—your aggression." He licked his lips. "I like that in a woman."

I laughed, I couldn't help it. "You like to be bossed around by a woman?" I stared wide eyed with blood running down my face. "Look at me, how sexy can I be?"

"Maybe I can help you rinse that shirt, somewhere more private. Then, you can take the necklace off for me." He shifted forward, rubbing against me. "I'll help you take it all off."

There were no words.

At my silence, he licked his lips, then stood tall, a sad attempt to appear unaffected. "Corbin. I got the girl. Keep D under control."

"But . . ."

"You heard me." He chuckled toward Dorian. "Can't have her all to yourself."

Dorain once again stepped forward. "Don't even think about touching her."

"It's okay," I muttered. "I'll be right back." I tried to meet his eyes, anything to let him know the man wouldn't get far with me, but I could tell it didn't work. Dorian wasn't comforted in the least.

Reynolds shoved me ahead of him, toward a small stream about fifty yards away. I searched the area around us, trying to think before he demanded more of me than I would give.

"You can rinse your shirt out here." He pointed toward the stream, smiling. He slowly slid to the ground, leaning against a fallen tree, watching me. Reynolds crossed his legs and waited. The amused smirk turned my stomach, but I knew if I didn't play my cards right, he could ruin everything. If he took my emeralds, I would never get home.

Swallowing my pride, I pulled the shirt over my head and dropped it into the stream, watching as blood mixed with trickling water, staining it red. With my back to Reynolds, I turned to face him. His eyes roamed my naked chest, and he reached down to adjust himself.

I think I'm going to be sick.

He crooked his finger toward me in a 'come here' motion and I took a deep breath before walking forward. I stood before him, not quite sure how to handle the situation. He gripped my hand, and jerked me into his lap—the evidence of his intentions obvious.

Yep. I just puked in my mouth.

I placed my hands on his shoulders, not wanting to touch him anywhere. He gripped my backside, pushing me into his hips, and leaned forward to kiss me. I tilted my head back at the last second, and his lips grazed my neck. He became more aggressive, and I knew I had to act quickly. He jerked the necklace from my chest and grinned, shoving it into his pocket. Then he began to loosen his pants.

I couldn't waste anymore time. I shoved my hand down the front of his pants and his head fell back against the bark of the fallen tree, as if overwhelmed by my touch alone. Then, with all of my might, I twisted.

He screamed, the highest pitch I'd ever heard from a grown man. I'm sure Dorian thought it could only have come from me. One more time for good measure, I twisted his balls the other direction and he scrambled, red-faced and fighting me with tears in his eyes.

"I'm going to kill you!" Reynolds dove forward, but something caught him around the neck, and his eyes bulged from the pressure.

I crawled away from him as fast as I could, covering myself in the process. Dorian stood behind him with something that looked like vine or rope, choking him to death. His hands twisted the vine over and over as Reynolds' attempts to free himself failed. His feet kicked, as if running in mid air.

I hurried toward the stream, snatching the blood stained shirt, and slipping it over my head. When I turned around, Dorian stood over Reynolds, staring at his limp body on the ground.

"Is he dead?" I asked.

He shrugged. "Is anyone ever dead in this place?"

"Good point." I searched the woods around us. "How did you get free?"

"The scream took us both off guard. I saw an opening to turn the knife against him and took it. Are you okay?"

I scoffed, attempting to look fine, although I was not fine at all. "Of course. I had it under control."

His eyes widened.

"I did. I had a plan," I lied.

He threw his hands up in surrender. "I believe you. Never seen such a violent testicle maneuver."

I leaned forward, pulling the necklace from his pocket. "We need to run. There will be others after this. If he knows, his men will too."

Dorian nodded. "Let's go."

We followed the river, searching for the crossing Dorian had taken so many times before. Large boulders and old wood crumbled behind us as we hurried to the other side, as if chasing us—a savage attempt to keep us from reaching our destination. Halfway to the mountainside, the river began to rise, flooding the valley within minutes. My thighs burned from the effort, but I never faltered as I followed closely behind him. If we didn't make it to higher ground, we wouldn't have a chance.

Water crept over my boots, up my calves, making it harder to keep pace. We could see a rock formation up ahead on the right and hope welled within me at the sight. The water began to lap at our thighs, slowing us down.

"We have to swim!" Dorian called out. He dove forward, disappearing underneath the dismal water, determined to reach the cave.

I followed suit, but the murky water made it impossible to follow him, so I continued coming up for air just to be able to find my way toward the entrance. About forty feet ahead of me, Dorian clung to the side of a rock, waving in my direction.

As I drew near, I could see fear in his eyes, and my chest grew tight at what it could mean. "What's wrong?"

"The only entrance I know of is at the bottom of this formation. I crawled through it when I arrived." He sighed, worry evident in his dark gaze.

"So it's underwater?" I asked.

"It's underwater," he replied.

"How long will we have to hold our breath?"

His eyes traveled over the flooded valley, continuing to rise. "Depends how long it continues to flood. We'll have to swim to the bottom, then up through the crevices until we reach the higher elevation," He sighed at the look on my face. "We could wait it out, see if the water recedes."

"I don't think it'll recede. The Oblivion is trying to keep us away, and it won't give up that easily." I didn't take time to freak out. Water had never bothered me before, but I'd also had the gift of elemental interference. If we were going to do this, we had to go right then. "I'll follow you."

"If it's murky, you won't be able to see well, just feel around for the openings in the rocks, okay?"

I nodded. "I'll be right behind you."

Dorian cupped the side of my face, then took a big breath, diving underwater. I followed suit, trying to keep the sole of his shoe in my line of sight, so I didn't get lost. The water had risen to at least twelve feet or so, and I kicked as hard as I could to keep up with his pace, as he swam toward the ground.

He felt around for a few seconds, but found the entrance he'd remembered from his arrival. A moment of claustrophobia seeped in as I squeezed through the small opening behind him, trying not to panic. He swam through what looked like a mossy tunnel, with twists and turns on a gradual slope upward.

There was no way of knowing how long I could hold my breath. I felt weak without the use of my power—useless and frail. I couldn't let it distract me from what we had to do though, so I put it out of my mind and pushed forward.

I stayed close behind him, but as I kicked my way through the water, the toe of my boot caught on something unforgiving, and no matter how much I pushed and pulled, I could not get loose. The need to cough became unbearable as the urge to open my mouth and breathe, tickled the back of my throat.

I bent down to free my boot, but the vine had completely wedged it against the rock, and every movement shoved it further into entrapment. I loosened the shoe strings, wiggling my foot until I could shimmy my heel up and out, then swam forward to catch up with Dorian, leaving the boot behind.

My lungs began to burn, and the pressure of the water pushed against my chest and back, daring me to take a breath. I reached a split tunnel, and didn't have a clue where to go. There was no sign of Dorian, but if I didn't move quickly, I would run out of what air I had left.

Bubbles began to escape from between my lips as I fought to keep my mouth closed. My heart pounded, and I decided to swim up the tunnel to my left, praying it was the right one. I kicked harder and harder, but my body struggled under the physical stress, begging me to give up.

Just when I thought I would drown, when I couldn't hold my breath any longer, my head broke the surface of the water and I gripped the side of a slippery rock, gripping anything I could find to hold onto. Tears filled my eyes as I gasped for fresh air, and I fought to control my emotions welling to the surface. I honestly didn't know if I would make it.

"Mercy! Mercy, are you there?"

I placed my hand on the wall and began to cry. "Dorian? Are you alright?"

"I'm okay. I lost you somehow, and we got split up. I'm inside the cave I arrived in, but I'm trying not to move. I really don't want to disturb the vipers on the other side."

"Lovely." I glanced around my side of the cave, suddenly nervous about slithery creatures close to me. Thankfully, I didn't see any. "I might be able to swim back down to the split, but I need a minute to catch my breath."

The rock around us rumbled, and a scraping noise startled me. A horrible feeling took root in the pit of my stomach—a feeling of dread. "Dorian?" I waited for a second, but there was no answer. "Dorian, can you hear me?"

"Ah, Mercy. I have a problem."

Once again, the cave began to rumble around me. "What's going on?"

His dark chuckle was anything but humorous. "The cave walls are closing in."

I looked around, but it didn't appear the rock around me had budged at all. "It's trying to keep him from escaping," I whispered to myself. I reached toward my neck, gripping the necklace. "Oh, no." I mumbled. "No. No. No!"

"Talk to me, Mercy!"

"The necklace. I have to get you the necklace!" I searched along the cave walls for an opening, a way to reach him before it was too late.

"Damn it!" he screamed. "It's pushing the snakes in my direction. They are not happy about it either."

"Have you been bit?"

"Once on my leg. We've got to figure out something, quick, before I lose feeling."

I dove underwater, feeling around the rocks for a way to get to him. The stone was solid all the way across, so I began to swim lower, hoping to find a break in the stone. About six feet under, bubbles from the other side of the rocks caught my attention. A tiny crevice, maybe a half inch wide, separated two rocks, a gap hopefully just large enough.

I swam toward the surface once again, full of hope. "Dorian! There's a crack, it's tiny but it may be big enough to get the necklace to you. You have to swim down maybe five or six feet. I'll push it through!"

"You want me to swim down with the water moccasins? Stick my hand in a pit of snakes? Is that what you're saying?"

I closed my eyes, hating myself for asking him to do it. "Yes. I need you to trust me. Can you do that?" The cave continued to shake around me, and I wondered how close it had gotten to closing in on him. "You have to try!"

"Okay," he replied, his voice trembling. "I'm ready."

I removed the necklace, and dove underwater, swimming toward the tiny collection of bubbles toward the cave floor. It took some work, but I turned the gem from side to side, pushing it through the crack to the other side. Just as my finger shoved it through, a sharp sting hit my skin, and I jerked my hand back in pain.

It was unlike anything I'd ever felt. I swear I could feel the venom traveling through my veins, creeping up my arm toward my neck and chest. With one arm, I swam to the surface, waiting nervously to see if Dorian found the emerald. If he hadn't, I wasn't sure what to do. After several seconds, I heard a gasp, and Dorian shouted, "I got it. Not gonna lie though, I've been bit more than I care to think about, Mercy. My arm is throbbing and going numb."

I held my finger under the small sliver of sunlight from a crevice above. It was already twice the size of the other one. I pushed myself up on a flat piece of ledge and slumped against the stone wall, my body fighting to stay awake. "You have to hurry. Use the necklace, Dorian. Maybe you can use your sensory gift to take the pain away. Change what you see, hear, and smell. Imagine somewhere other than the cave!"

"Damn. I'm trying. The bites aren't doing me any favors. I'm barely keeping my head above water over here." His gasps were audible, even through the cave walls.

"Don't do this to me, Dorian. We have to get you home!" I cried. "Please! Please, try again. I know it's hard but you can do it!"

Please, God. Please help him. Take him from this hell.

The cave walls began to slow, and I knew they were closing in.

"I want you to know . . . I'm grateful you were here with

me," he slurred, as if drowsy from the venom. "I'm sorry for the suffering you've gone through, but I'm thankful you were here."

"Dorian? Dorian!"

Tears ran down my cheek as the bright green glow I'd seen once before filled the cave, illuminating the walls around me. I gasped as the cave shook, as if fighting against Dorian's power. I could feel the vibrations inside my chest, the battle taking place on the other side of the wall.

All at once, the stone settled and the glow of green light dimmed. Relief turned my stomach, and I realized I had been holding my breath. My hand continued to swell and the vessels in my arm burned. I swayed forward then back, collapsing alone in the cave.

CHAPTER
TWENTY-ONE
MARLEY

Drake sat in front of me, holding his side, as if suffering from an injury or wound. I could see the toll the cave had taken on him, fueling the need for the dragon to be released. He closed his eyes as I pushed against his shield, eager to show him every memory I'd held onto for years. They may have taken his memories, but it wouldn't stop me from sharing my own. Every emotion. Every desire. I wanted him to *feel* it all.

The first time I met him—standing in our living room behind his father. He eyed me curiously as I reached for his hand. "I'm Marley."

He shook my hand, cutting his eyes toward his father as if nervous. "I'm Drake."

"We're gonna be good friends. I just know it."

Drake pushing me on the swing in the backyard, laughing at my squeal of delight.

243

"Higher, Drake! Higher!" I shouted. "Don't let me fall!"

He scoffed. "I would never!"

"Promise?" I asked, tilting my head back, as my long red hair blew across my face.

"Always," he replied.

SITTING AT THE DINNER TABLE, as Aunt Isla scooped a large helping of Macaroni and cheese onto our plates, and Drake reached for my hand under the table. He smirked, and I noticed he had a dimple on one cheek.

"Wanna take a walk after dinner?" he asked.

I nodded, unable to keep the goofy grin off my face.

HIS HAND OVER MINE, as he stands behind me, teaching me how to throw a baseball. Drake's breath blew across the back of my neck and I shivered. I could hear him chuckle behind me, as if he knew the effect he had on me.

"WHAT IS THAT?" I asked.

He looked over his shoulder, narrowing his eyes. "What?"

"On your shoulder. I've never seen it before."

Drake froze, and when his eyes met mine, I could have sworn they were tinted red. "It's nothing."

I stepped closer, inspecting the black speckle of dots collecting along his shoulder. "Is it a tattoo? I mean, it's cool if it is."

He swallowed, then mumbled. "Yeah, something like that."

I LEANED FORWARD, pressing my mouth against his underwater. He stiffened, as if unsure how to respond. Not giving him a chance to *pull away, I wrapped my arms around his neck and pulled him closer. His arms relaxed, and it thrilled me that he didn't pull away.*

We came up for air, and just stood in the water, staring at each other. I didn't know what came over me, but I didn't regret it. I grinned, but it quickly vanished at the sight of sadness filling his dark gaze.

"I'm so sorry, Marley. I really am," he murmured.

THE MONTHS *after Drake disappeared from my life, the grieving for my only friend and first love as the only thing I ever cared about vanished. The fights at school. The manifestation of a power I didn't understand.*

AN ALLEGATO MARK *that never came.*

I OPENED MY EYES, as tears rolled down my cheeks. His gaze roamed over my face, as if he needed a minute to sort through everything I had shown him. His eyes weren't as red, but still black as the night sky. He swallowed, but didn't speak.

"I know it's a lot to take in. I'm sorry I didn't tell you before. Your father wiped your memory to keep us safe."

Drake opened his mouth, but closed it again.

"Please say something," I begged.

"I don't know what to say," he admitted. "I don't understand."

"I think he was trying to keep an eye on me for my parents. He always asked about me—my interests, how things were going at school. He seemed like he genuinely cared."

Drake looked away, his gaze overlooking the valley of Seregalo. "I'm so sorry. I would have never left you, you have to know that. If we were close friends, I wouldn't have abandoned you." He took a deep breath, then leaned forward, wrapping his arms around me. His hands knotted in the back of my hair as I clung to his shoulders.

I closed my eyes, blinking tears away. I had never wanted anything more in my life than him. "I know you wouldn't have."

He held me for several minutes, then whispered, "This changes everything."

I nodded. "Yes it does."

Drake leaned back, cupping my face with his palms. "I don't know how I'm going to tell Mercy."

"She'll understand, she has to. We were together long before you met her."

He continued as if he didn't hear a word I said. "She's going to be thrilled."

I paused, unsure I had heard him correctly. "Sorry?"

"Yes," he continued. "Marley, all she's ever wanted is for you two to be family. Once she finds out how close we were as kids, hopefully it will make your connection stronger. This could change everything for you two."

"Um. You don't think she'll be jealous?" I asked, with one brow raised.

He laughed. "Of course not. We were just silly kids. We didn't even know what real love meant back then."

My stomach dropped as pain shot through my chest. I knew. No matter what anyone said, our connection was real. I knew what love felt like every time he glanced in my direction, and the pain I endured when he disappeared.

I knew.

"I sense her! She's alive, Mercy is alive!" Ren called out.

246

Drake broke away from my grasp and I slumped, defeated and heartbroken. How could he not see our connection? Did he not feel that our bond was stronger than his and Mercy's?

"Drake, you need to rest," Fitz called out.

"I can't sit back and rest while she's out there. I have to do something."

"Marley, Hillie has been at it for a while. We may need you to lend your power to Ren—give her a break," Fitz called out.

"No," Hillie argued. Sweat poured down her pale face as her hair began to fall from its intricate updo. "I can do this."

"You don't have to do it all on your own," he whispered.

I didn't know what to do. My heart had been completely shattered for the second time, and I stood there offering to help as if nothing had happened. "Fitz is right," I lied. "Let me help. I could use a distraction."

"I'm not turning her loose now that we've found her. We may not find her again. Plus, Ren didn't see anything but darkness when connected to Marley earlier."

"Ouch," I muttered, somewhat offended by Hillie's words. I vaguely wondered who I hated more—her or my sister. She grinned, as if she'd heard my thoughts.

I may actually hate her more.

"What do you see?" Drake asked. "Is she okay?"

Ren squinted, gripping Hillie's hand tighter. He shook his head, as if shocked. "I'm forcing my way into her subconscious, so I can only hear what she's thinking, feel what she's feeling. I'm not sure how much . . . Wait."

"What is it?" Fitz stepped forward, just as eager as the rest of us to know what he saw.

"She feels so far away, I can barely sense her. I don't think Mercy's with us anymore."

Drake leaned forward, and I feared his anger would cause him to lose control of the dragon. "What did you say?"

"She's in an in-between world. A land that exists, but not really."

"The Oblivion," Fitz whispered. "It's not possible." He paced the length of the cave, his mind on overdrive. "How can you be sure?"

"I can feel the darkness—a cold and desolate existence —the lack of life and purpose."

"But, how? How did she end up there?" Fitz pressed.

"I'm . . . I'm not sure." Ren took a deep breath. "She's confused, everything is hazy."

Drake's voice lowered, almost dangerous. "Is she hurt?"

Ren squinted. "I believe so. She's definitely weak."

The heat level inside the cave intensified as Drake's skin began to redden. He balled his fists, attempting to control the rage. "I will kill whoever is behind this. I will rip them from limb to limb. No one, and I mean no one will ever have the balls to lay a finger on her again. I swear it."

I took a step back as Ren opened his eyes, looking directly at me. He raised one brow, but didn't call me out. "Her arm is throbbing, she's going in and out of consciousness so I can't get a clear image of what happened."

"Can she hear you?" Colton asked.

"I don't know." He peered at Hillie, concerned. "This level of exertion could kill you. I'm not sure we should keep going."

Hillie swayed, her energy completely diminished. "We're not stopping." She blinked, giving everything she had to stay awake. She wouldn't last long.

A massive explosion shook the mountainside, throwing us to the cave floor. I jumped, and ran toward the entrance beside Colton, shocked to see black smoke and blazing fire wafting from the rubble of the Domicile. "This can't be happening."

"What is going on?" Fitz called out, pushing to his feet. He looked over my shoulder and gasped. "There's no telling how many have been killed. What could have caused the explosion?"

I knew exactly who caused it.

The sisters.

Thu Dang had warned me. He told me the sisters were unstable and impatient. I made a deal with the devil, and I didn't pay the price. Now I had to fix this mess.

"I have to go. That's what Mercy would want me to do," I told them, hoping they didn't see through the lie.

"Go, Marley," Fitz responded. He glanced back at Ren and Hillie, who were focused on connecting with Mercy. "We'll take it from here."

Colton stood at the mouth of the cave, watching me suspiciously.

My gaze traveled to where Drake sat, his eyes closed and head bobbing as if trying to tune out everything around him. I knew he fought the change—the beast begged to escape. Did he even hear what I said? Was he not worried about me going into a battlefield of blazing fire alone? What about the memories? Did they have no effect at all?

I kneeled beside him, placing my hand on his shoulder. "Hang on, okay? I'll be back as soon as I can."

He nodded, but didn't respond.

"We were just silly kids."

There were times during the last few days when I'd thrown myself into Mercy's world, trying to compete—a brief period of compassion or small lapse in judgement.

In that moment, watching the love of my life ignore me as I head into a burning building, I realized he would never love me like he did her. Did he care at all?

I balled my fists, turning away. More hurt than angry, I fought tears, refusing to let the pain weaken me. Aadya knew. She understood the agony of losing the one your heart calls out to when her own sister married my father. I hated being the product of my aunt's pain. She deserved more out of life, just like me.

I hurried down the mountainside, eager to escape Ren's knowing eyes, but dreading the psycho sisters' aftermath. I knew I should be more concerned with the innocent Regalians inside the Domicile, the ones who lost their life because of my poor decisions, but I wasn't. If I didn't know their name, it wasn't on my priority list.

After neutralizing their temper tantrum, the next thing would be to hand Ren over to the sisters, and convince Drake he belonged with me. I refused to give up. Mercy hadn't made it back yet, and there was a good chance she never would.

But I had to hurry.

Running toward the river, the screams grew louder, along with shouts for help. A ring of fire surrounded the Domicile, and several time interferers stood around the destruction, attempting to turn back time to reverse the destruction and death. But whatever spell the sisters had cast, refused the magic of time, unwilling to bend to the demands of others.

Dark magic had taken over.

One side of a tall tower remained as flames licked at the shambles. Trees splintered across the river with roots pulled up from the ground. My eyes burned from the smoke, and I fought to breathe through the fumes. After crawling across the trunk of a fallen oak over the river, I made my way toward the ruins of the Domicile.

I didn't get far before a firm grip latched around my ankle, tripping me up. I scowled, as I glanced down to find a man, laying broken and burned. The pieces of his clothes that were left melted to his skin, as raw meat bled and wept.

"Get off me," I shouted, kicking my boot to shake off his hold.

"Tell me," he croaked out.

Something about the shape of his eyes gave me pause, a familiarity in the downward tilt and gold specks throughout the lightest brown I had ever seen. "Tell you what?"

"Was it worth it?" He coughed, clearing the blood from his throat. "Everything you've done to us—to her—is it worth it to you?" His head fell back against the scorched grass, releasing his hold on my ankle.

Recognition flared, and I kneeled beside him. "Oh, Josiah. Does it hurt?"

His lips tightened, and I knew he refused to give me the benefit of reveling in his agony.

"Yes. As a matter of fact, it is worth it." I smirked, then leaned forward to whisper. "Maybe I'll get lucky and the Oblivion will take you, too. If so, tell Mercy I said hello."

His eyes widened, and his entire body began to tremble. "You will pay . . . for this."

I straightened my spine and stepped over his limp body. "Says the corpse."

I stomped past Josiah, hoping the suffering would last. Many more bodies lay scattered along the yard, some begging for help, others dead on impact. These were supposed to be my people, but as I hurried by them, I couldn't find the least bit of sympathy or compassion. They didn't love me. Their loyalty remained with my sister, and I would forever be the weak, temporary replacement in their eyes.

Up ahead, in the center of black smoke and sinister magic, the sisters danced among the dead, underneath the crumbling tower. Throwing their heads back, arms swung wide, reveling in the chaotic weeping of pain and loss. I envied their carefree nature. The ability to be who they really were, without apology, was something rare, even for myself.

Jules' head swung around as I approached. Stepping over crumbling stone and marble, I carefully avoided the dead at my feet.

I didn't want blood on my boots.

Jules paused, an excited grin breaking out across her pale face as if I were a long lost friend. "Marley! I'm so excited you joined us. Isn't this thrilling?" She spun around and around, breathing in the stench of ash and scorched skin. Her green dress ruffled around tall boots as she danced, as if all were right with the world.

"Why, yes. It's lovely. Is this your doing?"

She threw her hands over her heart, flattered by my words. "I'd love to take credit for this, but Creeky came up with it all on her own." She sighed. "Isn't she brilliant?"

Creeky held the sides of her brown floral skirt out, taking a rather proud bow.

I clenched my teeth. "You do realize, you've destroyed my home. Right?"

My words pulled Creeky from her interpretative dance of death. "Your home?" She cackled loudly, an odd contrast to those crying for their loved ones nearby. "This isn't home. This building is nothing but a symbolic power house, to remind others that they are not in control."

"Not anymore . . ." Jules sang over her shoulder.

"You have murdered Regalians!" I shouted. "Our people!"

"Who you care nothing about! Stop acting like you are different from us," Creeky shouted.

I lowered my voice. "What are you doing? You're destroying Seregalo—on my watch! Do you know how this looks?"

She shrugged, completely unphased. "We had a deal."

"With no time limit. I guess you'll learn to specify next time." I crossed my arms over my chest, daring her to argue. "I'm assuming Thu Dang told you the boy was taken from the dungeon this morning."

Jules nodded. "Oh, he did. He also said you've been holding on to him for days to make your boyfriend happy." She shrugged, innocently. "He said he tried to tell you . . ."

I raised one brow. "Is that right?"

Creeky began skipping through the rubble, kicking rocks and slivers of wood. "We can fix it you know—give you everything you've ever dreamt of. If you . . . cooperate."

I stepped forward, anger fueling my every move. "Do you have any idea who you're talking to?"

Creeky smirked. "A miserable excuse for a leader. A sad replacement for someone well respected and loved–in the community, and in Drake's bed." She grinned wide enough to display every black tooth.

"Shut your mouth!"

"Hurts doesn't it? Not getting what you want. . ." She twirled her hands in the air, and black clouds swirled overhead, creating a flurry of activity. "The only reason the mountainside is still standing is because the child is there.

Or else you and your beloved Drake would both be dead right now."

"I know Ren's powerful, I can sense it. But what do you want with him? There has to be more to this."

She tilted her head. "That boy is the only Regalian known to man who can naturally sift another's power."

"But . . . It's only for a short time. It isn't permanent," I explained.

Her eyes widened in amazement as she waved her hands in front of her face. "The things you can do in mere seconds . . . can you imagine?" She stepped forward, completely animated. "Imagine turning into a dragon, even for a few minutes? It's one of the few things dark magic will never be able to give us."

I gasped. "You want to use Ren to steal Drake's power?"

She pursed her lips, glancing toward the sky, as if in deep thought. "Think bigger, sweetpea. Mercy is out of the picture. I would be able to imprison Drake and use the dragon anytime we want. Not to mention he would be at your disposal." She winked, as if knowing my desire for him.

Another powerful explosion rocked the ground beneath our feet, and knocked me off balance. As I pushed up from the ground, pain shot through my palms, as broken glass burrowed further underneath my skin.

"Uh, oh," Jules sang. "That would be the river."

Creeky tossed her head back in peals of laughter, her silver curls bouncing as if laughing along with her. "Gives new meaning to the word tea-bombs, doesn't it?" They continued giggling, unable to speak.

My gaze traveled around the land, realizing quickly that they wouldn't stop with the Domicile. They were going to destroy Seregalo. They would rule our land, having Drake at their disposal. Through smoke and flames, a shadowy figure appeared, standing to the side, as if completely relaxed.

"Wonderful timing, as usual. Too bad everyone can't be as reliable," Creeky glared in my direction. "Any issues at the river, Dang?"

He stepped forward, his hands clasped in front of him, completely relaxed in the midst of chaos. "None at all."

I wasn't surprised in the least that his loyalty veered so easily. Thu Dang had never swore allegiance to anyone except Aadya, and even then, if betraying her had given him more power, he would have done it in a heartbeat.

"An Elder turning on his own people—why am I not surprised?" Heat began to rise up my neck, and pressure built to an unbearable level inside my head. I flinched at the intrusion, fighting to compose myself.

His beady eyes narrowed as he spat, "Don't speak to me about turning on the people of Seregalo. You aren't a leader. You were never meant to be a leader."

I hit my knees, pushing against his assault on my subconscious. "And you are?" I forced my power in his direction, and the shield protecting his mind cracked, if only for a second. "Everyone has a weakness, Dang. Even you."

His eyes widened at my gloating, refusing to be the weaker Regalian. "Aahh!" He screamed, stepping forward, flinging his hands toward my face. Vibrations intensified against my protective wall, and I fought to keep focus. I jerked my head from side to side, as if I could shake him off. I fought the need to surrender, but the pain in my skull became unbearable.

Drops of warm blood dripped from my nose as I kneeled on the ground in front of him. The sisters giggled, as they came up beside Thu Dang, leaning into his tall, thin frame. They watched with amusement as I writhed in pain on my knees, gripping the ash and rubble in my fists. Every part of my body shook as I put all of my energy into meeting his eyes.

"You will pay for betraying us," he promised.

I smiled, as blood dripped down my lips, filling my mouth. "You can't betray those you were never loyal to."

CHAPTER
TWENTY-TWO
MERCY

L oud humming intensified as I stirred, and my head pounded with every passing second. I began to wonder if the pain would ever end.

"Mercy? Can you hear me?"

A distant-sounding voice called my name over and over —a familiar anxiety-filled tone I'd heard before. Blinking my eyes, I fought to clear my vision, searching for another inside the cave, anyone who could have called out to me.

There was no one.

I relaxed my head back against the cold rock of the wall, figuring my sanity had left with everyone else. A dark cloak of loneliness settled over me, and fear began to trickle in at the realization I was on my own.

"Mercy. I'm here. I'm right here with you."

I jerked upright, shocked at how close the voice felt. "Hello?"

There was no one.

Just to make sure, I placed my hand on the wall and called out, "Dorian?" Silence met my words, and I closed my eyes, wavering between gratefulness and sadness.

The water had receded while I slept, leaving a layer of sticky wet moss in its place. The thin strip of light shined across my swollen hand, and bruising up my arm transitioned to brownish-yellow. I slid from the stone ledge, testing my balance, but stumbled to the right, forgetting I had lost my boot along the way. The slick surface made it difficult to get around, and I quickly learned it was easier to scoot down the declining slope, rather than walk.

Halfway down, I found my soggy boot, still wedged between rock and vine. I wiggled it free and slid my foot inside, knowing a wet shoe would be better than nothing at all. I eased my way down the tunnel, through the same way we entered. I stumbled as the sunlight blinded me, as if waking with a flashlight in my face.

"*Mercy . . .*"

Surprise coursed through me as I spun, searching for whoever called my name. "Who's there?" I swallowed, but dryness in my throat kept me from getting any relief. My gaze traveled across the field and mountainside, but not a soul could be found.

"You're losing your mind, Mercy. Get a grip," I told myself.

The swampy field slopped around my boots as I shuffled toward the river. The sound of fresh water running over rocks quickened my steps, eager to ease the discomfort in my throat. Sweat and grime clung to my skin, and it felt as though my shirt had melted to my back.

When I reached within ten feet of the river, I bolted forward, jumping in without another thought. I scooped up water in my hands, drinking until my stomach cramped. The crisp water enveloped me, washing away the dirt and blood, giving me a false sense of cleanliness. Leaning back, I ran my fingers through my hair, as if it could rinse the darkness from my soul and revive my energy—hopefully renew my spirit.

I floated on my back with my eyes closed for a few minutes, knowing the Oblivion awaited. It stalked me like a thief, eager to take anything I could offer, including my life.

"I'm here. I'm right here."

I jumped from the water, glancing around on guard. I couldn't have imagined the voice, it wasn't possible. Could the Oblivion be screwing with my mind? Of course that was always a possibility, but I didn't think so, not this time. Something about this felt real. Raw. Desperate. Standing in the center of the river, I closed my eyes and breathed.

"That's it. That's it, Mercy. Focus."

I gasped at the excitement in his voice, hope in a typically disheartened tone. A child I'd been burdened with for weeks. *Ren.*

Tears filled my eyes. "Ren?"

Like a broken radio, the signal went in and out, frustrating me. Could he really be inside my subconscious? Why couldn't he hold on to the connection? Who else was with him, if anyone? I knew I needed to keep moving, but I also feared I'd lose him for good if I moved in the slightest.

The burial ground in the forest was my only hope of getting home, and I couldn't waste any more time. Forcing myself out of the water, I crawled up the riverbank and trudged toward the treeline. Backtracking would be the only possible way of finding where I arrived, although I wasn't confident I wouldn't get lost. The burial site wasn't exactly marked.

The mysterious land seemed unusually quiet, as if thinking of the best way to knock me off my feet. Birds chirped overhead and the faint smell of honeysuckle surrounded me. At times like this, it was easy to forget this wasn't paradise and ignore the hell it had put me through.

Every now and again, I would pause, waiting to see if I heard Ren again. There wasn't anything he could do to save me, but his familiar voice brought comfort in my isolation. I knew it didn't matter though. This was a battle I had to go alone, and my desire to get home was just as strong as my determination to face my sister, once and for all.

A child's laughter echoed through the trees, quickly drifting past me like a breeze. I searched from side to side, but didn't see a soul. After a few more steps, I heard it once again, but closer this time.

"Hello?" I called out.

The sound of swift footsteps hurried through the trees on my left, and I turned toward the crunching of leaves in that direction. Then, I spun around at the sound of giggles behind me. I felt as though the presence circled me, taunting me from every corner of the forest. Whispers surrounded me—calling my name, telling me I would never make it.

I froze as the distant hushed melody of a lullabye reached my ears. I closed my eyes, the soothing voice calming my own chaotic nerves.

SLEEP SOUND TONIGHT, *my little one,*
  Darkness will not touch your light.
  I'll be here to watch you sleep,
  And protect you through the night.

KNOW *that you were always wanted,*
  Cherished, adored, and loved.

Even when I'm no longer with you,
I'll watch you from above.

I SQUINTED MY EYES, attempting to focus on the small huddle in the distance. A woman sat on the pine straw, a thick wool blanket completely covering her, with her back to me. Pale hands held what looked to be a newborn baby, wrapped in a thin blue cloth. I gasped at the vision of a woman, the love radiating from every whispered word, strength and determination in every touch.

She reached for the end of the blanket, gently wiping the side of the baby's face while she continued to sing. Dark, unruly hair, similar to mine, stuck up in all directions. I couldn't look away. All at once, the woman swooned, as if dizzy, and quickly sat the baby in her lap. She held her head, attempting to shake off whatever had weakened her.

Something obscure hovered around them, as if they were in grave danger. I wanted to run forward, to protect her from the darkness, but there wasn't anything I could do for either of them. I knew with all of my heart, the Oblivion was once again showing me a vision that would somehow affect me. I just didn't understand how.

How horrible, to be alone in such a weakened state with another to take care of. What must have happened in this woman's life to create such fear—such paranoia of the rest of the world? Was there no one to help her? Protect her? What did she hide from?

As if the child knew I watched from a distance, its little head turned in my direction and dark blue eyes met mine. Breathing became difficult and I gripped my chest, trying to relieve the ache from lack of oxygen. Exhaustion set in, and

I wanted nothing more than to lay down and sleep at that moment.

Then I remembered . . . sitting in Ren's bedroom, feeling as if life had been sucked out of me, leaving a void that took hours to recover from.

Could it be?

We never found out who Ren belonged to, only that his gift of Interference was quite different than anyone we had ever encountered. The sensation of my power being pulled directly from my source—I'd never felt that around anyone else before, not until now.

I wanted nothing more than to help Ren, to guide him as he grew up and teach him to control this unknown force he had been born with. But I didn't know how. The vision dissipated, breaking up into small particles that blew away with the breeze.

Stepping back, the break of a small branch under my boot startled me, and I jumped, realizing I had completely zoned out. The sun had risen only hours before, but there I stood in the middle of the forest at dusk, as if the Oblivion refused me the gift of daylight. Things would only get worse, I knew it.

I bolted through the woods, eager to leave this part of my life behind. I knew something would come along to distract me, a memory or nightmare would come alive and prevent me from getting home—back to my family and friends. Back to Drake.

Over the horizon, I watched as the sun dropped with astonishing speed, and the moon rose with a vengeance. I imagined an evil sneer on the cratered face of the blue orb, eager to terrorize me, and I hated if I made it out alive, I would never view the moon the same way again.

Crevices from the earthquake had long closed together,

and the pines stood tall, as if they'd never fallen. I ran for what felt like an hour, desperate to get through the thick of the forest. A stone structure appeared over the trees ahead, and I recognized it immediately as the cave Icy and I hid in after I first arrived.

Very little moonlight lit the path in front of me, and fatigue overwhelmed every part of my body. Something treacherous whispered, "Just rest. You need to rest." I refused, feeling as though everything I saw or heard was another distraction to keep me from getting out of there alive.

There was a moment when my thoughts drifted back to the swimming pool at Fremont. . .

You're selfish.

Don't quit.

You're lazy.

Push forward.

You're arrogant.

Just Breathe.

You deserve to die, just like your parents.

Just like that day in the water, I stalled at the last notion, the one thought that haunted me more than anything. Did I deserve to be in the Oblivion? Did I deserve to die? I stood, heaving for air with my hands on my knees. I stared at droplets of sweat and tears dripping to the ground around my feet.

"I can't do this anymore," I whispered. I closed my eyes as pressure built inside my head, and I suddenly realized someone was there with me. Someone was trying to break through.

"Don't give up."

"I don't think I can go on," I admitted. "I'm nothing without my power."

"We need you. Seregalo needs you."

Sobs began to wrack my body at his voice, and I hiccuped, trying to catch my breath as I let the meltdown take over. I'd never felt more lost in my life.

Ren repeated my mother's words, *"Stay strong. There isn't anything wrong with breaking down from the stress that awaits, but afterward you must rise up and take what is yours."*

"I'm trying, Mom. I'm trying."

I stood up straight, searching the forest, but I'd completely lost my sense of direction. Memories of how to get there hovered in the back of my mind, but were blocked. They hovered on the surface, teasing my subconscious.

"Ren? Are you there?"

"I'm here."

"I think it's trying to keep me from getting home. I need to see if you can help me find the way—the burial ground where I came in. Can you try?"

"Hillie is here with me, we'll try together."

I sat in the middle of the woods, closing my eyes and breathing slow and easy. I'd always had power to shield my thoughts, so the feeling of allowing someone free reign felt foreign and terrifying. Not like I had a choice. Ren was already in my subconscious, I was only giving him the okay to meddle around.

"I see you running through the woods. Most of it looks the same, though."

I sighed, disappointed.

"Stand up and look around, scan above the treeline."

I did as he asked, taking in every detail around me, but not seeing anything familiar.

"Stop."

"What do you see?"

"When you were running, the crest of the mountainside was

in front of you. And when you looked over your shoulder, the moon was behind you."

I nodded, understanding what he was trying to tell me. "So, now I need to keep the moon directly in front of me?"

"It's worth a try."

I found the crest of the mountain, and turned my back against it, facing the direction of the full moon. I continued for miles on that path, not seeing anything remotely familiar. I almost gave up, but remembered I wasn't alone. Someone was with me—guiding me home through my muddled memories.

Long red hair caught my eye between two pine trees up ahead, followed by the tail of an emerald green cape. Tears continued to fall, but I stood perfectly still, waiting to see what would happen next. Something about the scene felt obscure, as if I wasn't certain I wanted to see it.

A child screamed in terror, followed by a woman's cry. I instinctually bolted in that direction, but slid to a stop before I reached them. Aadya stood tall and proud, smirking at the sight of the dark haired boy in front of her, peeking out from behind a tree. *Ren.*

I continued watching the scene, knowing Ren's presence still hovered in my subconscious—knowing he would see this.

"Come out, young one. I won't hurt you," Aadya cooed.

Ren shook his head, as if sensing the evil inside of her. He couldn't have been more than three years old, if that.

His refusal only infuriated her further. "Bring him to me," she demanded.

"No! Please! Leave him alone!" a woman behind the trees shouted. "He's nothing to you!"

A Custos guard dressed in black jerked the boy forward by his arm. Ren pushed against him, and almost slipped away until the guard adjusted his grip and held him in front of Aadya. She leaned forward, grinning as if she'd found a new toy. "What's your name?"

My heart hurt at how small and innocent he looked—his wide confused eyes traveling from person to person, as if nothing around him made sense. Did he even remember this time in his life?

"Bits and pieces. It almost feels like a dream I can't quite piece together," he replied inside my head.

Aadya placed her palm on his forehead, as if attempting to discover his secrets, but it quickly backfired as her hands began to shake and the color drained from her face. She pulled back, but froze as if unable to escape his hold. I watched as she clenched her teeth, jerking hard, and finally freeing herself from his power.

She stumbled back, smoothing the lapels of her cape, fighting to hide the shocked expression on her face. "He's coming with us."

"No! You can't take him!" Another guard restrained the mother, keeping her from running forward. "Please!"

Aadya stared at the boy. "There's something different about him. His magic is warped and chaotic—a mutation in the Regalian bloodline, perhaps. Either way, I want him."

"No!" The child screamed and kicked, begging to be released. "I want my Mommy! Please, Mommy! Don't leave me!"

I gripped the front of my shirt, as if I could relieve the chest pain from seeing them separated—another family destroyed by Aadya's thirst for power.

Guards dragged him through the forest and the woman bolted forward in an attempt to save him. As soon as her hood fell back, her long red hair spilled over her shoulders, and I fell to my knees in shock at the sight of my mother, sobbing.

"Another child, hidden from the world. You're full of surprises aren't you?" Aadya cackled. "I'll have them all eventually. Your children are a threat, and I won't stop until I have every last one."

My mother rushed toward her, attempting to wrap her dainty hands around Aadya's neck, but the guards jerked her back. "You have nothing. No family. No one to love. That's why you crave what I have, but Noah will never love you," my mother spat. "My children will seek revenge. You've destroyed the lives of our family—keeping us separated for years. For what? Power?"

Aadya scowled. "Where is Marley? I know she's close."

Mother grinned, but there was no humor in it. "Who?"

Aadya stepped forward. "We can make this hard, if you want."

My mind drifted toward the trials in Stonedell, when I watched Aadya kill my mother in the woods. It all made sense now. She kept him hidden from the world, in fear of losing another child. Did she know something was different about him? I had so many questions.

Custos guards held my mother against a tree as she fought their grip. Her body sagged, tired and weak, as Aadya stood before her with her palm on my mother's head. Mom screamed against Aadya's intrusion.

"You might as well tell me where she is, Annabel. Don't you want the torture to end?"

My mother stayed silent, never breaking eye contact with Aadya. Her misery continued as Aadya dug deeper for information until mom's eyes met mine, almost apologetically, before she fell lifeless in their arms. An evil smile broke across Aadya's face.

"I know where Marley is. It's time to go home." Aadya stated, calmly.

They turned, leaving my mother's unmoving body on the ground.

Long after the scene vanished, I kneeled on the ground, thinking about everything I had seen. Not just me—but Ren. "Are you still with me?" I whispered.

"I am," he choked out. "I barely remember my time with her. I wish I had known her better."

"Me, too," I agreed. "More than you know."

"I don't know what's happening. I'm scared, Mercy."

Guilt flooded my heart at hearing the sad tone in his voice. "I'm going to take care of you. Don't worry, okay?"

"Please hurry."

Without another thought, I took off running through the forest, desperation fueling my every move. Aadya had taken everything from us, and I'd be damned if I allowed Marley to do the same. The bright light of the moon lit the path in front of me as I searched for the familiar burrows in the ground where people had crawled from, or at least tried.

Dirt and rock passed underneath my feet in a blur as I searched. I ran from tree to tree, scouring the ground for loose soil, but the Oblivion refused to make it easy. Panic set in. How would I find it? Could I get home a different way? What now?

"Look lost, you do."

I spun to find the old man, licking his lips before blowing into a harmonica. The high pitched melody traveled throughout the forest, and I stood watching him, my mind hazy and unable to concentrate.

"I've been lost for a long time," I admit. "What about you?"

He pulled the harmonica down and smiled. "Afraid so. Not sure I want to be found."

"You don't have anyone to fight for? Nobody waiting for you?" I asked.

He scoffed. "Maybe at one time. Nobody wants an old man around, right? Nah, I'll never get out of here. It will get easier for them, over time."

"Who are you?" I asked. "How did you get here?"

He smiled. "The name's Frank. Nobody important, I'm afraid. Came in through the ground, same as you."

"But you're Regalian?"

"I am." He glanced around the forest as if it were the most pleasant place he had ever visited. "Figured it out, I see. The necklace is gone."

I reached toward my neck where the gem had hung the past several days. I felt naked without it, as if I had forgotten something. I nodded. "I still have the ring."

Thunder rolled overhead, but the air didn't seem turbulent. It felt eerily silent.

"Best be gettin' home. There's something in the air tonight." He squinted toward the night sky, as if he could see the evil lurking nearby.

I turned to leave, but paused halfway. Something kept me from stepping forward. I couldn't think of anything except the poor soul sitting in front of me all alone. "What about you?" I met Frank's sorrowful eyes and something about his expression, the forlorn, vacant filled gaze, stopped me from going anywhere.

He chuckled. "I'm an old man. One day, this place will be done with me and I'll leave this world. I'll do right by people in the meantime, Regalians like you, and hope to make it to the good side when the time comes."

"Or it could torture you for a while longer," I replied.

"Maybe." He raised the harmonica to his mouth, playing a sad tune.

"Something feels off, Mercy."

The worry in Ren's voice tore my heart out, but so did the pitiful old man sitting in front of me, without a hope of ever getting back to his family. A soft voice whispered that my life was no more important than his, no matter the age or rank.

I didn't know what to do.

"Mercy . . . Someone else is in your head. I need you to listen to my voice."

I kneeled in front of the old man, taking his hand in mine. "It's time for you to go home."

His brows pulled together, as if confused. "Sorry?"

"I want you to have this," I answered, pointing to my ring. "You've been here far too long."

"But, what about you?" he asked.

"I'll figure it out. I always do."

He shook his head. "I can't let you do that. It's very kind, but I've made it this long, I can hold out a little longer."

"But what if you can't? What if you're killed, but this time you don't come back? What if this is your last chance to see your family?"

"That's a lot of what-if's."

I grinned. "I won't be responsible for you wasting away here."

"You're going to give me your ring? You're only chance to make it home?"

"Mercy, no! Don't give it to him!"

Fear hovered as I fought to ignore Ren's panicked voice in my head. I had to do the right thing. Above all, I swore to put Regalians before myself. "That's right," I replied.

Frank stood from his place beside the tree, standing slowly as if giving his joints a chance to loosen. He appeared frail and weak, leaning against the wide trunk of the oak. "I don't know what to say."

"You can start by showing me where those damn holes are. Let's get you home."

Frank limped in front of me, carefully stepping over broken limbs and roots. "Straight ahead, if I'm not mistaken. Not too far at all, now."

"*Snap out of it, Mercy!*"

Ren's voice sounded weak and distant inside my head, as if he struggled to reach me. I could barely make out what he was saying.

The night grew darker, if possible. Something about the forest felt dead, not the typical terror-filled atmosphere I'd grown accustomed to. I expected more as I approached the grave, more objection to another Regalian getting free—but there was nothing.

An odd haze of peacefulness washed over me, whispering that this was the right thing to do. My muscles relaxed, and my eyes grew heavy.

"I really do appreciate you giving up your chance to get home. Not many people in the world would sacrifice themself for an old man."

"You deserve a chance, Frank. Just like anyone else."

"Well, I won't forget you anytime soon, Mercy Monroe. I swear it."

My steps faltered, but I recovered quickly as I followed him into the forest. How did he know my name? I'd never told him. Something about this felt wrong, and I began to panic. The haze of peace disappeared as my mind reclaimed control over whatever dark magic he had used to trick me.

He looked over his shoulder and smiled, as if grateful for my generosity.

I sifted through everything I'd seen or been through. Storms, natural disasters, drowning, fractured spine, horrible visions . . . they never broke me. But leaving a weak old man to die alone—I couldn't do it. I swore I would do everything I could for my people and standing by while another suffers, knowing I could help, was something I couldn't live with.

The Oblivion knew it also.

I tightened my fist, refusing to let go of my mother's ring. I watched as he turned his head from side to side, in sync with the rolling thunder above. I took a deep breath, then I ran.

"Mercy! Where are you going?" He shouted from behind me.

Just as I expected, a second set of feet began to chase me, much faster than the feeble old man I'd followed minutes before. There was no man named Frank. There was only the Oblivion.

Trees began to fall from both sides, blocking my path. I jumped over the fallen trunks, and barely avoided another that landed only inches behind me. A crazed cackle echoed through the woods. The darkness hissed, "Smart girl, aren't you? I'm not done with you yet."

"Don't stop, Mercy. Don't look back."

Roots rose up from the ground wrapping around one ankle. I kicked, desperate to get free, but they tightened painfully, cutting through the top layer of skin. Blood dripped into my boot as I fell forward, clawing against dirt and rock. The roots held me like a shackle, refusing to give at all. I kicked, panicking, as I felt another hand grip my foot and jerk.

"Shh, now. Just a sec."

I twisted just enough to look over my shoulder at Marie, sawing through the roots with her silver knife. She muttered through heavy breaths as she cut. "Ye Mother was good to me. Always repay kindness, you do."

The root began to give just as more crept to the surface of the forest. "Marie . . ."

"She trusted me with your life, Mercy. I don't take that lightly." She cut faster, and eventually sawed through the thready piece of wood.

I kicked the frayed vine from my boots and jumped up, meeting her warm brown eyes. She handed me the long silver knife and nodded. "Keep it—just in case."

"What about you?"

"Don't you worry about me, lass. Run and don't look back."

Everything inside of me wanted to help her, to repay her kindness in a cruel and bitter land. Marie repaid a kindness for something my mother had done years ago, and although I didn't understand everything that happened between them, I could see the love and admiration in her eyes for my mother.

"Run, child."

I spun, tucking the knife in the back of my pants, and dodging every swipe of limb and root thrown my way.

Thunder rumbled overhead, as if the land itself were angry, growling at my escape. Freshly turned piles of dirt ahead caught my attention, and I recognized the over-turned soil immediately. Memories of the old man, leaning against the wider than normal oak on the right, as I dug my way through the ground—the Oblivion greeting me upon my arrival in hell.

Several golden sets of eyes gleamed in the darkness in

front of me, just as a large black wolf stepped out, snarling. He paced the length of the burial site, standing guard. I didn't slow my pace—I refused to back down.

I focused on one of the dark pits, the closest one to me. I couldn't use my gift, but before I had connected with my power, I could run faster than anyone. I could maneuver through obstacles with ease and ace a test without studying.

I needed to find myself once again, the strong and determined woman who survived without the knowledge of power. Before I'd learned about my six gifts, before Fitz told me I would be the chosen leader of Seregalo—I had to go back to the beginning and find Mercy Monroe.

The wolf jumped as I got within feet of the gravesite, a small hole, maybe two feet wide that someone had recently climbed through. I watched the spring in his back legs, the power he utilized to leap toward my body as his snout wrinkled, revealing sharp teeth. I could sense his desperation to rip out my throat, angry at my audacity for rebelling against the Oblivion.

As if time slowed down, the wolf hovered in mid-air, flying toward me. I waited, needing the timing to be exactly right, and when he hit his highest peak, I dove underneath, rolling toward the hole in the ground. I landed inches from where I needed to be, just as he spun to attack.

Feet first, I slid into the hole, wiggling down as quickly as I could. He snapped and growled above me, his razor sharp teeth within inches of my head. The ring on my hand glowed, as it had done so many times before, as if desperate to be of use. I closed my eyes, concentrating on the source, searching for a spark or flicker, anything to light the flame of my gift.

All at once, silence surrounded me, catching me off

guard. The wolf backed away, and the snarling ceased, replaced with a sorrowful melody from a harmonica above. I froze, not sure what to expect next, but fearful of what awaited. I closed my eyes once again, willing the power of the emerald to fuel me.

All at once, silence replaced the music from the harmonica, and pain shot through my scalp as the old man grabbed a handful of hair, attempting to pull me from the grave.

"This is your home now. You're not going anywhere!" He jerked as hard as he could, cackling at my panicked cries. I tried to pull my hair from his grip, but he was determined to have me, twisting my locks around his fist. I tried to reach the knife Marie had given me, but it was wedged in the back of my pants pocket, and I couldn't maneuver around to get it.

The dark hole made it impossible to see anything, but there wasn't a doubt in my mind as to the cause of the crawling sensation up my arms. I hated few things more than spiders, and the Oblivion knew it. Fuzzy legs brushed against my skin as I began to heave for air, still fighting his hold on my hair.

They began crawling up my neck, and I jerked my face to the side as I felt them tickle my mouth and nose. I fought to ignore it all—the prickling sensations on my body and the hair being pulled from my scalp. I couldn't.

He seeped into my thoughts, whispering, "You deserve to be here. This is where you belong."

The old man's voice became soft and distant, as clarity began to return.

"Focus, Mercy. We're trying to shield your subconscious from him."

I checked out completely as the memory of finding my

source at Fremont drifted through my mind. Searching for hours, to light the flame of my source, with Drake's hand on my leg, feeding the fire within me. I imagined the smell of rosemary on the rooftop patio of the Domicile. The sound of the Seregalo River flowing rapidly downstream. The heat of Drake's skin, warming me from the inside out.

"I can't hold him anymore," Ren groaned.

My ring glowed brighter as I fought through the pain. I closed my eyes, praying for strength as I began to weaken mentally. My head spun, and I started to lose consciousness as the hint of a flame sparked within my chest. As the flame grew, the light from the ring illuminated the black hole, and pain like I'd never experienced shot through my chest. My father's voice echoed over and over inside my head, *"Almost there, sweetheart."*

TWENTY-THREE
DRAKE

I couldn't hold on any longer. The dragon tore at my insides, shredding what was left of my control. I held my hand in front of my face, flipping it over, watching as the golden skin blurred into three-dimensional scales, tinged red.

I shook it off, groaning in pain, as the dragon angrily wailed at my resistance. Fitz kneeled beside me, one hand firmly gripping my shoulder. His attempt at invoking peace into my chaotic soul lasted for mere minutes. His face paled and he began to sway from the effort.

"Don't," I begged. "It won't do anything but weaken you." Pain shot through my spine, tendrils of agony wrapping around every nerve as if determined to break me. I arched back, resisting the change.

"Maybe you should let go, Drake. You can't keep it contained forever," Fitz whispered.

I clenched my teeth. "What if it kills you? Any of you? I won't put anyone at risk."

"What if it kills you? What then?" Fitz leaned forward, meeting my eyes. "What about Mercy?"

A green glow of power radiated throughout the cave, throwing Ren and Hillie back against the stone walls. I turned my head, shielding my eyes from the bright light as Fitz gasped beside me.

The bright light disappeared as quickly as it came, leaving a frightening silence in the dark cave. Colton stepped forward, cautiously. "What the hell was that?"

Fitz hurried toward Ren and Hillie. "Are you alright? What happened?"

Ren glanced around, as if confused. "Where is she? Where did she go?"

"Who?" Colton asked.

"Mercy!" Ren looked at me with wide eyes. "She was there. I could feel her getting closer to us! Where did she go?"

My chest tightened at his words. I pushed to my feet, unable to sit any longer. "Can someone please explain to me where she is?" I shouted.

Hillie sat up, pale and weak. "The connection—it was as if it couldn't hold. Wherever she is, I've never experienced anything like it."

"It's awful," Ren cried. "The pain and suffering . . . it's unimaginable."

"How do I get there?" I asked.

"You can't." Ren swallowed, his eyes full of tears. "None of us can."

Another explosion from the town rocked the mountainside, and I reached out to balance myself on the rock wall of the cave. Closing my eyes, I battled with the need to stay there in case we reached Mercy again, or join Marley at the Domicile. Uselessness was by far the worst feeling in the world.

I couldn't just sit there while Seregalo was being

destroyed. Knowing what I had to do, staggered toward the cave entrance, hell bent on protecting what was left of our home.

"Drake? Where are you going? Did you hear what Ren said?" Colton asked.

I nodded, as sweat poured from my face. "I have to go down there. That's what Mercy would expect me to do."

Colton stood straight and nodded. I didn't have to ask, I knew he would be by my side. "Let's go."

"I promise we won't stop trying," Fitz called out. "You have my word."

I looked back one final time. "I know you won't."

. . .

DISTANCE HELPED. The further we ran from the cave, the more I felt like myself. Devastation rocked me as I took in what was left of the Domicile. Everything except one free standing tower crumbled to the ground, partially covering broken and burned bodies of Regalians.

We drew near the river, but decided to cross upstream to remain hidden. Most of the villages were still intact, but a section of the river had been blown up behind the Elder's homes—fortunately not enough to cut off the flow of water.

"Drake," Colton muttered. "Who would have done this?"

I shook my head, "I don't know."

We kneeled behind a tree on the riverbank, assessing the property before rushing into a possibly dangerous situation. These weren't everyday people, they were powerful Regalians, and we had to expect the worst.

Colton jumped as a hand covered his mouth from behind.

Neela leaned down to whisper, "It's just me."

He slumped in relief. "Mom and Dad alright?"

She nodded. "Caleb is staying with them and Nora."

"Good." His dark brown eyes met hers. "You okay?"

She took a deep breath, and fought to control the trembling in her chin. "I don't know. I wish Mercy was here."

"Me too," I whispered.

Slight movement from my right caught my attention, and I shifted my position on the ground to get a better view. Through the forest close to the mountainside, I caught sight of Ren through the trees.

"What is he doing?" Colton asked. "He's supposed to be inside the cave."

I pulled from my sensory gift to look closer, but something about the dark magic muted my power, keeping me from seeing clearly. "Hillie and Fitz are there, too." Hope welled within me at the thought of Mercy being with them, but I didn't sense her anywhere.

"Does this mean they couldn't—"

"It doesn't mean anything," I snapped. "Let's go."

Neela and Colton followed close behind, quietly moving toward the center of the destruction.

Vibrations from dark magic rattled my source, fueling the need to break free from the chains of humanity and scorch whoever had been responsible for the dead at my feet. Lifeless men and women laid holding unmoving children on the ground. The claws of the dragon bit into the palms of my hands, drawing blood at the sight.

Heat radiated from my pores, and more than once, I met Neela's worried gaze.

"It's under control," I promised.

She narrowed her eyes, studying me. "Maybe it shouldn't be."

I ignored the remark, now close enough to make out the figures standing over the rubble and ash. Chills ran across my skin at the sight of Thu Dang in the center with his arms raised high, with two other women at his side. I should have known he would be a part of this.

"I'm going to make my way toward the river—maybe I can find Ren and Hillie." Neela glanced toward me once more. "You good?"

I clenched my teeth, glaring at the back of Thu Dang's head. My entire body shook as streaks of pain shot through my arms and legs. I fought to think straight, as if the beast first took over my mind, then my body. "Lovely," I growled.

Neela and Colton hurried toward the riverbank and I stepped forward, easing my way toward the destruction. A high-pitched scream caught my attention, and I spun, taking in the sight of the old schoolhouse in flames, completely collapsed in the front. Children cried as men and women fought to pull them from broken windows and demolished wood.

The Domicile forgotten, I ran as quickly as I could, the sight of frightened and bloodied children fueling my need to shift. Once again, my body seized as tendrils of snaking pain wrapped around my spine, radiating throughout my arms and legs.

Almost there.

I pushed through the agony, desperate to help. Pressure built inside my skull, and I ground my teeth as my jaw shifted forward. My vision blurred, and I fell to my knees, groaning through the inevitable change. My claws dug into the hard ground, and my ribs shattered against the force of the dragon.

I'd lost all control.

I growled at the onslaught of torture, desperate for it to be over. Inch by inch, red scales traveled down my body and heat enveloped my chest, suffocating me. What took seconds, felt like hours as I writhed in tortuous pain. Suddenly, the agony began to dissipate, and I blinked, my vision sharper than my sensory gift could ever master.

Within fifty feet of the schoolhouse, a woman turned and gasped at the sight of me. She pointed, yelling for everyone to run for their lives. I wanted to reach out and comfort her—assure her that I wanted to help, but I couldn't. Men and women began to bolt from the scene, the schoolhouse forgotten.

All except one.

He looked to be in his fifties, thin and frail. He fought to lift a collapsed beam off a small young girl with brown hair and large brown eyes. I could sense the confusion and fear inside of him, keeping him from utilizing his power. Pushing and pulling, he glanced over his shoulder in fear, but never abandoned her.

"Papa, please help me," she cried. "Don't leave me."

I lowered my head toward the little girl, and he gasped from shock. The flames surrounding us blazed, but the heat didn't affect me. I bit into the beam, easily lifting it off the child and into the air. The man pulled the little girl free and wrapped his arms around her, sobbing.

Immediately, I pushed my way into the crumbling building, lifting heavy pieces of splintered wood and maneuvering my way through the schoolhouse, freeing trapped children from the fire. Men rushed forward to help, carrying the little boys and girls to safety.

At least a dozen children were found alive, although injured. The ones I didn't reach in time, the small lifeless bodies who would never see the light of day again, would haunt me for the rest of my life. After we cleared the building, Regalians stood around the school house, the fear in their eyes replaced with awe and gratitude. Others, rocked their unmoving children in their arms, mourning the lives that had barely begun.

The older gentleman remained on the ground, holding tight to his granddaughter. He nodded in my direction—an acknowledgement for what I'd done.

Shrill cackling echoed around us, coming from the Domicile. With one swift jump, I flew through the air toward high-pitched laughter, determined to obliviate anyone who had a part in this massacre. Gliding toward the ground, I landed as gently as possible behind the fallen chunks of building.

The smell of smoke and blood assaulted my nose as I fought to focus on Thu Dang, the coward standing before me. The joke of an Elder who bullied those less experienced. The weak excuse of a man, threatened by those more powerful.

It ends today.

As I drew near, my eyes drifted to the woman at his feet —on her knees, with blood dripping from her nose and mouth. The red hair that hung limp across her shoulders . . .

Marley.

CHAPTER
TWENTY-FOUR

MARLEY

I wasn't powerful enough. On my knees in front of Thu Dang, Creeky, and Jules, the realization of how much stronger they were hit me harder than I ever thought possible. Aadya told me I would be more formidable than any subconscious interferer alive. She said my gift would go down in history as remarkable—an unrivaled power that would never be matched.

She *lied*.

First Hillie, and now Thu Dang. I could feel their power dampen mine, cracking the thin shield protecting my mind, one I thought was impenetrable. The same wall Aadya taught me to build, as if it would protect me against anything. Maybe this is why my family abandoned me.

I am weak.

Too vulnerable to defend myself. Too frail to lead Seregalo. My sister, the strong and notorious chosen one, she could have done it—all of it. But I took that away. I could have stood by her side. Supported her. Loved her. Been a part of all of the wonderful things she would have done for this land.

Instead, the pain and suffering of Regalians around me satisfied the darkness within. It put me on a pedestal, more powerful than I could have ever been alone. No, I needed others to fail before I could reach those heights. It had always been that way, but I refused to admit it.

Until now, just as death peeked its ugly head around the corner, welcoming me.

Blood dripped from my nose, and pressure behind my eyes increased as Thu Dang filled my subconscious with his power, delving and probing until my mind buckled from the intensity of it all. It wasn't physically painful as much as an emotional violation, knowing exactly how to hurt me in the worst way possible.

It was like standing on a track, watching as the train quickened, waiting for the impact.

The sisters paced around me, watching me writhe in front of them, excited for the moment my mind would collapse, followed by my body. Creeky wrung her hands together in anticipation, and Jules' eyes widened in excitement. Their emotions were so strong, I could sense the promise of death in the air.

Thu Dang stepped forward, his long pointed fingernails tipping my chin up, as if he yearned to look into my eyes when he killed me. He smiled, revealing short, wide teeth, typically hidden behind tight lips.

"You didn't think I would ever allow you to rule Seregalo, did you? You were a means to an end where your sister is concerned. That's all. You'll never be more than that."

I shook all over, fighting the need to fall at his feet. "What did you think? That you would be allowed to rule? You'll . . . never be more than—than Aayda's henchman. That is your legacy."

He tilted his head, narrowing his eyes at my words,

ones he didn't appear to appreciate. The tension in my head built, and my eyes bulged. It felt as if my head were in a vice, and I fell forward on my hands, unable to sit up straight. My arms shook as blood dripped from my face, and every muscle in my body spasmed from the strain.

As quick as it began, the pressure eased, and I found myself able to breathe once again. The relief caused me to collapse to the ground. I slowly raised my head, watching as Thu Dang's body transformed to ash in front of my eyes. His beady gaze widened, as flames licked his skin, devouring every inch of the evil man standing before me. He stumbled forward, wailing from pain as he hit his knees—his skin blackening, shriveling in a matter of seconds.

As his body fell to the ground, his high-pitched scream filled the air until fire spread over his lips, silence replacing his cries of agony. As the smoke cleared, a red dragon stepped forward, standing tall and fierce over a pile of ash.

"Drake," I whispered.

Drake's red eyes focused on me for a few intense seconds before narrowing on the sisters, who were backing away from his menacing glare. He stepped around me, prowling as the click of sharp talons raked through the rubble of the Domicile.

Creeky batted her eyes as if turned on by the beast, while Jules paled at the sight of him. I knew how hard he worked to control the dragon, and how it emotionally affected him every time he couldn't. Although he saved my life, I hated the aftermath he would have to endure, especially from his own people.

Movement to my left caught my attention as Hillie stood to the side, one arm in front of Ren, protectively. Colton and Neela ran forward, along with several other

Custos. A look of devastation crossed Hillie's face at the sight of Seregalo in shambles, then narrowed on me.

Creeky's eyes darkened, muttering toward her sister, "Get the boy."

Jules grinned, slowly stepping away from her sister, with one eye on Drake, as if not wanting to startle him. I stood, trying to find my balance, as I leaned against Drake for support, his scales sharp and hot.

"Hello there, big boy," Creeky called out. "You are something, aren't you?" She stepped forward, cautiously reaching toward him.

Drake opened his mouth, exposing long teeth as smoke trickled from his throat. He swiped at a boulder, tossing it toward her head as if it were a pebble. She threw her hand up, shielding herself with dark magic. The ripple of power shimmered around her as the hard rock slammed against it.

"Let's behave ourselves, shall we?" Creeky cooed. She took a step back as he prowled forward.

Jules studied Ren, and smiled. "Hi, there. I've been so excited to meet you."

Hillie stepped in front of him, protectively. "Don't even look at him."

She continued to move closer, not paying Hillie any attention. "Why don't you come over here with me? I know we'll be the best of friends."

As if hitting a protective glass wall in front of her, Jules jerked back, scowling. Once again, she stepped forward, but couldn't get any closer to Ren. She sneered, glaring in Hillie's direction. "You are a feisty one." She shrugged. "I do hate killing the fun ones."

Hillie's blue eyes seemed to brighten as she stepped forward, as if thrilled by the chance to brawl with the psycho sister. Taking the multicolored hair tie from her wrist, she wrapped her blonde hair in a messy knot on top of her head and rolled her shoulders back. "I'd like to see you try."

Drake's talons clawed the rocks under his feet, growling as if warning the sisters. His red gaze traveled between them and Hillie, as if contemplating an attack without injuring the innocent. I could see the turmoil in his eyes.

Throwing her arms up, Jules twisted her wrist and began pulling at the air, her fingers snapping together in a gripping motion as Ren fought against her invisible pull. He shook his head, clenching the back of Hillie's shirt.

The air thickened, and energy pushed against Jules every time she demanded it bow to her demands. Neela focused on the evil sister from across the rubble, blocking her advances.

"I said . . . Don't. Look. At. Him." Hillie's body vibrated from head to toe as Jules gasped, holding the side of her head.

I'd never seen her use her gift defensively. Not the typical push and pull from a nosey interferer—actual pain and suffering inflicted on another by her hand. Dark blue veins darted across Jules' face from the pressure of Hillie's intrusion, easing into her mind, tormenting her every thought.

I watched, hypnotized. I'd witnessed plenty of deaths by subconscious interference, but none quite so intense. Hillie took her time with the crazy woman—making her an example—demonstrating her strength. Creeky screamed at the sight of her sister, quickly dwindling in front of her. All at once, thunder roared overhead, and wind swirled around us, knocking me off my feet. The ground shook and the river began to rise along with her temper.

Creeky's wild curly hair stuck up in all directions, as her

bloodshot eyes focused on Hillie, struggling to stand against the raging storm—her instability fueled by angry, torrential gusts, carrying a hind of bloodlust and rage. So many emotions swirled around me; anger, jealousy, protectiveness, rage, and desire clashed together in an unbearable war of power.

Ren stumbled back, as if overwhelmed by the energy around him. Hard rain pelted the side of my face as lightning struck above. Jules raised her head from the ground, weakened after Hillie's assault. Blood filled the whites of her eyes as she swayed back and forth, as if she'd fall over at any moment.

Creeky walked steadily through the midst of the storm, as if she were a goddess, unaffected by its ferocity. The wind continued to spin around us, filled with Creeky's anger and violence. Hillie weakened under Creeky's rage, no match for the dark magic suffocating her. Neela stepped forward, attempting to control the force of energy around them, but it was no use.

I stayed close to Drake, watching the scene unfold around me under his protection. I knew I was too weak, and I refused to risk my life for people I cared so little for. I'd let them kill each other, let them die as a result of my actions, ignorant of the one who set everything into motion.

I could smell the stench of death in the air, a wretched combination of blood and charred bones. Screams of terror and pain echoed around me, begging for mercy, as Regalians cried over their family, their gifts useless in the fight to save their lives.

Drake growled, stepping toward Creeky with a murderous glare in his red eyes. He was determined to kill her, just as he did Aadya.

Colton ran forward, wrapping his arms around Ren and

pulling him away from the massacre. Creeky raised one brow as she caught sight of them, attempting to protect him. She turned away from Hillie, dropping her limp body to the ground, as if she lost interest, slowly sashaying toward the boy.

The air around me felt different, as if it bowed to her command. She tilted her head forward and raised her hands in front of her. Fitz shouted Colton's name, but it was too late. All at once she jerked her hands in opposite directions in a breaking motion, and Colton's head snapped to the side—his body immediately falling to the ground.

The dragon roared, throwing his head back in pain as Neela bolted toward her brother. Creeky's eyes widened in shock as she looked over her shoulder at where we stood. Dark red flames licked the rocks around her, but couldn't penetrate her protective shield.

His rage-filled growl sent chills up my arms. I backed up, mesmerized as inch by inch, the beast transitioned from red scales to golden brown skin. In a matter of seconds, Drake had taken control once again.

Sweat covered his body as he heaved, running to where Colton lay, unmoving in Neela's arms. "Colton? Can you hear me? Colton!" Drake lifted his head, clutching at the man that had become one of his closest friends. "Don't do this to me."

I knew Drake depended on Colton like a brother, and I hated to see the agony in his eyes as he clung to his dead body, unable to save him.

Psychotic giggling reverberated through the rubble of the Domicile, as Jules fought to breathe through her laughter. She slapped at the ground, as if delirious.

Drake cut his eyes toward Creeky. "You will pay for this, he growled.

Fitz eased Ren away from the war zone, behind a large piece of stone from the Domicile.

Creeky put one hand on her hip and frowned, baiting him. "I wonder how you'll feel when you find out what I did to your precious Mercy."

He rose to his feet, taking a menacing step forward. "What did you say?"

My stomach turned at her words. I eased toward the last remaining tower of the Domicile, trying to keep from drawing attention.

Her voice brimmed with confidence. "There isn't any hope, you know. She's never coming back."

He took another step forward, then another, completely unfazed by the dark magic pulsing around her, eager to be called upon.

Creeky watched him closely, as if trying to decide how to handle him. With a flick of her wrist, lightning struck the crumbling stone mere feet from where he stood. I jumped, wanting to run to him—help him, but knew I would only be a distraction.

He didn't so much as flinch. "You're going to die for this," he promised. "You're going to bleed and cry for compassion as I watch you take your last breath."

She cackled, amused by his confidence. "You're going to kill me?" Creeky tilted her head back, unable to keep a straight face. All at once, her body jerked forward with wide, shocked eyes—her mouth open as if wanting to speak but unable to form words. The reflection of a long, silver-handled knife gleamed under the sunlight as it deepened, embedded in her back, then traveled up her spine at a slow, agonizing pace.

"No," he responded. Drake clenched his jaw, his muscles tense as he took a deep breath. "She is."

Creeky stared at Drake as dark red blood spewed from her lungs. She hesitantly looked over her shoulder, falling to the ground at the feet of Mercy. My blood turned to ice as my stomach clenched from the shock of her presence. How could this have happened?

My sister didn't use her gifts to destroy Creeky. There was no power involved at all. She had just proven she was a survivor—a strong leader who didn't rely on her gifts for revenge, and I hated her even more.

My gaze traveled to Drake, but his eyes were only for her, drinking her in as if dying of thirst. He knew our history. He knew that we made promises as children. Did they mean nothing to him?

Mercy stood in bloodied jeans and a stained cotton shirt, her hair knotted on top of her head, with wisps of fallen strands surrounding her face. She had lost weight, but appeared stronger than ever—not only physically, but mentally.

Mercy glared at Creeky, bleeding out in front of her, but didn't react at all. She looked toward her left, and threw the knife to Neela. She caught it in mid-air, then casually leaned forward and slit Jules' throat, as if she'd done it a hundred times before.

Jules fell to the ground, smiling as blood bubbled from the gaping wound.

I should have been shocked, or even disturbed by the brutal display of power, but I wasn't. Something about it intrigued me, and I wished I'd been the one to hold the knife. I didn't even care who the victim was.

Neela ran toward her brother, as Mercy kneeled beside Hillie. I watched as she lovingly guided her to a sitting position, making sure she wasn't injured. Drake stood a few feet away for several seconds, but what felt like minutes, before rushing forward, wrapping his arms around Mercy, clinging to her as if he never thought it possible again.

A horrible wail echoed around us as Neela sobbed by the body of her dead brother. She pulled him into her lap, apologizing for not being able to save him, as she placed her cheek against his, rocking back and forth.

I had to admit, I felt slightly bad for her, but it only lasted a moment.

Mercy ran toward Neela, immediately throwing her hand out to turn back time and save his life. Right as the energy around us began to pulse, Neela placed her hand over Mercy's and lowered it.

"You can't," she cried. "It will deplete your power, plus you'll bring the sisters back. Look at what they've done. We can't risk it." Neela palmed the side of Colton's face.

Mercy glanced around the Domicile with tears in her eyes. The crumbling buildings, dead Regalians, and loved ones suffering surrounded her, and I thought she might fall apart herself. Before I realized it, her gaze focused on me, cowering behind the stone tower. Restrained rage seeped across the distance, as she slowly stood.

"I'll be right back," she whispered to Drake.

I eased back one step, then turned to run.

CHAPTER
TWENTY-FIVE
MERCY

There were few times in my life I had experienced a hatred so strong, I lost all control. Agony for those we had lost fueled the turmoil and rage, begging for release. My sister peeked around the tower like the coward I knew her to be.

She wasn't strong enough to defend herself, but that didn't stop her from ruining the lives of everyone around her—just like Aadya. They were one and the same, never satisfied until they fed off misery seeping from the pores of everyone around them. They thrived off heartache.

Not anymore.

Her long red hair swung through the air as she turned, hurrying up the stairwell of the solitary standing tower of the Domicile, desperate to get away from me. I didn't rush, there wasn't anywhere she could go that I wouldn't find her. Step by step, my blood boiled as I followed.

"Mercy?" Drake called out. "Where are you going?"

His voice sounded distant, as if calling out to me in a dream. It reached the deepest part of me, pulling at my heart, begging me to turn around, but my mind refused.

I reached the first step, and the memory of climbing out of the grave came rushing back, choking on dirt as my nails broke from clawing through the ground.

Another step . . .

Drowning in the river, held captive underneath the ice as I fought Asher for my life.

And another . . .

Falling, breaking my back on jutting rock, tumbling to the ground where death refused to free me, only prolonging my suffering.

Step by step, the painful visions rushed forward, reminding me of what she put me through. For what? So she could destroy Seregalo, the only home most of these people have ever known. The land that would keep them safe, so their families could thrive among those who were born just like them.

She not only stripped away their security, but their faith in me as leader of this land. This wasn't only a crime against me, but to anyone who depended upon me. I took each step with ease, not once feeling winded or weak. After ten or so floors, I reached the top where the building had collapsed around it, a tower standing tall and isolated like a lighthouse.

Marley stood, waiting, knowing I would come. For a moment, we stood across from each other and stared. Her shoulders heaved, short of breath from the exertion, while I felt more alive than ever.

"I guess we have a lot to discuss," she muttered.

"Do we?"

She tilted her head. "How'd you do it? How did you get back?"

I balled my fists at her words. "How'd you do it?"

Marley scoffed. "What? What are you talking about?"

"Poison your sister. Destroy our land. Make a deal with the devil. How could you turn your back on your own family? Do you even know how many were killed?"

She scoffed at the question. "Collateral damage."

I threw my hands out, gesturing toward the mountains and valleys surrounding us. "I love these people. I want them safe and happy, even if it means sacrificing myself! This is why you were never chosen!"

Marley's nose wrinkled, her teeth clenched in anger as my words hit home. She dove forward, catching me off guard, immediately grabbing for my hair. She jerked my head forward, then slammed it against the stone, getting two good hits before I righted myself. I punched her as hard as I could, sending her flying backward. I jumped up and kicked her in the ribs, rolling her to the edge of the tower.

She laid on her side, holding her weight on one elbow while shaking off the dizziness. With her head down, she cut her eyes toward me, palming the side of her face. "I hate you," she mumbled.

I shook my head at her nerve. "Was it all for power? Is my seat on the council really that important, you would sacrifice your own sister? Please, tell me what I did to make you hate me this much!" My voice cracked from emotion.

She clambered to her feet, swaying back and forth. "It's always about you, isn't that right?" She spat blood at my feet. "You stole him from me."

"Stole who?"

"Drake. He is supposed to be with me." She slapped her chest. "Mine!"

I laughed out loud, I couldn't help it. "Is that right?"

"You think it's funny? We fell in love when we were only children! His father ripped him away from me to protect

296

you! He was all I had!" Marley's scream echoed off the tower.

I shook my head, sifting through every word, not quite understanding.

"Tell her! Tell her, Drake!"

I glanced over my shoulder at Drake as he walked up behind me.

Marley continued to scream, hysterically. "Tell her that you were my first kiss. That we were the best of friends. You know the truth! You saw the memories!"

"Shut up!" I screamed, unable to think with her screeching like a banshee.

She pointed once again, stomping her foot like a spoiled child. "Tell her!"

"It's true," he muttered. "Someone erased my memories of Marley."

I tilted my head, trying to wrap my mind around his words.

Drake continued, "My father checked on Marley for your parents. I would go with him to visit from time to time."

"He is all I had!" She sobbed.

I seethed inside. Did she think she was the only one with a sad past? That she was the first to feel unloved? Unwanted? Now she wants to lay claim to the only person who has ever been mine, body and soul? I stepped toward her, slowly.

Her eyes took in every detail, and I could feel her feeble attempts to sift through my subconscious, to understand what went through my head, but blocking her was second nature. I stood mere feet in front of her, eye to eye. With all of my strength, I slapped her across the face, spinning her body in a complete circle before landing on her stomach.

"Mercy!" Drake shouted.

"Do you seriously think I care about some childhood crush that happened years before I met him? Have you really spent half of your life dreaming up a fairytale that didn't exist? Did you?" I snapped. I stepped over her, straddling her back, then jerked her red hair back so she could meet Drake's eyes. "Tell him," I demanded.

"Mercy, that's enough!" Drake stepped forward. "You've proven your point."

I jerked a handful of hair once again. "Tell him!"

Silence enveloped our small inner circle on the tower.

She shook her head, refusing to relent.

I leaned forward, whispering, "Why don't you tell him who sent me to the Oblivion on my wedding day?"

Drake chuckled, dark and deep. "That's not possible. Marley wouldn't do that to us. Tell her, Marley. Tell her it was Creeky and Jules!"

Marley nodded. "It was them," she choked out.

Drake's shoulders relaxed, "See. I told . . ."

"I made a deal with them," she continued. "It was the only way."

Drake's body tensed, and the outline of his eyes flamed red. "What did you do?"

"It was the only way," she pleaded.

He stepped forward, and I could feel the intensity of his anger vibrate around me. "The only way for what?"

Marley began to cry, pleading with him to understand. "For us to be together."

I released her hair and her body fell limp at his feet. He stood over her, shaking with anger. She fought to stand, pulling at his arms, begging him to see her side. "Please, Drake. You are everything to me."

He stepped forward, menacingly, and Marley shuffled back. "How many Regalians died today, Marley?"

She shook her head, eyes wide with fear and confusion. "I . . . I don't know."

"And Josiah? Colton?" He advanced once again.

Marley stumbled back, mere inches from the edge. "That wasn't supposed to happen!"

I stood to the side, listening to her excuses. Nothing she could say would change my mind about her. Not anymore.

"What did you offer them?" Drake whispered. "They get rid of Mercy, and what?"

She swallowed. "I—"

"Answer me!" He demanded, his entire body shaking.

"Ren," she admitted. "I promised them the boy."

I froze, not quite believing my ears. "You didn't."

Marley continued to stare at Drake, as if I didn't exist. "I only wanted us to be together, Drake. You have to know that," she pleaded.

He leaned forward. "And you have to know there isn't a chance in hell I would spend the rest of my life with you."

Marley gasped, shaking her head as if she couldn't believe it. "You don't mean it. What about that day on the beach? The sandcastles? Baseball?"

"What about the day you tried to kill my mate on our wedding day?"

Marley snapped. "She isn't your . . ."

"I'm in love with her!" He shouted. "Not you!" The gold skin of his arms sparkled under the sun, transitioning to deep red. He rolled his shoulders back, loosening his joints as if allowing the dragon inside of him to take control and finish this. *Finish her.*

"No," I snapped at Drake, who stood heaving, never

taking his eyes off Marley. "This is between me and my sister."

He stepped back, suppressing the beast that begged to be released. Drake was in complete control.

Marley hiccuped from uncontrollable sobs. She swung her head toward me. "This is your fault!" Blood dripped from her lip and oozed from a small cut over her eye.

"You were going to trade an innocent child," I replied.

"I don't care about a stupid child!"

"You were going to hand your own brother over to those psychotic women," I whispered.

Her eyes widened in shock, but there were no words.

I shook my head, disgusted with her. "It's over, Marley."

She sagged in defeat, her gaze drifting to where Drake stood, as if longing for him to turn and look at her. He didn't. Sadness washed over her, dimming the bright green of her eyes. I felt sorry for her, even after everything she put me through. She loved Drake, and whatever she had conjured in her mind about their relationship, it was real to her.

She stumbled, blank-faced as if she were slowly accepting the fact that she'd lost everything. Marley met my eyes and whispered, "I hate you."

I watched, as if it were in slow motion, as she threw herself from the tower, her arms out by her sides as if completely resigned to end it all. I jolted forward, but froze as my heart battled with my mind.

Marley hated me. She blamed me for everything that happened in her life. She would never love me, and always see me as competition. Honestly, I could live with that.

My palm flinched as I threw my hand out to break her fall, but I still wavered. The noise around me transitioned into a dull hum, and my heart pounded.

What I couldn't live with is the heartless massacre of hundreds. Regalians, suffering and dying because of her jealous temper tantrum. That would never change. The people of Seregalo would always be at risk as long as she lived. How was that fair? How could I, as their leader, allow such a callous, bitter woman to live among the innocent, just because she was my sister?

I couldn't.

Marley made her choice, and I refused to interfere.

I quickly turned, burying my head in Drake's chest as her body slammed against the stone below. Silence filled the air as he held me tighter, as if waiting for me to break. My chest tightened as I fought to breathe, and I almost collapsed from dizziness.

But I didn't cry.

I had always heard a part of you died when your twin left the earth, that your spirit dwindled right alongside of them. I didn't feel that way. There was sorrow for the woman I never knew, sadness for the daughter my parents fought so hard to protect, and hopelessness that a sliver of humanity remained inside of her.

But I never shed a tear.

TWENTY-SIX

TWO WEEKS LATER

The overcast sky darkened above me, as if following me wherever I went, matching my emotions. I stood, hand in hand with Drake, leading a large crowd of Regalians toward Cormadel Memorial, where we would bury two-hundred and fifteen men, women, and children.

Creeky and Jules had been cremated, their ashes, along with what was left of Thu Dang's, had been buried in an undisclosed location. Some of the Elders refused to allow Marley's body into the Cormadel memorial, knowing her part in the destruction of Seregalo, but eventually relented out of respect for me.

I didn't voice my opinion on the matter either way, partially out of respect for those who lost their lives, and also my confused feelings from losing my sister.

Small arched headstones rolled over the hills in front of me, and my heart ached at the sight of family members rushing forward with flowers, sobbing over the gravesites. Drake and I stopped first at Colton's, where Neela and her family bowed their heads out of respect for his heroic efforts. Nora clung to Caleb, who stood quietly over his brother's grave. Drake took a moment of silence, gripping a handful of dark soil.

I knew it would be difficult for him, he didn't grow up surrounded by many people he could trust, and they had grown close over the past couple of months. I stood between Drake and Neela, wrapping my arms around my best friends, invoking as much peace as I possibly could into their broken hearts.

Neela pulled back. "No, Mercy. We need to feel it. We'll never get past it until we do."

"Can I do anything?"

She shook her head, her bottom lip trembling as her father wrapped his arm around her shoulders.

I laid white roses on the ground, then Drake and I shuffled through the crowd, stopping every now and then to pay our condolences or offer a kind word to other mourning Regalians. I stopped at the feet of Josiah's grave, covered in red and white roses. I added to the flowers—what felt like a small offering considering everything he had done for me.

Many nights, I thought of what I would have said to him if we had one more day together. Would I have thanked him? Hugged him? Tell him how much his support meant to me?

I honestly didn't know.

Drake ran his hand up my back, and my spine tingled, the memory of hitting the sharp rock jolting me.

"You okay?" He asked.

I hadn't been able to talk about the details of the Oblivion to anyone yet, for fear of breaking down. Since my return, I had been consumed with reinstating order throughout our land, and taking care of the injured who had no one to tend to them. Sometimes at night, I could feel

Drake's eyes watching me, taking in every scar that ran down my spine.

The small white scar of the two-sided arrow on the back of my neck, identical to Icy's. I remember her telling me how she woke up with the raised mark when she arrived home—a reminder of her time there when her fingers ran across it.

I would forever have those reminders, and there wasn't anything he could do for me.

"Just a little overwhelmed today," I admitted.

He gripped the back of my neck in support, the heat of his palms relaxing the muscles across my shoulders. I leaned into him and closed my eyes.

"Do you want to go home? You don't have to do this today," he offered.

I swallowed, hating to admit the thought crossed my mind. "No. Let's go."

Several minutes later, we arrived at the back of the cemetery, where a single headstone stood off by itself, part of the memorial, but not quite fitting in.

Just like her.

Grandma Monroe stood in the distance with Hillie at her side, and I knew the battle she fought, wanting to pay respect to a family member you had no respect for. She was currently fighting her own battle, mourning a grand-daughter she didn't know, and hearing of a grandson she didn't know she had. It was a lot for all of us.

The isolated grave sat bare and lonely, and my heart hurt to know her afterlife was no different than the years she spent alive. I gripped a single red rose, welcoming the sting from the thorns.

"I wanted so much more for her—for us," I admitted.

He sighed. "I don't think you can change someone who doesn't want to be different, Mercy."

"Do you remember your childhood with her?" I asked, not sure I wanted to hear the truth.

He shook his head. "I saw it in her memories, but that's all. I could feel her attachment to me in her subconscious when she let me in. I'm not going to lie, it was strong."

I laid the single red rose on the grave, hoping and praying Marley was at peace. No matter what she had done to me and everyone else in Seregalo, I didn't want anyone to suffer.

I felt someone behind me, and I turned to find Ren, staring at me with watery blue eyes. Fitz stood several feet behind him.

"How about I take Ren for a walk?" Drake offered.

I nodded. "Thank you."

He swept his lips across my forehead, then patted the side of my hip as he walked away.

Fitz stepped forward, looking down at Marley's grave. "How are you holding up?"

I shrugged. "Holding steady."

"Feel like chatting for a moment?" He looked over his shoulder. "If it isn't a good time, we can do it later."

"No, maybe it will distract me. What's up?"

"Ren. I've been spending some time with him, working with him. His control is improving, and I think his system has been in shock from being locked up."

We turned, walking away from the memorial, to keep anyone from overhearing us.

"He's spent his entire life being told he's dark, and his magic is abnormal. He's terrified of hurting someone."

"He told me he hears voices, Fitz. That worries me."

He nodded. "But I don't think there's anything wrong

with him. Just because we've only seen six gifts, doesn't mean there isn't a seventh or eighth. I mean, look at Drake. It's rare, but it can happen."

I took in a deep breath, then exhaled, my gaze traveling over the lush green hills in front of me. "What do you recommend?"

"I'd like to keep working with him. The child has something special, just look at how he was able to reach you with Hillie's help."

I smiled. "You know I almost quit a couple times. He kept me going. I wouldn't have made it without them."

"This has been a lot to take in. How are you handling it?" He asked with raised brows.

"I have to be better than he is," I replied.

Fitz nodded. "I can't imagine what he's gone through. We have a chance to make a difference in his life, and I'd like the opportunity to help change his story."

I grinned. "You know when I first met Hillie, she told me when my mother was pregnant, if it was a boy, she wanted to name him Fitzgerald."

Fitz's eyes filled with tears. He pursed his lips, trying to contain his emotion. "The boy likes the name Ren. Plus, it's an honor. He's named after a fine young man."

"You mean two fine men, right? Ren Fitzgerald has quite a ring to it."

He chuckled, shaking his head. "You remind me so much of Annabel."

"I'm going to take that as a compliment."

Drake sat on the side of the Seregalo River with Ren, tossing rocks into the water. Fitz was right, he needed a chance like everyone else, but he also deserved a choice. "Let me talk to Ren. For once, someone needs to ask him what he wants."

As we made our way toward the river, Drake turned, as if sensing my presence behind him.

Fitz called out, "Drake, do you mind helping me with a few things?"

Drake cut his eyes toward me, then to Ren, not missing a beat. "Sure thing." He ruffled Ren's hair, then he and Fitz made themselves scarce. Ren blinked, wide-eyed, waiting for me to begin the conversation. It continued to amaze me how intuitive he could be.

"How are you?" I asked.

He bent his knees to his chest, wrapping his arms around his legs. "The man who saved me, he died?"

I nodded. "Colton's a hero, Ren. He died with honor."

"Why would he do that?"

"What?" I asked. "Save your life?"

He nodded.

"Why wouldn't he?" I nudged his shoulder. "You're pretty awesome."

He fought a smile, but didn't answer.

Then it hit me . . . I wasn't drained or weakened by his proximity. The power and energy around me wasn't pulling from my body into his like it usually did. I wasn't sure if he had stabilized after the trauma, or if Fitz had helped with his control. Maybe both.

"Ren? What do you want?"

He blinked several times, as if taken off guard. "I don't think anyone has ever asked me that before."

"I'm asking you now. It's okay if you don't know, we'll figure it out together."

Ren looked out over the water. "I keep thinking about your visions, when I was in the woods as a baby. I wish I could remember more about my mother, maybe under-stand her better."

I watched the sunlight gleam off the dark strands of hair, the exact color of mine. The way the reflection of water rippled in his blue eyes, identical to my grandmother. "I never met our mother, but somehow between Stonedell and Oblivion, I feel close to her, as if I know exactly who she was. Amazing, right?"

He nodded.

"I met Dad in New York. Although it was only a short time, I'm so grateful for those moments spent with him. Maybe I could tell you about them sometime."

"I'd like that."

"We aren't as lucky as some, Ren. There were people who loved us, but others who were determined to make our life a living hell. I think they would be proud to know we found each other."

He grinned, but didn't reply.

"Listen, I'm mature enough to admit that I'm not ready to raise a child. I can't give you what you need right now. I want you to have everything a young boy should have and more."

He nodded, sadly.

"But I also want to spend as much time with you as possible. You're my brother, and I'm looking forward to bossing you around for years to come."

He laughed, immediately in brighter spirits. "I wasn't sure if you would want that."

"Want it? I'm excited about it. You have to be more pleasant than my last sibling."

He snickered. "I want that too, but I also want to go home."

"Home?" I asked.

"With the Hughes family. Before everything went bad, we were happy, you know. Madi and Kenz took me fishing, and Aly made the biggest cinnamon rolls I've ever seen! Gary would read to us at night. It felt like a real home."

"Do you want me to talk to them? I heard they were pretty upset when you were taken away."

He nodded. "Do you think they'll take me back?"

"They'd be crazy not to."

. . .

I LEFT the memorial needing some alone time.

Time to think.

Time to breathe.

I often woke in the middle of the night, plagued by nightmares, thinking I'm back inside the Oblivion, screaming for help. The first couple of nights, I woke with Drake on top of me, holding my hands above my head, trying to calm me down. It wasn't lost on me that he woke the next day with scratches down one side of his neck, but he never brought it up.

I walked down the sidewalk, thankful for the neighborhoods that were still intact, and grieving for the houses in shambles. Creeky and Jules' neighborhood appeared as pristine as ever, but the small lot where their house stood had been replaced by a pile of ashes—burned to the ground.

I only wish I'd been the one to throw the match.

After another couple of blocks, I found myself in front of Icy's door, unable to knock. I knew she wasn't in the best health, and hadn't been able to attend the memorial. Part of me wanted to see her, but what would I say?

"You gonna stand there all day, or you gonna come inside?" The Elder raised one brow, leaning against the front door.

I never even heard it open.

"Aren't you supposed to be in bed?" I asked.

She scoffed. "Aren't you supposed to be dead?"

I cracked a grin. How could one, frail old woman break through the wall I'd constructed around myself the past couple of weeks? "Aren't you?"

Icy turned, hobbling inside the house on a cane. "I wondered when I'd be seeing you."

I closed the door behind me and sighed. "I'm sorry, Icy. I needed some time."

Her sitting room looked exactly the same, the neatly folded quilt on the back of the couch, and figurines stacked neatly across the mantle. I knew she didn't use the room often, and it likely sat untouched for most of the day.

Icy led me toward the back porch, where she often sat, looking out over the water. "So where are you staying now?"

"My parents' old cottage. The Elders have asked about rebuilding the Domicile, but I'm honestly liking the idea of staying in the cottage, just the two of us. It feels right."

She nodded. "Do you want to talk about it?"

I couldn't meet her eyes for fear of crying. "Not sure I can. Not yet anyway."

"I get it. It took me a while, you know. Sometimes I can still feel the thrash of the river, the grim visions in the cave. But, we've seen the other side, Mercy. A side that most will never know truly exists. For that, we are stronger."

"Why didn't you tell me? Beforehand, I mean."

"Several reasons. Mama always told me not to mess with the natural order of things, and I wish I could say that was the reason, but it isn't all of it. If I told you and you didn't go, would I have made it back? Would Dorian have survived? Would something worse have happened with those crazy sisters and Marley? Hell if I know."

I nodded, letting her words sink in. After several seconds of silence, I asked, "What happened to you? You were such a sweet child."

Icy gasped, then a smile broke through the emotionally injured facade. Giggles quickly turned into cackling, and I held my stomach from laughter as she leaned forward, tears running down her cheeks. We took a moment, a few minutes of unrestrained bliss, to appreciate what we'd been through, and that we were alive to talk about it.

"Seriously, though. Thank you."

"I should be the one thanking you, right?"

"Maybe, but still. I do have a question for you."

"Go for it. There isn't much about me that you don't know."

"Well, it isn't necessarily about you."

She sat up straight, loving the thought of gossip. "I'm all ears."

"Does the name Marie sound familiar to you? Maybe an old friend of my mother's?"

Icy's face fell, and her smile quickly turned sad. "Where did you hear that name?"

"The Oblivion."

She closed her eyes for several seconds and shook her head as if surprised. "I haven't thought of sweet Marie in a long time. I always wondered what happened to her."

"Who was she?"

"Marie Morgan, Annabel's best friend. They were closer than sisters—it drove Aadya crazy. Always together since they were kids, even stood by Annabel's side when she married Noah. She was yours and Marley's true godmother, but it was too dangerous for them to leave either of you with her. That's the first place Aadya would have looked."

"She just disappeared?"

She nodded. "Marie helped your mother escape Seregalo."

My mind sifted through everything, and Marie's words drifted through my mind.

"She trusted me with your life, Mercy. I don't take that lightly."

"Marie saved my life."

"In the Oblivion?"

I nodded. "I might not have made it without her. When I woke up in the cave with Ren and Hillie, it was her face I saw. I couldn't get it out of my mind. She also gave me the knife we used to kill Creeky and Jules."

Icy sat back against the chair in shock. "She was caught helping your parents, Mercy. Aadya showed no compassion."

"I don't want to even think about it, Icy. It breaks my heart."

"You have a chance to change things for these people, Mercy."

I sighed. "Ren was there with me, you know, in my subconscious. We saw a vision of Aadya taking him away from his mother. My mother."

Her eyes widened, but she didn't speak.

"I've never seen you so quiet," I muttered.

"It's a lot to take in. At least offer me a drink before you throw that at me."

"Imagine how he feels."

"What about you? Or has anyone asked?"

I smiled. "I'm happy, but I hate what he's been through.

I hope he is young enough to mold into the wonderful young man my parents would have raised."

"I'm sure he'll be fine. He has you after all."

I slumped into the rocking chair. "Sometimes I wonder how much I should tell him."

"Everything. Might help the boy to know his mother was a brave and kind soul, one who gave her life for his. First, give him time to settle. He has been through a lot and there will come a day for that conversation. Then, me and Mrs. Monroe can tell him stories about his mother as a child. He might enjoy that."

"I bet he would."

"How's Drake?"

I nodded before answering. "Better. He's learning. He's gone every morning when I wake, usually in the mountains by himself, shifting and practicing control. He seems more like himself now that he's accepted his other side."

"What about you? You finally gonna marry that fire-breathing, sexy man of yours? Because if you're having doubts, I'm available."

I narrowed my eyes, pretending to act jealous. "Seems like a bad time to be celebrating, Icy. I'm still looking over my shoulder, waiting for something bad to happen. I want it to be perfect, you know."

"Perfect doesn't exist, Mercy. Stop waiting for perfection. Take the moments you're given and make them perfect."

I knew she was right. "I'm scared, Icy. Every time things are going well, something terrible happens. I don't want my life with Drake to be filled with fear."

"Never trust your fears, they don't know your strength."

Tears filled my eyes at her confidence in me. "Anything else?"

"Yes," she replied. "Be wary of advice from an old woman who drinks before lunch."

I laughed, shaking my head. "Noted."

. . .

I SPENT the evening with Icy, finally gaining the courage to talk about our time together in the Oblivion. I didn't realize how much I had held inside since returning, and there wasn't another soul I could talk to who would understand. Not like her and Dorian.

The shadows around Icy's eyes had darkened since I saw her last, and her bright blue gaze had dimmed. I didn't know how much time I had left with her, but I wanted to make the most of it. I promised to return the next day, then walked home in the dark, giving myself some time to think.

The moon hovered high above Seregalo, and memories of the blue-cratered orb in the Oblivion rushed back, causing chills to run across my skin. The sensation of being watched hovered beneath the moonlight, and I would never look at the moon the same way again.

I focused on the bright stars, twinkling against the blackest sky I'd ever seen. Stars over the city I had grown to love—the land we continued to rebuild. There were moments I couldn't believe I'd made it home, because part of me doubted I ever would.

A single light lit the inside of the rock cottage up ahead, and I couldn't help but smile. After returning, Drake refused to spend another night away from me, so we found a small home away from town, close to the mountainside and river.

It had been a nice change from the enormous Domicile, filled with the hustle and bustle of staff.

It was exactly what we needed.

I walked up the cobblestone sidewalk and into our quiet home, Drake nowhere in sight. Just as I entered our bedroom, the shower faucet groaned from the bathroom and the spray of water silenced. I laid back on the bed, throwing my arm over my eyes. I felt as though I hadn't slept in weeks.

"There you are. Do you know how many times I almost went looking for you? I talked myself down—didn't want to look like an overprotective, unbalanced shifter. Everyone is already frightened as it is."

I laughed, raising my head to meet his eyes. Giggles caught in my throat at the sight of him freshly showered, in nothing except a pair of gray sweatpants. All of a sudden, I wasn't so tired anymore.

"I can sense your pheromones," he shook his head. "You're not subtle about it."

"Sense this," I muttered. I closed my eyes, imagining Drake having his way with me in several rooms of the cottage, then used my sensory power to show him.

He walked toward the bed, stalking me. Raising one leg up, he removed my shoe, then began to massage the arch of my foot. "Maybe we should wait until you marry me. I'd hate for you to steal my virtue and take advantage of me."

My eyes rolled back in my head at the feel of his hands, kneading the tender spots on my feet. "I think it's a little late for that."

Drake scoffed, as if insulted, then increased the pressure on my foot.

I moaned. "I'll do anything you want, just don't stop."

"Anything?" he asked.

"Um, hm," I mumbled with my eyes closed.

He leaned forward, kissing the side of my foot, on the sensitive side of the arch. "So you're going to walk down the aisle this time?" Gently relaxing one leg on the bed, he picked up the other foot, easing my shoe off and showing it equal attention.

"Maybe we should take some time to let the dust settle, you know?" I asked, my eyes still shut tight. I knew if I looked up at him, it would be game over for me.

"I think having to wonder if I would have to live without you made me edgy. Forgive me if I'm anxious about finally getting you down the aisle."

"I'm sorry," I murmured.

"It's fine, I mean I had Marley to keep me company."

My head shot off the pillow and I pushed up on my elbows, glaring. "That was low."

"Just making sure you're listening." He let go of my foot and began crawling up the bed, hovering over me. "Marry me, Mercy. You are the only one I love—have ever loved." His lips gently kissed the side of my neck, then my jaw. "You are the only one I want to wake up to in the morning, and kiss goodnight before bed."

He settled his weight on top of me, and I wrapped my legs around his waist. He teased my lips, but when I leaned toward him, he pulled back just a bit. "Marry me."

"I'm scared," I admitted.

He knew how hard it was for me to admit. His eyes softened and he leaned down to kiss me, soft and sensual. "Anything that comes our way, we'll fight it together. I swear."

Icy was right, there would never be a perfect moment, we had to create perfection out of the moments we were given. I refused to waste another minute in fear.

I mumbled around his lips, "Can it be a small ceremony?"

He leaned back to meet my eyes and smiled. "It can be anything you want, as long as you're mine."

"Til death do us part?" I asked.

Drake's eyes flashed red at the thought. "It can try."

EPILOGUE

My deep red dress hung on the door of my bathroom, ruffles upon ruffles flowing down the length. The seamstress had brought it from their shop that morning, considering the original had burned with the Domicile. I hadn't stopped staring at it since. It was everything I'd ever dreamed of having. The perfect day. The perfect man. The perfect dress.

But I couldn't wear it.

My hair wasn't fixed, and I hadn't touched my makeup. Every time I had ever prepared for a ceremony, it turned into a nightmare. Something didn't feel right. I shook my hands, as if I could rid myself of the nerves, pacing the hardwood floor of my bedroom from one side to another.

"Mercy, honey?"

I turned at the sound of Hillie's voice and sighed. She peeked into the room, her hair intricately braided into a fancy updo. A bright orange and yellow dress hung from her shoulders. "You look beautiful," I told her.

Her gaze traveled down my body, scowling at the loose tee and denim cut-off shorts. "Can we come in?"

"We?" I asked.

All at once, my door swung open and Neela pushed her way inside, followed by Hillie and Nora. Neela stunned in a red asymmetrical dress and four inch heels, while Nora wore a pink babydoll dress with a ruffled hem. The blush in her cheeks matched the shade of her dress perfectly.

"Wow. You ladies look lovely."

"Is there a reason you don't?" Hillie asked.

I teared up, and Neela elbowed her, stepping forward. "What she means is, what can we do to help?"

I turned away from her, throwing my arms into the air, then faced her once again. "I don't know. Maybe nerves. Something doesn't feel right."

Nora wrapped her arms around me, and peace settled over my anxious mind. "Tell us how we can make it right."

My eyes filled with tears. "I don't know."

Hillie ran over, a tissue in hand. "Now, now. We'll figure it out. All this running around, Oblivion and funeral chaos. Maybe you need to just sit and . . . not think. Hell, that's how I get through most of my life."

I stared at her as if she were the most intelligent person I'd ever met. I nodded slowly, pondering her every word. "I think you might be right."

Neela pushed me into a chair and the three women went to work, combing and pulling, brushing and curling. Neela hummed a relaxing tune behind me, as Hillie shoved a dark chocolate brownie in front of my face. I closed my eyes, devouring the treat, pretending like I didn't know what she'd put inside.

I wasn't even sure how long I'd been sitting there when someone knocked.

"Just a minute," Hillie called out sweetly.

They knocked once again, as if they didn't hear her.

"I said just a damn minute!" Hillie turned back toward me and smiled.

Everything felt slow, as if no one seemed to be concerned about the ill-mannered dragon waiting for me down the aisle. I snickered, picturing a red dragon in a tux. Nora raised one brow higher than the other, then continued swiping shadow across my eyelid.

"Who was at the door?" I asked.

"What?" Neela asked.

"The door. I heard someone knock."

Hillie scoffed. "That was almost an hour ago, Mercy. They were dropping off champagne for you."

"Pop that bottle, what are you waiting for?" I grinned, excited.

"Well, we already did." Hillie had the decency to look ashamed.

"How much did you give her?" Nora asked, scowling at Hillie.

"You can't even look mad, Nora. Stop trying." I snorted. "You're like a koala bear that didn't get a nap."

Neela's hands shook in my hair as she laughed behind me. "You're going to mess up my work of art. Stop moving."

Hillie and Nora stepped aside, and I blinked several times at the mirror in front of me. Neela had swept my hair to one side in an elegant bun with a thick braid wrapped around the crown of my head. My makeup was fresh and light, with smokey gray eyeshadow and pink lip gloss.

"I think you should wear these," Neela whispered. She held her hand out to reveal the fire stone earrings that Mrs. Williams, Ren's mother, had given me. It felt like such a long time ago.

"Your grandmother was holding onto them for you. She sent them over yesterday."

"They're perfect, Neela."

She smiled. "Do you want to wear your emerald necklace?"

I reached for the necklace around my neck, remembering it was gone. I knew Dorian would make sure I got the necklace back one day, probably when I least expected it. "No, I don't think so."

"You are beautiful with or without it," Nora said. "Are you ready to get dressed? It's almost time."

I looked over toward the red dress, custom made. Something about it felt wrong, but I didn't know why. Right as I started to tell them I couldn't wear it, Grandmother Monroe knocked, slipping into the room, and closing the door behind her.

"I don't mean to interrupt." She shifted from foot to foot, nervously, clutching a white box.

"Please, we'd love for you to join us," Hillie called out, smiling brightly.

"I have something for you, Mercy. Please don't feel like you have to wear it today, but one day you might want to hand it down to your daughter. I never had girls of my own, you know."

I stood from my chair, taking the box from her hands without a word. "Can you give me a minute?" I asked.

"Of course," she whispered.

I took the box into the restroom, where I could open it alone. The thought of my grandmother giving me something she loved brought emotions to the surface I wasn't used to dealing with, especially in front of an audience.

I opened the square white box and pushed the wrapping to the side. Immediately, I looked away, fighting the tears I knew would ruin my makeup.

It was my grandmother's wedding dress.

I couldn't believe how perfect it was—long, clingy lace over ivory fabric, with lace sleeves. But it wouldn't have mattered what it looked like. I needed to wear something with meaning, a dress that had been handed down by someone who loved and supported me. A tradition that didn't mean anything to some girls, meant everything to me.

I slipped into the gown and stood in front of the mirror, unable to keep the smile off my face.

Now everything is perfect.

My grandmother knocked on the bathroom door. "Mercy, everything alright?"

I opened the door and she covered her mouth in surprise. Tears fell freely as she fought to find the right words. "You don't have to wear it. I know you wanted the red dress."

"I wouldn't dream of wearing anything else."

"You're glowing," Neela whispered. "I think you're ready."

One by one, the ladies shuffled out of the room, making their way outside. My grandmother kissed me on the cheek, then followed them out. I turned to the bedroom window of the cottage, pulling the sheer curtain to the side. White chairs were lined beside the river, with my closest family and friends waiting patiently.

Small and intimate, exactly what I wanted.

I opened my door to find Fitz, leaning against the wall across from my door. "How long have you been out here?"

He grinned. "Just making sure you aren't trying to make a run for it."

I laughed. "I think I'm ready this time."

Fitz escorted me outside, where our guests stood at attention. Most of them weren't used to a traditional wedding, so I was thankful they participated in something so special. Drake, dressed in a black suit and white dress shirt, stood in front of the water, beside Neela's father, who agreed to officiate.

Drake's eyes lit up as I walked down the aisle, the glow of the setting sun lighting the mountainside behind him. My knees shook, and I clung to Fitz's arm, afraid I would collapse at the sight of him waiting for me. I wanted to run my hand through his messy hair, graze my lips underneath his jaw, exactly how he likes it. Wrap my legs around his waist...

Neela cleared her throat, glaring in my direction, and I realized I'd projected my feelings to every single person at the wedding. They all shifted in their seats and looked away, extremely uncomfortable. Drake smirked, shaking his head. Ren stood beside him, wrinkling his nose as if disgusted.

"She always has to make things interesting, doesn't she?" Fitz whispered.

"That she does," Drake responded, taking my hand, and wrapping it around his arm.

Mr. Parker recited a lovely poem that was read when he and his wife married in Seregalo. Fitz prayed over our union, and Drake and I exchanged traditional vows, and followed with Regalian mating ceremonial oaths. It was everything I could have hoped for.

Mr. Parker announced, "You may kiss..."

Drake pulled me into his body, cupping the back of my head, and devoured my mouth before Mr. Parker could finish his sentence. I clung to his suit, lost in the warmth of his skin. Everyone stood clapping and laughing at Drake's reaction to me officially becoming his wife.

A large white tent had been set up behind the cottage. A

band played softly in the corner as Regalians filed in, eager to lose themselves in a night of celebration. I considered foregoing a reception at all, but Neela encouraged me to have it, saying the people of our land needed something to celebrate after such a devastating loss.

So we danced, and drank, and danced some more. Even after cutting the cake, I continued to swing by the tables, shoving hors d'oeuvres and bites of cake in my mouth. I licked the icing from each one of my fingers just as I glanced up to see Drake watching me with smoldering intensity.

He walked toward me, grinning, as I attempted to regain a sense of control. A waiter hurried by with a tray of red wine and I snatched a glass before he even knew it. I turned it up, never taking my eyes off Drake.

He took the empty glass from my hand and set it on the table. He then swiped the icing from the side of my lip, and I watched hypnotized as he stuck it in his mouth.

"Hungry?" he asked.

I took a deep breath, but didn't respond. I didn't know what I wanted more—him or the cake.

Hillie busted up our private moment with an ungraceful twirl toward the dessert table. "Woo wee! These munchies are something else. How are you not devouring these goodies?"

Drake's eyes widened at her words. "This is going to be a fun night."

"This wedding cake is something else, but the groom's cake . . . now that's where it's at."

Drake frowned at the red dragon cake at the end of the table. "It's something else alright. Who's idea was that?"

Hillie paled at his tone. "Well, um, I, do you hear that? Someone is calling me." She turned, running into the dessert table, before righting herself and shuffling away.

As much as I wanted cake at that moment, he looked too good to ignore. "Would you like to dance?"

His gaze traveled down the tight lace dress and he smiled. "I'd like to do a lot more than dance, Mrs. Moreno."

Drake wrapped his arms around my waist, lifting me until my feet dangled in mid-air. He held me tight against him, swaying to the soulful melody of a saxophone. For the longest, I closed my eyes, consumed with the feel of his arms tight around me.

My thoughts drifted to our parents. Would they be thrilled for us? Proud? I hoped so.

"What are you thinking about?" Drake's finger rubbed across the wrinkles on my forehead.

"Our parents. I think they would have loved this."

He smiled. "Dad used to say he became a man when he married my mother. She made him want to be a better everything."

Knowing Dorian, I could hear him saying that. The thought made me tear up. "He sounds like a good man."

"I've been thinking about him lately. I know this seems premature, but if we ever have a son, I'd like to name him after our fathers—Dorian Noah Moreno. How do you feel about that?"

My eyes filled with tears. "I couldn't love anything more."

Drake cupped the side of my face and kissed me softly.

A sweet, timid voice called out. "May I cut in?"

We turned toward Nora, who stood blushing beside us. Drake raised his brows. "I'm guessing you mean her, not me?" he asked.

Nora grinned. "Sorry."

He put his hands up in surrender. "I don't blame you.

She's a better dancer anyway." He kissed my forehead, then whispered, "I'm going to get a drink."

Nora wrapped her arms around me and we began to sway to the music, reminiscing about how far we had come since our days at Fremont. I could feel the intensity of Caleb's gaze across the tent, watching Nora's every move.

"How is he?" I asked.

She frowned. "He misses his brother, but he's trying hard to move forward. They all are."

I searched the dance floor until I found Neela, dancing with her father. "They've been through so much. I envy their relationship, especially today."

"You have family all around you, Mercy. Just look around."

I met her eyes and nodded. "You're right. I do."

She smiled, a tight-lipped grin full of emotion. "Plus, our family just keeps growing and growing, you know. One day, we may have more than we can handle."

Nora continued dancing, her eyes hazed over with dreams of the future. My feet slowed and she glanced up at my change of pace. "You look so happy," I told her.

"I really am. Our ceremony is planned for next month. I keep thinking this is all just a dream, you know?"

"I know exactly how you feel. But I think it's time we all enjoyed our life, don't you?"

"I think so, too. And one day, we'll have children. We'll make our own family, right here together, Mercy. Everything we've ever dreamed of."

I laughed. "I'm not sure when I'll be ready for that, Nora. I have some growing up to do."

"Not me," she said proudly. "I can't wait until the day comes. We've already talked about names."

I knew they would want to name their child after Colton, but I asked just the same. "Tell me."

"If it's a girl, we want to name her after my grandmother, but I think he wants a boy so he can name him Colton."

I smiled. "No matter what you have, that baby is going to be so loved, by all of us."

"I know, but you have to admit, Analise Parker has a ring to it."

I froze, and my heart pounded against my chest. "What did you say?"

Nora's brow furrowed. "My grandmother's name, Analise. Do you not like it?"

I stumbled back, my vision blurring from the adrenaline. "Can you excuse me?"

"Mercy, are you alright?"

I nodded, waving her off. I rushed off the dance floor unable to think. Dorian's words repeated over and over inside of my head.

"My true love and Allegato match is a beautiful and smart woman named Analise. I can't put into words how funny she is." He chuckled, then grew serious. *"All I want is to grow old with her. It's all I've ever wanted since I laid eyes on her."*

I searched the crowd for Drake, finding him talking to Fitz and Neela in the corner of the room. I smiled politely at them, but pulled at his arm to follow me outside the tent.

"Mercy, what is going on? Are you okay?"

I spun to face him in the dark. "What is your mother's name?"

"What is this about?"

"I need to know."

"Victoria. I think I told you that before, right?"

"Victoria? Not Analise?" I knew he thought I had lost my mind. Maybe I had.

Drake shook his head, confusion and worry filling his red-tinged eyes. "No."

I closed my eyes, struggling to come to terms with the truth.

"If we ever have a son, I'd like to name him after our fathers —Dorian Noah Moreno."

"Our son," I whispered. "He was our son."

"What are you talking about? Did Hillie give you another brownie?"

I bit my lip to keep from crying, unsure whether I should divulge the information or keep quiet for fear of changing our future. Drake pulled me against his chest, rubbing up and down my back to soothe me. "I got you. Everything is okay."

Stars gleamed brightly overhead against a pitch-black backdrop as the trickle of the river flowed over smooth rocks. I let out the breath I'd been holding as tears streamed down my face, over my lips. "You're absolutely right."

The End

ACKNOWLEDGMENTS

A huge thank you to my husband for his never-ending support and proofreading capabilities. Without you, I wouldn't be able to do this.

Isolette, "Icy" for her love of reading and support of authors such as myself. It has been a joy to meet you.

To the friends who randomly message me saying, "You've been on my mind, and I said a prayer for you this morning." You know who you are, and I love you so very much.

ALSO BY A.F. PRESSON

Women's Fiction

Blind Trust: The Trust Series Book One

Broken Trust: The Trust Series Book Two

Fragile Trust: (Coming Soon!)

Young Adult Fantasy

Interference: Book One

Oblivion: Book Two

Prequel: (Coming Soon!)

Inspirational

Chronicles of a Lost Boy on Christmas

ABOUT THE AUTHOR

A.F. Presson's career in writing began in 2021 with a women's fiction novel titled Blind Trust, soon followed by Broken Trust and Interference. Blind Trust was awarded Distinguished Favorite in Women's Fiction from the Independent Press Awards and also a finalist for the Annie McDonnell Book Award.

Amanda, born in Chattanooga, TN, resides in North Alabama with her husband Brian, and their two sons, Roman and Isaac. When she isn't writing, she is working in a local electrophysiology lab and spending time with her family. An avid fan of music and Broadway, the arts have always played a large part in her life and she embraces the opportunity to enter the world of literature.